SATAN'S VENGEANCE

Carroll John Daly

SATAN'S VENGEANCE

THE CASEBOOK OF SATAN HALL

CARROLL JOHN DALY

ILLUSTRATED BY

JOSEPH A. FARREN

COVER BY

LEJAREN HILLER

STEEGER BOOKS • 2020

CHAPTER I

A MISSION OF DEATH

THE COMMISSIONER OF POLICE was a little man who sat painfully erect at the end of his chair. He avoided the eyes of Detective Satan Hall when he talked.

"So it's Dan Gargan again," he said at length. "That's it, isn't it, Satan? Dan Gargan!"

Satan nodded, said it was, waited. The silence was long. The Commissioner finally broke it.

"Bentz is dead. Halpin is dead. The Greek is dead. It's gang-killing, of course. You've got to admit it, Satan, the city is better off without them—any of them."

Satan ran a hand across thin lips; his green eyes bright. He said:

"There were two children killed; shot right down on the street. The city street! Is the city better off for that?" And when the Commissioner looked toward the window and the towering buildings beyond Satan continued, "It's not like you, Commissioner. You had me on Gargan's tail almost before his name was even known to a head-waiter; then the murders and my lay off. If I didn't know you so well—"

"I know. I know." The Commissioner came to his feet by sliding off the high swivel chair. "There's no evidence, Satan, and there are big people behind Gargan—the biggest."

Satan's green eyes narrowed.

"Bigger than you, Commissioner? Bigger than your job? Bigger than the millions of people you represent?" And very

1

slowly as he tapped a finger beneath his right armpit, "I don't know anybody that big. I never met anybody that big."

The Commissioner coughed and turned from the window.

"It's witnesses, Satan. Men who will swear to an alibi for Gargan. Yes, a man who'll swear to it the night you saw Gargan after the Greek was killed. It would be his word against yours on the stand."

"He must be a fine crook." Satan shot his chin forward. "I'd like to know his name, Commissioner."

"Glenwood E. Nostrom!" the Commissioner said suddenly. And as Satan's head jarred back, "Yes, a real leader in the party. No more honest man in the City of New York."

"Nostrom!" Detective Satan Hall said in a loud, dull voice. "That's right, Commissioner. I'd believe him against myself on the stand; but I can't believe he'd alibi Gargan."

"You've got to." The Commissioner nodded. "He told me himself. Yes, I said you were there, that you saw Gargan plainly—

*Another man stepped
from the coupé. "All right,
Jerry, let him have—"
That was all Satan heard.*

and the machine-gunner who was with him; and Nostrom said you must be mistaken."

"You believed him?"

The Commissioner said, "I had to believe him, and I've never known you to be wrong. I've got all your facts, Satan. There is something big stirring and Gargan is only the 'front.' He's the display window for all the crooks and racketeers and politicians in New York. He's the man who stands out, representing a power—a great power for criminals to see. A power which is eliminating racket leaders for the purpose of taking over those rackets. Gargan can't be touched because someone says 'No.' It's the biggest thing the city ever had to face."

"*Someone* has never said 'No' to me," Satan told him bluntly.

THE COMMISSIONER walked slowly across the room, laid a hand on Satan's shoulder.

"Law and order had a break, Satan, when in that twisted brain of yours was conceived a hatred for criminals. There are times when I'm frightened of you myself. Oh, not personally." The Commissioner's smile was a very tired one. "Afraid for you; for the people you serve. You've got a good head, Satan, a fine active brain. I'm not denying that. Others of us with less have gone a great deal further. But it isn't that brain the criminal fears. It's your direct and violent method of dealing with crime. They fear what they give—and death by violence!

"You have had to work straight from me because no one else could give you orders you'd listen to. I've appreciated you; maybe, in a small way, understood you—if anyone can understand the killer instinct. The killer hate in a man whose code, or rather, honesty, is the highest I have ever known. You can't be bribed. You can't be intimidated. You can't be forced. I've always stood behind you. I've defied the editorials: LEGALIZED MURDER, THE KILLER COP, and—"

"Rot!" Satan said suddenly, and the word had an odd sound coming from such grim lips. "I want the truth or nothing, Commissioner. The G-men have changed all that silly sentiment against killing the criminals rather than trying them. I knew then, just as I know now, that all the criminal ever feared was death. You were fighting for something then; fighting for me before the G-men knew what a gun looked like or that the smell of powder didn't burn the nostrils. Now the papers are behind the law of 'death by violence for criminals.' It's just that the other cops haven't my advantages. To work straight from the Commissioner of Police and be responsible only to him! That's every cop's dream of Utopia."

The Commissioner looked surprised. It was a very long speech for Satan and there was something very serious about it, something that the Commissioner understood, or thought that he did. But he said abruptly:

"There's an insidious thing in the city, Satan. Far beyond the ordinary rackets, as we understand them. Someone is taking control. Not trying to take control, understand, but actually taking it; leaving me helpless. It's crept into the Department. It was going on for months before I was fully aware of it. What influence can make men—big men, even prominent men—perjure themselves? I found the answer to that question."

"How," asked Satan, "is it in the Department? Did it have anything to do with the dropping of Inspector Carson, the retirement of Captain Rooney, Chief Inspector Burke's sudden departure, and the scandal concerning the policy racket and Lieutenant Stevens?"

"It did!" The Commissioner was emphatic. "I was forced into dropping Inspector Carson and retiring Captain Rooney. Yes, and into letting Burke go too. It had nothing to do with me. All three of them were able, fearless men. They were doing more to stamp out crime—especially rackets, in the city than—" The Commissioner paused. "I thought their records were perfect; but they had made mistakes in the past, things they have lived down since. Someone sent me information about them, and with it, the threat that if they did not leave the Force, exposure would follow. I laid that evidence before them, Satan; let them make their own decisions. They were not young men. They had wives and families. So—three of the deadliest enemies of the present day rackets were taken from me by the man, or men, who must be behind Gargan. Those notes with the evidence were signed 'The Other Man.'"

" 'The Other Murderer' is more like it," Satan said slowly. "It's simple enough, but it's the deadliest thing to fight. Extortion, blackmail, hunting things in men's pasts. It must be someone who knows the city well. These witnesses, these alibis for Gargan; all the same thing. Just a knowledge of criminal, social or business ruin, that is in the hands of 'The Other Man.' That's what makes men perjure themselves."

"Yes, Satan. But how deeply is the thing rooted, even in the Department? Who is behind the thing? Who is behind Gargan?"

"Someone for years associated with the rackets, with politics, with crime, must be behind Gargan. Good God, Commissioner!

You don't think, through some threat of exposure, Glenwood E. Nostrom was influenced. There could be nothing in his past life."

THE COMMISSIONER turned again and looked out the window.

"There are things in all our lives the exposure of which might make us ridiculous, small—or perhaps, even criminals. I often wonder, Satan, if there is any man who can stand before his glass and look back into his own soul and not find something hidden there. I know that I can see many mean and petty things in mine; things that I wish I could destroy, and try perhaps by future actions to destroy. Just as Inspector Carson and the others hope to destroy the past by the future good they did."

"But, Nostrom! Surely there could be nothing in his life that would cause him to perjure himself under the circumstances. Two little children were shot to death."

The Commissioner said, "Nostrom's testimony would acquit Gargan at the trial, if we could force through an indictment. Yes, Nostrom assured me that he would testify to Gargan's alibi."

Satan nodded slowly.

"I understand." He took his heavy thirty-eight from beneath his left arm-pit, turned it over in his hand. "The city wants vengeance, not justice. Is that it?"

The Commissioner tapped a pencil slowly on his desk.

"You put things rather bluntly, Satan," he said. "Gargan, of course, is only the 'front.' It's the man back of this thing we want. The man with such accurate knowledge of the city; of its rackets. The man who wants power. If you killed the front man, Gargan, another man would take his place. But that would give us time." He looked long and intently at those green eyes. "It would give me an opportunity to find out how deeply rooted this power is." And when Satan said nothing, "Don't misunderstand me, Satan. I'm not suggesting—anything."

Satan's lips twisted grimly. The Commissioner, who knew him well, didn't think it was a smile; and he was sure it wasn't after Satan said:

"We could make the front's existence very short and perhaps force the man behind the show into the way of a few bullets." And when the Commissioner shook his head, "Then what do you want of me? Why did you send for me? You laid me off Gargan, and now—"

"Now," the Commissioner's hand went on Satan's shoulder, "I need you. Tonight! I need you to save a man's life. I don't want anyone to know it's you; I don't want Gargan, or whoever is behind him, to know it's you. They're afraid of you, Satan. There's been influence, pressure—surprisingly strong pressure— brought to have me lay you off. There's to be a murder tonight. The chances are very good that the murderer will be Gargan. In saving this man's life you might—"

Satan's tongue moistened his lips.

"I understand," he said. "Just an accident that I was there. Just a mistake that Gargan took the dose of lead. I'd like Gargan to know I gave it to him, but I can let that go. Whose life is threatened?"

"Eddie Greer."

"That rat!" Satan spat out the words. "I'll wait until after he—"

"No!" The Commissioner cut in. "That rat has been selling me information. It's been worth the price. Gargan has discovered he's a stool-pigeon. Greer doesn't know this, but Gargan knows Greer's plans for tonight. Greer will leave the basement of—" and he gave a number in the Seventies. "He'll walk toward Central Park West, turn left at the corner. If he reaches it, he will deliver a message to a man; a man of mine who'll be waiting for him— Sergeant Peters. I don't know how it will happen, but Greer is to meet death sometime during that walk."

"Why doesn't Gargan go get him where he is? It sounds queer. Commissioner."

"Because Gargan doesn't know which house he'll come from. Gargan only knows that he'll appear on that street; that he'll be wearing a black felt hat, a tan raincoat with a large belt, and tan shoes. Remember. He'll leave those basement steps at one-forty-

five a.m. exactly. I don't want Greer killed, Satan. As for Gargan
or his associate or bodyguard. Razor Young, or whoever is set
for the job—I don't care what happens to them."

"Nor I." There was no doubt of Satan's agreement. "I have
never seen Young; that is, to know him as Young, but I wonder
if he was the other face in that car. The machine gunner who
actually got the children. If I'd been there a few minutes, even a
few seconds, earlier that night!" For a moment Satan's face was
a hideous mask.

The Commissioner spoke quickly.

"I know. I know. But never mind that night. Carry the hate
in your heart if you wish, Satan; but be sure—"

"I'll be sure tonight. If the death car comes down that street
I'll see that the driver winds it around a pole." And coming to
his feet, he said almost sheepishly: "Thanks for the job, Commissioner."

FOR THE first time the Commissioner actually smiled.
Satan was like that. There wasn't another man on the Force the
Commissioner would send alone on such a mission; more than
one man would give his plan away. Yet Satan thanked him for
the job; thanked him for it, and meant it.

Before he left, Satan turned; green eyes narrowed. He asked:

"Greer doesn't know—then who gave you the information
that he was to be killed tonight?"

The Commissioner hesitated. Wrinkles formed in his forehead, faded as his eyes narrowed.

"A woman!" he said suddenly. "Over the telephone. A voice
of refinement and culture. A frightened woman, Satan." And
before Satan could voice the question, "She telephoned from a
booth in a drug store on Fifty-seventh street. She called me at
my home. I tried to hold her on the wire, but by the time I got
my secretary to put a call through to Headquarters she was gone.
Her last words were: 'This may cost me my life, but I can't—can't
permit murder.'"

Satan stared at the Commissioner for a long time. First,

Glenwood Nostrom; then a woman of refinement. It didn't quite make sense. Or did it; a lot of sense that he couldn't understand? He didn't question the Commissioner further. It was twelve o'clock and Satan wished to be on the job before Gargan—or Gargan's men.

"Don't miss, tonight," said the Commissioner; and it was not with a feeling of Satan's marksmanship, nor even with a feeling of hatred toward Gargan. It was simply with a feeling that he couldn't afford to lose Satan.

Satan's only answer was twin balls of green fire peering through narrow lids, just before the door closed. Things had changed in the city; changed considerably. The Commissioner had sent him on a mission of death. Satan grinned evilly. He liked it. Yes, by God! he liked it a lot.

CHAPTER II

THE MAN IN THE
TAN RAINCOAT

IT WAS WELL before one o'clock when Satan crouched in the sunken areaway of the house next to the empty brownstone one in the Seventies. He didn't know just how the attack would take place. It might be a murder car spewing lead down the street, or a single man. Perhaps Gargan himself, for Eddie Greer was a rat. There wouldn't be much of a squawk about his death either. Yes, Gargan could pull that job; let the boys know he handled his own traitors, and strut his stuff some more along the Avenue.

Again, it might be just a ride. Screeching brakes, screaming tires, a huge car at the curb and the trembling Greer dragged into it to be dumped out dead in some vacant lot in the Bronx or up around Van Cortlandt Park.

Satan didn't have a bit of doubt he'd get the men who got Greer. Gargan or his men wouldn't be expecting any trouble. Satan would be just another figure moving in the darkness; a citizen of a great city who'd be glad that he was still alive after the shooting took place. No, there was nothing to worry about along that line. If Greer didn't know he was suspected, Gargan would feel pretty sure of himself.

Satan thought of Gargan too. No special hatred there. No more than that Gargan was the man he was after and that Gargan had shot down, or caused to be shot down, two children. But the racket was a good one; a new and greater power. Yet, the same old racket. The collection of money through fear! The poultry, the laundry, the building, the policy, and most despicable of all—the milk racket. Honest men paid tribute to the criminal to be allowed to make a living. Hundreds of millions of dollars each year. Crooked judges, crooked lawyers, crooked politicians. Criminals with long records dragged in today, turned loose tomorrow. Murderers, gunmen, big shots, who ran high priced cars and lived in penthouses. All lived at the expense of the honest citizen.

Satan wondered. He gripped his gun the tighter. Blackmail or extortion would not save the killer or killers tonight. No amount of fixing or intimidating or political influence ever took a bullet out of a man's stomach and put it back in Satan's gun. He grinned in the darkness. Then he shook his head. The Commissioner was right. This was the biggest thing that had ever struck the city. Someone was uncovering the weakness of strong men and was turning that weakness into his own strength. Yes, Satan could see how easily that someone could not only control the rackets, but shake the whole foundation of the city government itself.

Suppose Greer should get suspicions and not appear! But that couldn't happen. Satan tried to figure, out his plan of action. It was simply a death car and it came down the street facing Greer, then Greer would take the dose before Satan could go into action.

That the Commissioner wanted Greer to live didn't bother Satan. That was just the Commissioner's way. Greer had worked for him and he had promised him protection. Certainly, from now on Greer would not be much good to the Department. And if he wasn't much good to the Department he might just as well be dead. He was a rat. A tall muscular man who should have had—

SATAN'S THOUGHTS blanked. He stiffened, raised his head, ducked it almost at once. A figure was ascending the steps from the basement next door.

One-forty-five? Satan looked at his watch. Hell, no! The dial showed one-fifteen. The Commissioner had been wrong about the time or it wasn't Greer. But it was Greer! Satan saw him plainly as he stood on the next-to-the-top step, looking up and down the street. He didn't see the man's face, but he knew it was Greer. Tall—just about Satan's size—but more of a stoop to his shoulders when he walked, and more of a shuffle to that walk than Satan's heavy determined stride. But there was a black felt hat, the tan raincoat, and the large belt. Satan couldn't see the shoes then.

Satan opened his mouth to call softly, then decided against it. No one would know better than Greer just what time he was to start. Satan would be right behind him, holding close to the buildings; close to the shadows. It was going to be a hard job after all, because Greer was nervous; plainly very nervous.

Greer made a sudden decision. He stepped quickly up that final step, turned, and walking in the opposite direction of Central Park West, started toward Broadway.

Satan was up those steps and after Greer, had a hand on a shoulder; on a shoulder that sagged as the man's knees gave and Satan, half supporting him, said:

"Easy, Greer. It's Hall—Detective Hall." And clapping a hand across the man's mouth, "I didn't come to rub you out."

Satan saw the man's face there in the darkness. White; a cream colored sort of white, with blotches of yellow in it. He saw the man's lips moving too—just moving. No words came. Little drops of saliva formed on those lips.

Satan half carried, half supported the trembling, terror stricken Eddie Greer back to that basement, down those steps. He had some difficulty in locating the key in Eddie's pocket but he finally found it, spun it in the lock and pushed Greer through the door.

Inside, Greer recovered somewhat. At least, he was able to walk, able to talk too; mumbling incoherent words. There was a strong smell of liquor when Greer led Satan into a room in which the shades were so tightly drawn that no light could show outside.

It was Satan who found the light button and pressed it. But it was Greer who stumbled across the room, tore open the door of a small cupboard, tried twice to pour himself a drink with shaking fingers, and finally put the bottle to his lips.

"So that's how it is!" Satan said. "You've been hitting the muscilage and it played you false." He walked across the room, took the bottle from Greer, placed it back in the cabinet. "There isn't enough courage in a case of it to help you, Greer. You've got a date tonight. You leave here at one-forty-five sharp. Trying to run out on the Commissioner and Sergeant Peters?"

"No, no." Greer tore at the collar of his shirt. "It isn't that; isn't that at all. They're going to kill me tonight. I know. I know! I saw it in Gargan's eyes, heard it in his voice." He clutched Satan's arm. "You don't know Gargan, Satan. You never met him. He kills for pleasure, like—like—" and the "like you do, Satan!" died on Eddie Greer's lips. He wasn't drunk enough to say that, wasn't terror stricken enough either. He went on. "He gripped my shoulder, Gargan did. Gripped it tightly, said, 'We like you, Eddie. We're going to take care of you, Eddie. Aren't we, Young? Maybe a month from now; maybe tonight.'"

Satan's green eyes widened.

"There wasn't any harm in that. It's just your conscience, Eddie." And seeing nothing incongruous in his following words, he continued, "Buck up, Eddie. Be a man! You've got nothing to worry you. All rats feel like that."

GREER DID buck up. He braced his feet, grew sullen, said:

"I'm not going. I tell you I won't go." And seeing Satan's eyes "They're going to kill me, and you—you—" His voice raised now.

"You're here to get them for murder—my murder. You know too."

Satan said, "I'm here to protect you. There's no danger, Eddie; none at all." And seeing the terror creeping back into the blood-shot eyes, he lied easily. "I've done it before, Eddie; followed you for your own protection. There's nothing wrong tonight."

Greer laughed. It was not a pleasant laugh, not even an

hysterical laugh; more like the growl of a cornered animal. He leaned upon the urn painted table, looked at the plain kitchen chair beside it, half glanced toward the open drawer of that table. He wet his lips, looked at the cupboard.

"I won't go. You'll have to drag me screaming down the street. I've been drinking but I know what I'm doing, what you're doing." And suddenly. "Of course it was the woman. She telephoned me, warned me to skip town." And raising his voice, "That's right; that's it! It was the woman."

Satan took a step forward. His eyes narrowed, his hand stretched toward Greer's shoulder, hung a moment in the air and dropped to his side. He remembered the Commissioner's words—"the cultured, refined voice." He said simply, and as if with knowledge:

"What of it?"

"What of it?" Eddie straightened, his eyes widened. "If Gargan knew, he'd kill her. She ain't a bad dame, Satan, and filthy with money. She heard them talking and told me to leave town. She likes me maybe." Greer shook his head, ran a hand through his hair. "She's been paying through the nose, that's why she still lives. But she's too bright for a dame with dough; too wise. Gargan would have killed her if it wasn't for money,"

Satan said cheerfully, "Don't we all, Eddie? Where is she keeping herself now?"

"Why, at the same—the same—" Eddie steadied himself, gripped the table. His eyes rolled, grew steady as he looked at Satan. "Gripes!" he said. "It wasn't the dame then. It— You don't know her."

"Of course I know her." Satan took another look at his watch; time was passing. "Where does she live, Eddie?"

"Ask Gargan." Eddie drew away from the outstretched hand. "He'll be seeing her. I—I—" And drawing back and his voice going shrill, "She's just a dame, just a skirt. No, no. I ain't going, Satan. I ain't going!"

Eddie Greer was sober enough now. Sober enough to know

that he had made a mistake. Sober enough to know that when Satan went on a job he completed that job.

Satan moved toward him.

Eddie Greer went cold. Great beads of perspiration broke out on his forehead. The alcohol streamed down his face disguised as sweat, sobering him, leaving him broken, trembling more now as he looked into those green eyes. It must have been the thing in those eyes that got Greer; certainly not the voice, for Satan said simply:

"You're going through with it tonight, Eddie; as planned."

EDDIE GREER'S dull mind flashed a mental picture; a crystal clear picture. He would precede Satan down that street, a gun covering his back; a gun held in the hand of a man who killed. Yes, Greer thought, who killed for the very pleasure of it. And that gun would be forcing him straight into other guns; the guns of Dan Gargan or his boys. That was right. Satan wanted Gargan; wanted him for murder. And he planned to get him for murder; for the murder of Eddie Greer.

Eddie dove straight for that open drawer and the grip end of the gun he could just see. It wasn't courage that drove him to that gun; courage neither in nor out of a bottle. It was desperate terror. A rat cornered, fighting for his life. For he saw death; saw it sure and certain in that sudden forward lunge of Satan. The outstretched hands; the empty hands, with long strong fingers that clawed toward his throat. It wasn't courage. Eddie Greer didn't know what he was doing when he clutched at that gun, tore it from the drawer and swung.

He hadn't seen Satan's right hand lower. He hadn't seen that hand go in and out and up. Nor did he see Satan hesitate that split second that his finger half tightened on the trigger. Eddie Greer saw nothing of that. He only knew that he turned and that something struck him. Just a black shadow in the air! Then darkness as Satan's gun crashed against his head.

Eddie Greer hit the floor pretty hard. He wasn't dead. Satan was sure of that as he stood over him. But he was sure of something else when he knelt beside him. Eddie Greer would never leave that house at one-forty-five exactly and walk toward Central Park West.

Satan knew that as he came to his feet. Then his green eyes widened. He stared a long time at the crumpled man. He stared at the length of his body, the width of his shoulders. He stared at the black hat, the tan coat, the big belt, even at the tan shoes.

He nodded his head very seriously. Eddie Greer was about his size and weight. All that was needed in the darkness of that street was stooped shoulders and shuffling steps. And Satan could supply both of them since Eddie could supply the rest.

Satan's lips set grimly, parted. His eyes flashed. He was wrong after all. As far as Gargan was concerned, Eddie Greer would walk the street that night.

A different Eddie Greer. An Eddie Greer who carried death in both hands; a death that he knew how to use—would use.

A desperate chance on Satan's part? Maybe. But Satan's eyes didn't show that, nor did his lips show that. The boys were coming in for a bit of a surprise! Satan rather enjoyed the change. If things broke right that night, there wouldn't be any Dan Gargan.

At exactly one-forty-five a stoop-shouldered figure, wearing a black hat, a tan rain-coat with a big belt mounted the steps from the basement of the house in the Seventies and turned toward Central Park West. The shuffling movement of the man's feet was not entirely assumed, for the shoes were a light tan and slightly too large for the wearer. All was dark on the basement floor of the house behind. All was silent too. The lone figure who lay so close to the table did not move.

Slowly Satan shuffled down that street. The scene changed slightly. Far down the block, before brownstone fronts gave place to the towering stone sides of an apartment hotel, a small coupé was parked. There were no lights on it. It was as if a careless or a saving motorist had left it so.

SATAN DIDN'T turn his head as he approached that coupé.

He didn't look back over his shoulder. No car was following him; none was approaching him. No pedestrians were on that street.

Satan tried to think things out. His life might depend upon that. The death of Gargan might depend upon that. And it wasn't of his own life that he was thinking now.

Certainly the attack, if there was to he one, should take place before he reached Central Park West. That was a prominent street. People would be passing along it, cars would be flashing by. A blast-out didn't seem to be the solution to Satan now. Eddie Greer didn't call for such action. Any gunman could do the job easily enough. No. The attack should take place just about where that coupé was parked. Just about? Well—maybe exactly where that coupé was parked.

Where the area ways leading to the basements of houses could easily hide a killer, so could the coupé. But the coupé had an advantage over the area-ways. A coupé can move away and carry a killer with it. An areaway must stay where it is and the killer leave as best he can.

Satan moved both his hands beneath the tan coat. They remained there. He didn't know the play. But he did know that until he reached that coupé the attack could come only from one direction. From the brownstone houses. When he reached that coupé— And he did reach it. That is, he was almost beside it when the door opened and a man slid out.

There was nothing suspicious about the man's movements. Indeed, his back was toward Satan and be was slowly turning his head; slowly turning his body. His right hand was across his chest. Satan knew that from the position of his elbow.

Was this just a late home comer or was this the blow-off? Satan didn't know; wasn't sure. He liked to think that it was the blow-off and that the man was Gargan. But the man wasn't Gargan. The face was a strange one. Not an evil one either. Hard, determined, yet with a sort of cheapness about it.

"Got a match, buddy?" The man gripped Satan's left arm just as Satan was squarely alongside the coupé. Then the man swung, and Satan saw the gun; saw the gun as feet beat lightly on the sidewalk. Another man stepped from an areaway, shoved a gun against Satan's side and spoke.

"We want you to know, rat." The newcomer jeered. "We want the whole mob to know-cops and regular guys—to know how Gargan pays off squealers. All right, Jerry; let him have—"

That was all Satan heard. Two shots rang out as one. Two more! The man who had stepped from the coupé seemed to jump upward. His right hand shot straight into the air. His gun exploded once, as if he fired in salute. Then the second slug tore a hole in his chest and threw him back against the coupé, onto the sidewalk. He never would move.

The man at Satan's right never finished his words. His body slumped against Satan, jarred erect, then slumped forward again. But this time Satan was not there. He had stepped back.

The gunman's knees gave. He tried to turn his body but only half succeeded. His right hand waved a gun frantically. His left hand clawed at the hole in his chest.

SATAN WAITED, uncrossed his arms from beneath the raincoat where the two burnt holes showed plainly. His hands appeared, twin guns flashed black against the white of bent fingers. His lips pasted, trembled slightly. Points of green: watched the twisting man. Watched him stagger once, fall to his knees, try to rise, hang so a moment, his body weaving in and out.

Windows were going up. A woman screamed, then another. A police whistle shrilled, a siren screeched, feet beat down the block toward him. And Satan still watched the man on the sidewalk.

Finally the man swung his head directly toward Satan. His eyes were moist, uncertain. Then they stared; stared as Satan gasped in astonishment.

"Hell! You're not Gargan; you're—you're—" Satan stepped forward as the kneeling killer raised his gun. It was in Satan's mind to kick the gun from the man's hand. But he didn't.

He simply finished his sentence. "You're Razor Young, child killer." Then he shot the gaping gunman right in the center of his open mouth.

It was then that Sergeant Peters was upon him. He spoke rapidly.

"Satan!" Peters gasped. "I saw it; saw you half raise your foot and then—then—did you have to kill him?"

"No, no," said Satan very slowly, "I didn't have to kill him, nor did he have to kill those two children when the Greek went out. It's your party, Peters. Keep your mouth closed about me until you talk to the Commissioner. Gargan and his boys will think Eddie Greer did it."

Sergeant Peters stretched out a hand and clutched Satan by the arm, then dropped his hand almost at once. He knew, as every cop on the Force knew, from the newest rookie to the oldest inspector, that Detective Satan Hall didn't like hands on him. But Peters said:

"Did-did he recognize you before—before he died?"

And Satan laughed. At least, a queer gurgling sound came from thin lips and Peters thought it was a laugh, or meant for a laugh.

Satan said, "If he didn't recognize me, Sergeant, there will be a lot of boys in hell who'll fear the coming of Eddie Greer." He pushed the dead head, with the glaring sightless eyes of Razor Young, aside with his foot to make room for himself to pass. "I didn't have to do that either, Sergeant," he added. There was no irony in his voice; just a peculiar sort of vehemence.

A patrol car roared down the block. Satan spun quickly, passed into an alley beside a house, hurried down the length of it, crossed the yard behind, and hopping a fence made his way to the street beyond.

A stranger would have marked him for a late merrymaker returning home, for he was humming softly to himself. But then, a stranger would not have seen his face nor the two holes in the burnt raincoat that was Eddie Greer's.

CHAPTER III

NO SEX IN MURDER

DAN GARGAN SAT in his private office at the Café Wellington. He was a tall, broad-shouldered man. If he rose from his chair, picked up a pen or even lifted his hat from a rack, he did it in a sudden quick movement. With a gun, Dan Gargan was the same active man. He spoke now, and his words tumbled out as fast as he could speak them. He said to the quiet, sharp-faced lawyer:

"Listen, Maxie. You're the big mouthpiece when the jury turns a man loose or the judge knuckles down, but to me you're just another shyster with a yen for cash. The telephone call was baloney then. You couldn't fix it; couldn't dump an ordinary dick off the Force."

Maxie Rosen played for a moment with his glasses before he placed them on his nose. He both admired Dan Gargan and was amused by him. That is, he was amused when the young racketeer didn't fly off the handle and want to fix things in the only way his kind knew. There was nothing finished or polished about Dan Gargan. That is, in a mental way. Outside— well, perhaps if money accounted for the final decision, Dan was the best dressed man on the Avenue.

Maxie Rosen smiled, waited, finally said:

"There was nothing I could do for the moment. You misunderstand politics and the workings of a great machine of a city this size. You must sit tight, learn patience and wait—"

Dan Gargan laughed.

"I never wait," he said simply. "You brought me on here to give you action. You got it from the day I stepped off the train at the Grand Central Station. I've been giving it to you ever since. Bentz is out. Charlie Halpin is out. The big lad, the Greek, is gone. I've split things wide open. The city is ready to dump the treasury into—" He straightened suddenly, looked defiant. "Into my hands."

"Into *your* hands," Maxie Rosen said very softly, and there was only the slightest hint of a question in his voice. "You mean, the 'Other Man's' hands."

"Maybe. Maybe." Gargan's voice was doubtful. "The 'Other Man' isn't so bad. But it's the truth, Maxie. I don't like, never did like this melodrama stuff. This 'Master Mind of Crime,' the 'Power Behind the Throne.' The unknown lad who sends messages through you. No—I don't like it."

"You liked it," the lawyer said slowly, "when I made you the offer. You've had money. You've had men; the best in the city. The 'Other Man' looked you up, picked you as the right one to clean out the small fry and put things in order for him—for us. That took cash. You didn't have that, Dan. That took brains. You didn't have that either, Dan. That took knowledge of the workings of the city; of politics, crime. It took years of watching and studying and being closely associated with the right people. You came in as a stranger, Dan, and simply obeyed orders." And for a moment Rosen's voice became even lower and softer, with perhaps a warning in it. "And will continue to obey orders."

Gargan's wiry body swung quickly, his mouth snapped open, but the words didn't come. Dark smoldering eyes seemed to lose their fire, but not their sharpness. When he did speak, he said:

"That's right. That's right, Maxie. You've got a head; a head for such things." And in a voice that was almost pleading; or at least, anxious, "This 'Other Man' guy! He isn't on the ground, can't see the opportunities."

MAXIE NODDED and smiled before he shook his head.

"You're young, Dan. You're impulsive. But you've got the

stuff. The 'Other Man' was right." And more seriously, "But you've worked a little too fast. The 'Other Man' would have been glad to have given you a year, even more for the job; and you've been here only a little over six months." A moment's hesitation. "There were a few who died suddenly, though they were not on the list the "Other Man' gave you."

Dan Gargan dismissed the complaint with a deprecating shrug.

"Killing is a business," he explained. "The boys who took the dose would have made trouble later. You wanted my name well known, and it is. You've got brains, Maxie, but any punk mouth-piece could have sprung me if I dragged in."

"But," said Maxie Rosen, "you had to know where to be and I had to know who'd say you were there. Men with names that meant something. A good alibi! That's why you have never seen the inside of a jail here in the city."

"Or any other city." Dan Gargan laughed. "I'm not complain-ing, Maxie. You know your stuff. But I've always kept a little 'fall money.' I'd buy my own alibis if I didn't have you to fix it."

"And that means—?" asked Maxie.

"Nothing. Nothing." Gargan crossed the room and ran his hand through Maxie's falling hair. "Just don't over-rate your own importance. You're just the go-between for me and the 'Other Man'. It's his head talking through your mouth. I've learned things. You were once a big criminal lawyer, but you're washed up. You've had your day. I'm coming." Gargan thought a moment. "Yes, I'm coming. Remember that! It may be worth something to you!"

"I'll remember it." Maxie Rosen nodded. "Now for the busi-ness of the moment. Detective Satan Hall!"

"Hall—Hall. Satan Hall." Gargan shot out the words. "I've heard about him ever since I've been here. You and half the lads along the Avenue. One dick. One common flat-foot who has had some luck with a gun. What does he know? Why all this waiting until you can gather enough influence to get him tossed from the Force? That's what you were working on; that's what was supposed to be straightened out a week ago. And you did nothing!" And seeing the glint in those colorless eyes of the lawyer, "So that's how it is. You've come to me to fix it, eh?"

Maxie nodded.

"I'm afraid that's it. Yes, I'm afraid you'll have to fix Mr. Detective Satan Hall." A long moment of silence. "Do you think you'll like that job?"

Gargan went back to the big desk and sat down.

"This Satan's a killer, eh? A cop that can't be bought. A cop who'll take a chance and shoot it out with any man who draws a gun?"

Rosen shook his head.

"Just shoots, Dan. As you might shoot, as any man you might hire would shoot. Yep, that's right." Maxie nodded at the surprised look in Gargan's eyes. "He's just a killer. The Killer Cop."

"You mean, he wouldn't—doesn't give a man a chance? Goes in for—for murder?"

Maxie Rosen smacked his lips.

"That's correct, Gargan. If he wasn't a cop, they'd call it murder."

GARGAN SET his lips tightly. "Just what do you mean—that I'll have to fix Detective Satan Hall?"

"Why—" Maxie Rosen let his eyebrows go up, "you told me a month ago that would be the easiest solution to the job. You told me you had a man from Philly—Chopper Regan. A man who would blast out Satan and—"

"You told me to wait; that things would be fixed. Sure, I remember. I brought this lad from Philly on and you wouldn't have it. The Other Man wouldn't have it."

"That's right." Rosen was very serious. "But things have changed since then. You see, Satan's got all your 'action,' as you put it; but he hasn't your weakness. I mean—women."

"Women!" Dan Gargan grinned. "I can take them or leave them alone."

"I was thinking of one woman. Elsie Stone!"

"Oh—her!" Gargan turned away, half whistled a tune. "I was thinking of having her take me around a bit. Right people! It's an 'in.'"

"It's an 'out,'" Maxie Rosen snapped. "And you have taken her around. And what's more, you have shaken her down." Maxie Rosen took out a little book, turned the pages slowly, paused, put his eyes on Dan Gargan. "You had her downstairs here twice, once at the Gold Room of the Terrace Garden. And twice you waited outside her bank while she cashed large checks."

Dan Gargan came to his feet. His fist pounded on the desk. He snapped out the words viciously.

"So you've had a tail on me. I have a damned good mind to smack all your teeth down your throat, you dirty little—" He paused, looked shrewdly at Maxie, said sullenly, "Well—what of it?"

Rosen closed his book, held it in his hand a moment, then put it in his pocket.

"The Other Man," he said slowly, "doesn't like it. He has gathered together certain names, certain information. Things to hold over people's heads. Respectable people, Gargan, like Glenwood Nostrom, who is now saving you from the electric chair. Like Mrs. Elsie Stone; wealthy, social leaders. They are the havens for men like you; for friends and leaders of the Other Man, who are in distress. Alibis that are respected so much that the police will not dare to make an arrest."

Maxie shrugged his shoulders. "Of course, if they forced a trial we could not use the same people over and over. When Elsie Stone is no longer an ace-in-the-hole, a means of protection, then the Other Man will make the shakedown; make it himself. And it will not be in the form of petty larceny."

"Hell!" Dan Gargan shook his shoulders. "I just let her think

I was trying to help her buy back the letters. It was soft money. I hated to see Eddie Greer grabbing it off."

Maxie nodded very slowly.

"The Other Man hated to see Greer grabbing it off too. That's one reason you had your orders to kill him."

"One! One reason!" Dan Gargan looked at the lawyer shrewdly. "Greer's a rat, and he's nosey. He's been trying to find out who the Other Man is."

"That's right," Maxie said solemnly. "A man who works for the Other Man is very foolish to try and find out who he is."

"Why?" Gargan demanded.

"Because it would be the last things he ever did find out."

DAN GARGAN'S mouth snapped open, hung so, then closed. He did not think it advisable to utter the hasty and bragging words that were on his lips. He finally did say:

"So I'm not to see the Stone woman any more."

"On the contrary," said Maxie Rosen, "the woman, who was an asset, has become: a liability. If it was you bleeding her or Greer bleeding her, I don't know. But she's become slightly defiant. I am afraid she has misunderstood the visits I have made in her interest. And I'm afraid of something else, Dan. I'm afraid she knows too much to live."

"With all her dough, you—you want her knocked off?"

"I think," said Maxie very slowly, "that she'll be worth only money now. After that, you wouldn't mind killing a woman, Dan?"

"Me? Me?" Dan's face mirrored surprise. Not at the foulness of the crime but at the indifference of Maxie Rosen. "Me? Hell, no!" he finally said. "There's no sex in killing. Is it a quick job, Maxie?"

"No, no." Maxie settled his eyes on the ceiling. "I must have the money first, if possible." And seeing the greed in Gargan's eyes, "But the money is only secondary. You haven't any vision, Dan. Don't you see what the Other Man is trying to accomplish? Control of the entire city. And you are to lead it, Dan; be the head of the entire organization."

"Figurehead?"

"Active head." Maxie went on, a brightness in his eyes. "Even the law is with us. The investigation is driving men who have long controlled things to cover. You and your boys are driving the more daring and less brainy out with lead. That's it, Gargan. Human knowledge and brute force working together. That combination cannot be beaten. Because the human knowledge protects the brute force from legal retribution. Don't you see? Don't you understand? It's hunting into men's pasts, finding the flaw in the armor of respectability with which our bankers, our politicians, our public office holders, and even our great private citizens clothe themselves.

"All strong men have a weakness. It is those weaknesses that the Other Man finds—and discloses if these men will not serve him. We must find what human agency has seared each soul. So did we drive from the Force such menaces to our power as Chief Inspector Burke, Captain Rooney, and Lieutenant Stevens." A long pause. "They were fools. If they had listened to reason they might have made huge fortunes, but they would not be bribed. But all public servants are not so foolish and many whose pasts were unsavory have listened to reason and—"

Dan Gargan yawned.

"I've heard all that," he said. "It's hot stuff, but not up my alley. You fix. I strike. The Other Man is clearing the way in great shape. Every obstacle is going."

"Every obstacle but one," Maxie Rosen said. "And that one obstacle is the greatest possible menace to our success. Just a single man. Neither an influence nor a power. Nothing in his past but the dead bodies of men he hated and the city feared. He has no past that can be touched. His murders are legal murders. We waited too long to strike through influence, political pressure. The papers are already back of him. He needs no knowledge, has no interest in evidence, respects no alibis. He simply kills, and no amount of influence can help the dead."

"You mean—"

"I mean the only man or machine or organization that the Other Man fears. I mean Satan Hall. He's got to die, Gargan— *got to die.*"

"Sure! Sure!" Gargan looked at Maxie Rosen as if he doubted the sanity of the man. He couldn't understand the fear of a single "cop" whom he had never met; had never even seen since he came to the city. His shoulders shrugged; he said almost indifferently:

"It's nothing to me, Maxie. If you want him dead I'll lay him out deader than hell for you. The trouble with the boys here is—this cop has their numbers; he puts the sign on them. Well, tell the Other Man that I come from Chi, where they like them tough."

DAN GARGAN stood for a long time after Rosen had left. Once or twice he rubbed his chin. He wasn't afraid. He had never known fear in his life. He wasn't thinking so much of the woman, or even of Satan Hall. He was thinking of Maxie Rosen, and if the word "respect" was not in his mind, the meaning of it was. Yes, he had never thought so much of Maxie before.

He thought too of the Other Man and thought that perhaps the unknown, with the fancy moniker which struck him as silly, knew a great deal. Not only when he arranged to hook Gargan up with his racket, but when he made Maxie the go-between. And he thought too that Maxie might not be a bad man to know better—a hell of a lot better.

Yes, Maxie was a bright lad; so was the Other Man. Gargan nodded his understanding. The Other Man was well protected. Gargan didn't have any idea who he might be. Maxie Rosen was well protected too. No one knew that Maxie brought him instructions. Gargan chewed on his lip. The word, of course, was "orders," but he didn't like the sound of that.

It was clever, but Gargan understood the protection it

afforded both Maxie Rosen and this unknown Other Man. Damn it! He was made to see so many different men in the course of a day—some even well known men—that no one could even hazard a guess as to whom he was associated with. Well, what of it? That might be their way of doing business; their way of getting protection.

He rubbed his hand across his face. Some day he mightn't need that advice. Some day, when he knew his way around better, he too might find it impossible to remember having received "information" from the Other Man.

If they wanted Satan rubbed out, so did he. Most of Gargan's enemies were dead, and his axiom was that dead enemies were good friends. Satan Hall, eh? The tough dick. Well, he had been in the city for six months, made his name known from Brooklyn to the Bronx. Where had this Commissioner's pet been during that time? He had been where all of them had been—skulking up a back alley. He'd give his right arm to meet Satan face to face. No, there wasn't a dick on the Force who wanted any part of Dan Gargan.

CHAPTER IV

BLACKMAIL

DAN GARGAN CLIMBED from behind the wheel of his big expensive car and ran easily up the steps of the pretentious stone dwelling. He leaned against the bell, stepped back, and slipping his right hand beneath his left armpit straightened out his shoulder holster. He frowned slightly. He liked the new gun harness and he didn't like it. It was awkward when he moved around quickly, but it was handy—damned handy. And that was important to a man who enjoyed life.

The butler who opened the door a crack was more shocked than surprised at the force which drove the great wooden door in, sliding him across the polished floor with it.

"Mrs. Stone is not receiving tonight," he said, and his stiffness was less pronounced because of the quickness with which he got the words out.

"She's receiving me." Dan Gargan crossed to the stairs, turned. "In the sitting room upstairs, Albert? Well— yes or no?" He advanced two or three steps menacingly.

"Yes," said the butler. "In the sitting room upstairs."

He followed Gargan to the stairs and part way up them. The whole thing puzzled him. He didn't know why he was told to keep Mr. Gargan out, yet to admit him if he seemed forcible. The butler nodded his head. Certainly he had been forcible. He wished Mrs. Stone would be done with the man and call for the police. Even in America, with its loose social habits, Mr. Gargan by no stretch of the social standings could be called "people."

Dan Gargan reached the upper hall, turned right as one familiar with the house, stopped by the nursery door and looked in at the sleeping head. He could see a curly tousled head and grinned his appreciation. Kids like that were a help in his business. It made people soft—especially women.

Elsie Stone, known in the phone book and to her more formal social friends as Mrs. Robinson E. Stone, was standing in the center of the sitting room, facing the door. Her right hand was gripped tightly at her side, her left hand against her chest. She was a small delicate young woman-hardly more than a girl, with deep rings beneath her listless blue eyes. She spoke the very moment Gargan entered the room.

"I'm not going to give you any more money. I am through paying."

Gargan's broad generous smile was wiped off his face as if a rag was drawn across it.

"Okay, sister." He kicked the door closed with his foot. "We understand each other then. Is that the racket?"

"I don't know if you understand me or not." The woman's chin raised slightly as she forced out the words. "But I understand you."

"Good!" said Gargan. "So I don't have to talk like a friend of the family any more. Get your things on and we'll see the town. I've got words that will interest you,"

"You can't interest me." She closed the fingers of the hand at her side. She felt that they were trembling. She didn't want him to see that.

"No?" Gargan let his eyes rest steadily on her. She wasn't bad tricks. Just a little pale. Washed out from worry. "But your husband might be interested in those two letters. I've been trying to buy them for you." He made no attempt to hide the sneer on his lips. "Today I got a look at them. You must have been some baby when this lad, Bert, took you to Virginia. Your husband can thank me you're behaving yourself this time while he's away."

THE WOMAN swayed slightly. But she said, "That's in the past. That's forgotten."

"Now, is that nice? What'll Bert think? No romance in your heart. Just a little trip, a couple of letters of fond memory—and you forget him. Bert wanted to forget too, but we—they put the screws on him for a crooked paving job and he hollered 'Uncle' and delivered your letters. Hot stuff!"

The woman said, "I didn't know I loved—loved my husband then. And I didn't have my—my baby. Give them to me; give me the letters! I'll pay. I'll pay what I can."

"The baby! Not a bad looking kid." Gargan nodded. "He'll be proud of his mother in years to come if his old man keeps the newspaper clipping of the divorce as a souvenir. Tough on the kid, Elsie." He walked over, put a hand on her shoulder. She shuddered slightly. "Haven't been talking, have you?" He grabbed her suddenly by the shoulders, peered closely into her face. "Didn't listen to anything the other night?" And pushing her roughly from him, "That rat, Greer, with his oily hair and his oilier tongue! Well, what do you say? You read your papers. He shot two men to death last night."

"No, no!" Both her hands went to her mouth now. "No, he couldn't."

"That's what all the boys thought—that he couldn't. But he did. It was just down the block from here. I told you he wouldn't bother you any more."

"You were going to have him killed—have him killed! I knew that. Oh, God! I knew that. Why don't you leave me? Why don't you leave me alone? I won't go with you. I won't go out with you again. The shame of it!"

Gargan raised his right hand, flipped the back of it suddenly forward. It struck her across the mouth. She staggered slightly, stepped back. He followed her. She reached out her right hand, felt along the wall, found the push button that would summon a servant, placed a finger upon it, swung toward Gargan.

"They have orders downstairs to ring for the police if I press this button. If—if—"

"Press it!" Gargan sneered. "Press it, and I'll let you tell the police your story." He was close to her again now, and this time his flipping fingers were more a push; knocked her back against the window sill, away from the bell she did not press—dared not press. She was confused, bewildered. No man had ever struck her before.

Gargan was stung by the look in her eyes—not of fury or of hate, not even of fear. Just a loathing. He said: "What did you tell Greer? Come on, talk!" He raised his hand again, and when she did not shrink, only stood there, "Shall I go in and smack the kid? Come on!" He took her by the arm, dragged her toward the door.

It wasn't real; it wasn't true. It was a horrible-dream. She'd wake up and find him gone and Robinson, her husband, back. God, how had she become mixed up in anything like this? A fit of jealousy, of self pity; the imaginary neglected wife. Now—now—a few days, a few hours even of folly, and—

She held back. She tried to talk but she could not speak. Her baby! Yes, she knew. This man would strike the baby just as he had struck her. She said:

"Greer telephoned me. He wanted money. He was like you; but I couldn't see him die. I—I told him not to come, to go away, to— Don't you see? I wanted him not to come."

"That's a lie. You thought he'd get the letters." Gargan gripped her arm tightly and she cried out. He clapped a hand across her mouth, a few flicks of blood stuck to his fingers when he drew his hand away. "All right, we'll see how the kid likes it."

"No, no! I'll tell the police. I'll— What do you want to know? Don't—don't go near him. Don't! Don't!" She set her heels into the floor.

"Rosen!" Gargan said. "You told him you paid me. You told him, didn't you?" He bent back her arm, but he didn't need to.

She said, "Yes, I told him. He wanted to know." And suddenly, as if things cleared, "Is he like you, too; just—just a common blackmailer, who preys on women?"

And this time Gargan brought his hand up—raised it. She watched it, her face puzzled, bewildered. Watched it turn from a hand into a fist. Waited for it to hit her.

Then she didn't watch it any longer. She was looking over Gargan's shoulder, looking at a door that had silently opened and the figure that stood there.

That face; that diabolical face! She screamed; a low smothered sort of cry. Gargan dropped his hand, swung. Then his hand jerked up again, under his left armpit. The man in the doorway spoke.

"Dan Gargan, eh? It would be quite a coincidence if our first meeting was our last."

And Gargan knew; knew though he had never seen the man in the doorway before in his life. Knew just as well as if the man had handed him a card with his name engraved upon it. He was facing the Other Man's greatest menace—Detective Satan Hall.

CHAPTER V

ON THE STAIRS

DAN GARGAN DIDN'T have to ask himself why the name "Satan." It was there in every feature, every line; right to the V shape of the entire head. Sinister, cruel lips! He could see the ears, too, tapering. Even the jet black hair seemed to creep down the forehead, to come to that V point—come naturally to it.

Dan Gargan knew that the eyes slanted and that they were green. But it was the thing behind those eyes, a sinister something that he had never seen in a man's eyes before. It was that something that made him drop the hand that he had raised to his left arm-pit as the door clicked closed.

Gargan couldn't make himself believe he was looking at a cop. A cop who gave you lip or threatened to drag you in or touched you for a few grand for an imaginary benefit. No, Dan Gargan was looking into the eyes of a killer and he knew it.

Satan didn't move and he didn't speak.

Gargan let his tongue run around inside his mouth, dropped his eyes down Satan's arm to the long, muscular looking fingers. Fingers that might be quick on a trigger. But those fingers didn't hold a gun. Those white hands were empty, absolutely empty. Gargan's eyes raised to Satan's face again, and his hand remained at his side.

Evil was in that face; a malignant sort of hate.

Gargan jerked his body slightly, blinked his eyes. His voice sounded false when he spoke; rang tinny to his own ears. But his words were clear enough. He said:

"What do you want, copper? You can't bust in on me like this." And forcing the words out, though he knew they were better unsaid, "I've killed men for less."

"Sure! Sure!" Satan took five slow steps forward, until he was directly facing Gargan. "There was Bentz and the Greek, and a couple of others. The department owes you a vote of thanks for that." And when Gargan grinned, "Then there were the children; innocent kids playing in the street. Two of them died."

"Now isn't that just too bad." Gargan was fast becoming himself again, and now he was resentful that for a moment he had been shaken. Shaken by a mask; a mask of Satan stamped permanently upon a human face. He went on.

"People have got to die, you know. You didn't come here to break my heart!" And when Satan just looked at him, "It took you a long time to come around. There's been others more interested. They ain't working the same jobs now. Cops that talk out of turn—either inspectors or first grade detectives—have got to learn their lesson. You're not talking to a common hood now. I know my way around. I've heard about you, Hall. You never stepped on my toes before. Your tin badge and your ugly face doesn't give you the right to bust into a private house; Mrs. Stone's house. I think you've stepped into something this time. I think you've put the skids under yourself." And turning to the woman, "Mrs. Stone, this is a police detective. Do you wish to make a complaint?"

"There's no complaint," she said slowly.

Satan's lips parted but his eyes remained hard and cold. He spoke to Gargan. "I came to see Mrs. Stone. The butler let me in, told me where she was and I came up. Tell that one to your smart friends."

"She doesn't want to see you." Gargan straightened, tried to play the gentleman. "You have no right here. Mrs. Stone can make trouble for you."

"Mrs. Stone has enough trouble of her own." Satan looked directly at the woman, said to her, "I want to talk to you alone."

"You can't." Gargan stepped between Satan and the woman.

GARGAN HARDLY saw the hand move until he felt it strike his shoulder, and though he was a powerful man it drove him hard against the wall. His lips quivered slightly, his eyes narrowed, his right hand raised, went under his coat. Satan's hands were empty, Satan wasn't even looking at him; he was staring at the woman. Self-defense! Satan had come into the house; the woman had seen the blow. Besides, there were her letters. They'd serve a good purpose now. She'd make a good witness on the stand. His hand crept higher up, and Satan spoke:

"That might solve the problem, Gargan."

And Gargan's thoughts changed. This wasn't the time or the place for it. He remembered suddenly the Other Man. He owed something to the Other Man; to Maxie, too. He couldn't shoot Satan down like that. The whole nasty story of the blackmail might come out. Not that they could prove anything on him, but a good lawyer, with that woman on the stand, might—

Satan was talking.

"Mrs. Stone," he repeated, "I want to talk to you alone. I can't believe that you could possibly be even acquainted with this common hoodlum. If he's blackmailing you, the Department will protect your interests and punish him. If—"

"Tell him to get out." Gargan looked at her, jerked a thumb toward the nursery. "It'll be too late in another minute—too late."

The woman cleared her throat, said:

"Mr. Gargan is visiting me here on business." And when those steady green eyes remained on her, "He's a friend of my husband."

"It's your house and you can have who you want in it," Satan said bluntly. "But I wouldn't libel my husband if I were you."

The woman recovered now, the haze went out of her eyes. What good would it do to tell the police? What could she tell the police? How would it harm Gargan? But most of all, how could it help her? She said:

Satan's hand shot up from his knees. "After you, Mr. Gargan," he said.

"I'm afraid you've made a mistake. Albert should not have permitted you to come up. Please go." There was command in her voice, the voice of a woman used to giving orders. And then her voice changed; there was only appeal in it. An unconscious appeal. "Please go," she said again.

"Very well." Satan turned toward the door. "You're a woman of refinement and culture." He unconsciously took the Commissioner's words. "You can't possibly be in any doubt of the man you're entertaining. I hope you'll never be sorry, for your child's sake."

She moved quickly, clutched his arm.

"What do you mean? What do you mean?" she demanded.

And then Gargan was between them. He was calm now. His voice was low as he talked to Elsie Stone. But if Satan knew that the fingers that gripped the woman's arm bit painfully into the flesh in warning, he made no sign.

Gargan was saying, "Mrs. Stone is worried. I am here to help her. Elsie, let me see the officer to the front door."

Gargan was surprised and a little more sure of himself when Satan simply nodded and backed into the hall. He gained confidence, too, when Satan walked slowly down the hall toward the stairs. Satan's steps were long, even, heavy. And Gargan's confidence turned to anger; anger at Satan, he thought. But it was anger directed at himself, though he did not realize it. He had not acquitted himself well. He had allowed Satan to bully him; put that Satanic face upon him and throw him as it had the others.

AND WHAT had happened? Nothing; absolutely nothing. Satan was like the rest of them when they ran up against Gargan. Just a mask and a sneer and a threat. And Gargan gave vent to rising anger. His voice was soft but his words were hard; hard and foul. Satan's head turned. He had never had anyone talk to him like that before. He turned his green eyes on Gargan and smiled with his lips.

Gargan misunderstood that smile and talked on. When they reached the head of the broad flight of stairs, Gargan paused. He was a little proud of himself. He had let himself out and Satan had taken it. The feared Satan Hall, the man who shot tough criminals to death at the least provocation, or without any provocation at all.

Gargan saw the butler at the foot of the stairs, looking up. He was pleased. He wished Frank Wheeler was there, the man who wanted his job as head man for the Other Man. Frank, who had warned him again Satan. He wished Maxie Rosen was there, too, to see how Satan was acting now when Dan Gargan told him exactly where he got off, and exactly what he was.

He bowed in exaggerated grandeur there at the top of the stairs, said to Satan in a loud booming voice:

"After you, copper."

"After you, Mr. Gargan."

Gargan was surprised to see Satan bow, too. He didn't think there was any humor in the man. Perhaps, after all, he was wrong and Satan had not followed him to the house but had come there not knowing he was there. Then he wondered—was Satan making fun of him?

Satan was standing right on the edge of that top step, his legs spread far apart. Gargan had a sudden impulse. Just a push to start him going! And Gargan gave him that push. In fact, he slammed his hand against Satan's back as he said:

"After you, copper. I insist."

For one moment Gargan was surprised that Satan did not even sway upon that top step from the force of his hand against Satan's back. Then Satan was speaking; repeating his words.

"After you, Mr. Gargan. I insist." Satan's hand shot up from his knees, turned into a fist and landed flush on Dan Gargan's jaw.

The astonished butler at the bottom of those steps saw the feared and despised Mr. Gargan shoot up into the air; saw him hurtle out over the stairs, and landing halfway down them, turn over twice and stretch himself on his back on the floor below.

Dan Gargan didn't move. He lay very still.

Satan Hall slowly descended those steps, stood looking down at the most feared racketeer and killer in the city.

Then he spoke to the butler.

"It isn't often I go in for light comedy. You'll excuse it, I hope."

The butler looked into that hard, cruel face, and stepped back a bit. He didn't speak. He just stood there with his mouth open as Satan Hall stooped down, lifted the unconscious Gargan as if he were a small child and tossed him over his shoulder. Nor was the butler sure that, when Satan turned before he sought the front door, it was an accident that Gargan's head struck the newel post at the foot of the stairs.

But he did distinctly hear the crack of bone against wood, and thought it was a very pleasant sound indeed.

The butler closed the door but stood for a long time looking through the squares of glass. He saw Satan cross the sidewalk, approach the expensive car, heave his shoulder and toss the limp body of Gargan through the open window of the car.

CHAPTER VI

A HAND FROM THE DARKNESS

MRS. ELSIE STONE sat for a long time in her room with the door closed. She sat very still, with her hands clasped over her knee. She heard the crash distinctly. She got up and went to the door and listened. The police? What could they do for her? Simply bring to light the very thing she would give her life to hide; had given part of her own inheritance to hide.

Then she heard the front door jar, waited. Would Gargan be coming back? What would she do then? Surely he wouldn't want to take her out now. He wouldn't expect her to listen to his promises and plans to get those two letters back for her. She knew now that she had never really believed him. But somehow she had believed Greer. She had seen the greed in his eyes; the fear, too. The fear of what he was doing, what he was planning to do—not for her but for money.

No feet came up the stairs, though her heart stopped beating while she listened for them, even imagined them, felt them pounding, along the hall outside. She shivered slightly and thought of her laughing habit of saying, "I feel as if someone were walking over my grave." She had never thought what that meant, if it meant anything at all. But now she thought of it; felt that she knew exactly what it meant.

There were steps; real steps, slow steps, feet she was long familiar with, yet she did not recognize them. She clutched at her throat, came to her feet gripping the chair. There were three separate knocks on the door before she said, "Come in." And then, in relief when the door opened, "They've gone, Albert; both of them?"

"Both of them." Albert cleared his throat. "The man who looked like the devil himself, if I may be permitted to say so, Mrs. Stone—he mistreated Mr. Gargan in a way that was a pleasure to see." And suddenly, "I can't bear it, Mrs. Stone; I can't bear it any longer. You're too good a woman; too fine a woman. I know there's something terrible behind it all; behind this Mr. Gargan's visits, and I've heard you in the nursery crying at night. You—you—you might as well be dead, ma'am."

Mrs. Stone opened her mouth to speak. She had always liked Albert, always trusted him. Now, for a moment he was no longer a servant, but a friend; a very old and dear friend. She had to grip her fingers tightly into the palms of her hands. Only long training held her back. But she did say:

"I understand, Albert, and you are very kind." And after a moment, "We won't discuss it further."

Albert held his ground, stiffened slightly, finally got the words out.

"I think you'll have to, Mrs. Stone," he said. "That man, the one who said he was a detective; he hates Mr. Gargan as you hate him and I hate him, but he don't fear him as you fear him and I fear him for you. Good night, ma'am. I'm quite certain Mr. Gargan will not bother you again this evening."

"Thank you, Albert." Elsie Stone bobbed her head very slowly up and down. "You're very kind, but I'm beyond help." And when the butler would have spoken again, "That is all, Albert. Good night!"

WHEN THE door closed behind the butler she thought only of a few words he had said. "You might as well be dead!" She wondered. She had sinned, of course; but did all people who sin pay the penalty so horribly—so terribly? She had just been foolish. A mistrust of her husband! Anonymous notes that had later proved to be lies. His trips were just business ones. And she—she had been a fool; just a fool. She hadn't loved anyone but her husband. It was more a childish impulse of revenge. A silly, stupid, foolish thing. But now it was tragic; the most tragic thing in her life. Her husband loved her, adored her—and she had ruined it all.

She might just as well be dead. More, she might better be dead. Criminals cannot make use of the dead. There is no threat that carries fear to the dead. She tried to think. She couldn't think. She didn't want to think. And the sudden thought that if she were dead, she wouldn't have to think.

She crossed the room quickly, opened the door, started into the hall, stopped. She thought she saw a shadow there by the open door to the nursery, but it wasn't there when she looked again. It was just her mind; an active mind that was growing dim, confused, breaking under the strain.

Mrs. Elsie Stone went directly to her husband's room, opened the bottom drawer of his dresser, reached in beneath some shirts and took out a large gray steel automatic. She held it in her hand, her finger avoiding the trigger. Then she gripped it tightly, placed a finger upon the trigger, closed her eyes and raised the gun slowly to her head—placed it against the side of it.

The nose of the gun felt cold and she shivered slightly. Her finger felt numb and did not at once tighten upon the trigger. She remembered the discussions she had had about suicide and how she had said it was a cowardly act, and now— She couldn't do it!

Her firm lips set tightly; her chin came out. She opened her eyes and closed her finger tightly upon the trigger. Nothing happened, and she remembered the safety catch. With a quick determined movement she snapped the tiny catch back, jerked up the gun again—and then the face of the baby danced before her blurred vision. Her hand dropped.

She must see her baby first. She was freeing her husband and the baby from the horror those letters would disclose. It wasn't a cowardly act; it was a noble act. She had a right then, the only right she asked, to hold the baby in her arms just once—just for a moment before she died.

She didn't turn on the light. She could make out the curly head by the dim light from the hall. It nestled there upon the pillow. She could even see one chubby arm outside the tightly pinned covers, and her only thought then was that the nurse had been careless and that the baby would catch cold. She didn't realize that she laid the gun down on the bed. She didn't realize that she tucked in the white arm just before she drew the baby from the crib and held him close to her breast. He didn't wake up but he gurgled in his sleep, ran thick groping fingers along her face, muttered unintelligible words.

SHE HELD him very tightly to her, talked softly to him. She was crying when she put him back under the covers. If she held him a moment longer she couldn't do it; couldn't bear the thought that she would never hold him again; never hear the baby prattle that rang in her ears like words of great wisdom. She pinned the blanket about him, lifted the gun from the bed. He wouldn't understand; he was too young to know. If she left the room now her courage to act would leave her.

Elsie Stone stood up straight. Then she placed the gun against her head. Her finger tightened—

Strong fingers gripped her wrist, turned the gun from her head, twisted it from her hand. A voice behind her said:

"So you're the kind of a woman who'd duck out on the kid!"

The woman swung. In the dim light she saw the man. It was Detective Satan Hall. Elsie Stone didn't speak; she couldn't speak.

"It takes courage," said Satan, "to do whatever you don't want to do; whatever you are afraid to do. You wanted to do it, and you were more afraid not to do it than to do it. It's blackmail, isn't it?"

"Yes," she nodded. "It's blackmail."

"I'm not going to ask you what it is because I don't care." Satan sat facing her. "Is it letters—written stuff of any kind?"

"It's letters," she told him. "Two letters."

"And if you had the letters, there wouldn't be anything in a man's head; anything that could convict you of a crime?" And when she didn't seem to fully understand, "I mean that if you had the letters, there is nothing that could come out of anybody's mouth that could hurt you?"

She spoke as if she were in a trance.

"No! No! Nothing that could come out of anybody's mouth that could hurt me."

"Good!" Satan nodded. "I'll get those letters for you."

"How will you do that?" There was doubt in her voice.

"I hope," said Satan very slowly and very seriously, "to take them from the body of a dead man—Dan Gargan."

"You—you will do this for me?"

Satan stared coldly at her.

"I'll do it for seven million people; seven million people who pay me to do it. Your trouble, Mrs. Stone, is that you see only one life; only one sufferer—yourself. I'm not saying that the rest of the seven million don't look on life and death in the same way. If they looked on it differently; if they rose in a body and looked on it as a crime against the State instead of a crime against a single individual, most of our crimes would be wiped out in a year. Now—did you telephone the police commissioner about Greer?" And when she hesitated, "Yes or no!"

"Yes." She raised her head now and faced him squarely.

"Why?"

"Because I thought that if I paid Greer enough he would finally help me, and because I could not see a man murdered."

"How did you know?"

"I was told that Greer would bother me no more. And I was told that a man named Frederick Young and another named Jerry Lock would be at my house from eleven o'clock to five in the morning." She paused. "At least, I was to swear that they were here last night and this morning. I was to say, if the police questioned me, that I could not sleep, and at one o'clock came downstairs and stayed with those two men in the library from one o'clock until ten minutes of three. I knew that Greer would be coming to see me; I knew that he was helping the police. I knew that, for a price, he would get me those letters, if he lived."

SATAN NODDED, and whistled softly. The Other Man's organization was strong for alibis. Not the alibis of professional crooks or even people of shady reputation, who might not be believed on the witness stand. But honest people; respectable people, that a jury would believe. Still, Razor Young and Jerry Lock, at the home of Mrs. Stone, would not be easy to explain. Satan asked:

"How would you explain their presence?"

"I was telephoned that my child was in danger of being kidnaped. I did not want the police notoriety, as the threat might have come from a crank. So I asked the Preston Protective Agency to send up a couple of men, and they sent those two."

Satan's eyes opened wide. The Other Man was organizing things faster than he had thought and organizing them on a business basis. Of course Satan knew that the Preston organization was crooked; but then, a great many such detective agencies were. There was no secret about that in the police department. An ordinary copper just wondered why they were licensed to operate and had been wondering for a long time past, and probably would wonder for a long time in the future.

Mrs. Elsie Stone was saying:

"I don't know any more, except that there is someone who speaks of the Other Man. A lawyer who first came to see me about those letters. He seemed honest enough; said he hated to be mixed up in such a thing but that someone had to protect my interests."

"A lawyer, eh?" Satan jarred to the end of his chair. "What is his name? There are hundreds of such shysters in the city."

"His name is Rosen—Maxie Rosen."

Satan was pleased. He knew Rosen; knew that he had been quite a criminal lawyer in his day but had dropped out of things lately. He knitted his brows, tried to remember. Something to do with the Bar Association. He couldn't exactly remember. But he did know that Maxie Rosen was seen very often with Dan Gargan. It was rumored that he advised Gargan. And Satan thought, with the thrill of an animal who finds the right scent, that he might even have located the go-between; the man who brought the messages from the Other Man to Dan Gargan.

Satan leaned forward when he spoke to the woman.

"Did you give him any money?" She shook her head.

"We'll trap him, Mrs. Stone. You'll offer him money. We'll mark bills and have someone ready to arrest him after he takes them."

"But he won't take any money. He told me it wasn't legal for him to do that. He said, once he's sure he can buy back the letters, then he'll tell me the price I must pay, and whom to see."

Satan sat back. His disappointment was plain. He spoke very seriously.

"I know your troubles are big to you, Mrs. Stone. But they are very small compared with the menace the entire city faces today. You are a valuable asset to a great crime ring; a crime ring that is already formed and ready to strike—to strike every place at once, perhaps. An unknown man controls it; the one "called the Other Man. You are simply one of many into whose past he has gone. Some, for the purpose of driving them out of his way. Others, he will force to aid him and betray their trusts. Some, like you, he uses simply for alibis for his murderers."

"And you?" she said. "Are you not—is there nothing in your past?"

SATAN'S LIPS set to a single red line, green balls glistened through narrow lids.

"There is nothing in my past but a list of dead. Dead men whose names were known and feared in the night; dead men that this Other Man knew and admired for their influence and their daring. He sees nothing in my past but the death of his own future. You are a bright woman. You are a clever woman, whose brain has been stunned and twisted and dulled with fear.

You may be able to help. The Other Man may try and make use of you. This lawyer! What did he tell you last?"

"He told me to pay no more money to anyone."

"Not even to Gargan?"

"Not even to Gargan."

Satan was surprised. His slanting eyes showed it. He thought a moment, then spoke his thoughts aloud.

"Gargan, then, was working on his own. That is the greatest asset of the police. These men cannot trust each other. It means that the Other Man is prepared to shake you down or use you in some large way." Satan hesitated. "I think you can help me. They don't suspect you?"

"I think they suspect me about Greer. Gargan was different tonight. He struck me. Gargan looked at me as if I—as if he intended to kill me. I'm afraid! I'm afraid!"

"Afraid of death?" Satan's eyes opened wide. "But you wanted death a few minutes ago. Now you must help me. The future of seven million people may depend on it. Listen, Mrs. Stone." His words came through tight lips. "The price of milk has already gone up. The reason is that the dealers have to pay protection to get their milk delivered to their distributors. The distributors have to pay protection to get it delivered to their customers. You know who those customers are. They are babies; just like your baby. But unlike your baby, they will be starved for milk if the price goes up a few cents. A cent even! You've been raised in luxury. You can't understand that."

"But what can I do? What can I do?"

"They must need you; they must want to use you. Whatever they ask you to do, order you to do—you must tell me. Then I'll know what you can do about it."

She put her head in her hands, began to cry softly.

"I can think of only one baby," she said. "My baby."

"In return," said Satan, "I will deliver to you those letters. Get Gargan to have them on him. Promise him anything—but you must see the letters. He must have them with him when you act as he wishes."

"A body—a dead body." She repeated the words Satan had used before. "You want me to lead Gargan to—to his death."

Satan smiled. His lips parted and the woman noticed that his teeth were sharp, pointed; V-shaped, like the rest of his features. He said:

"Gargan will know I talked to you tonight. Gargan will plan to lead me to my death. I want you to help him."

"You want me to help him lead you to your death!"

"Yes," said Satan. "That's exactly what I want. I want you to help Gargan lead me to my death." He walked to the door, said, "If the thought is not in his head, I want you to put it there. Offer him my life for those letters."

ELSIE STONE stared at Satan. His face was so hard and cruel! She wondered why she had such confidence in him. Why she had confided in him. Perhaps it was just that she had to talk to someone. She didn't know what it was. She followed him to the door, said:

"And you are doing this for me; risking your life for me?"

"I am thinking of you," he said, "as just one of the seven million who pay me."

"Then you don't care if I live or die."

"I am the law," Satan told her bluntly.

She looked at him a long time. Fear seemed to leave her then. The suppressed feeling as if her head was being crushed in by a giant vise seemed to go. She thought of all she had read about this man in the papers, and knew that it was true. She straightened, said:

"And I suppose the law will keep that gun."

Satan stretched out his hand, pushed the gun into hers.

"If you want to run out on the kid I can't stop you; the law can't stop you. There are windows, there are bridges, there are ropes, and there are poisons that can be bought at any corner drug store. I don't think you'll do it now. You may have a chance to pay for the past; be proud that the past gave you the chance to aid the future of the city."

"But it's you—the man who is going to count on me." She was no longer the frightened girl of a few minutes before.

Satan hesitated, looked into her eyes. They remained steady beneath his piercing, searching look.

"I'm going to count on you," he said. "Good night!"

She said, "Good night." She stood there when he walked out the door. There was something about the man that gave her a new confidence. But she didn't know if she feared him, loathed him, or liked him. For a moment she felt almost sorry for Gargan, but just as she might feel sorry for some beast that might have to face this hunter.

She didn't hear Satan speak to the butler downstairs nor did she hear Albert's answer. Satan said:

"Thank you, Albert, for holding Mrs. Stone's attention until I got upstairs. I'm sure it will do a lot of good."

"I hope so, sir," said Albert, "and thank you, sir," he added as he opened the front door and watched Satan go slowly down the steps.

A devil had entered the Stone residence and taken away a lot of evil with him. At least, that was the way Albert looked at it as he put the heavy chain across the door.

When Satan reached the street the expensive car was gone. Satan frowned. Gargan had not been hurt much then. He had recovered and driven away.

CHAPTER VII

AN ORDER TO KILL

THE COMMISSIONER MOVED about the room. His steps were uncertain. One moment he looked out the window, the next he straightened a huge volume in his bookcase. Everything physical about him was uncertain. Yet Satan knew that his brain wasn't. It was clear, as it always was clear. He waited for the Commissioner to speak. Finally the Commissioner dropped into a chair behind his desk, said:

"Gargan is still alive, eh? Things worked out wrong."

Satan's shoulders shrugged.

"Jerry Lock was identified as a bad man from Cleveland. Razor Young did the actual killing of the children. I wouldn't say it was all wrong."

The Commissioner laughed mirthlessly.

"And what happens? It's through the underworld like fire. Greer is no longer a rat to the boys. They think he shot Gargan's closest men to death. I can't roast him for that crime, knowing he didn't do it. Gargan doesn't even suspect you were there?"

Satan grinned.

"No. It's a surprise to him as well as to Greer, though Greer is hiding out. It isn't pleasant for Greer to think that Gargan wants his—well, his body. Greer doesn't happen to think he's as dangerous as the boys believe; at least, as yet he doesn't."

The Commissioner said:

"I'm sorry it wasn't Gargan, Satan—damned sorry. It would have given me a breathing spell; a chance to find the man back of it all; the Other Man. Now, the Greek's racket has been taken over uptown. The morale of the Department is not so good. Inspector Burke was out to kill the rackets, and what happened to him? As far as the men on the Force know, he was tossed out of the Department as soon as he stepped on Gargan's toes. It's true, too. He was. But I can't tell the men it was because of something in his past. I've got to have time. I've got to, Satan! I'm sorry it wasn't Gargan the other night."

Satan said very slowly, "I never wanted to be, never asked to be more than a first grade detective. I take my orders directly from you. Are you giving me an order now?"

"Just what do you mean—an order?" The Commissioner stared hard at Satan. He didn't realize it then, but his lips were slightly puffed out, his voice deep with a warning. Other men, the biggest on the Force, knew the sign. It meant that the conversation along that line was closed.

Satan knew it, too, but he ignored it. He said bluntly:

"I mean, are you ordering me to kill Gargan—to murder him?"

The Commissioner straightened, puffed once, glared directly at Satan, bent his head forward and seemed to think for a long moment. Then he looked up.

"No, I'm not." And suddenly, "But *someone* is ordering your death—your murder."

Satan grinned evilly.

"Someone has been doing that for years. Just sit tight, Commissioner. Dan Gargan has something to think about now."

"I know! I know!" the Commissioner said irritably. "But why did you go in for that sort of stuff? Knocking him down a flight of stairs! I don't like it, Satan. I don't like it one bit. It doesn't make sense. What made you do it?"

SATAN LOOKED over at the ceiling, smiled pleasantly.

"It seemed like a good idea at the time, Commissioner. Maybe I shouldn't have told you. But I thought—" Satan paused. "He turned over twice in the air before he hit the floor. He didn't complain, did he?"

The Commissioner made a wry face, said:

"No, no. He hasn't complained."

"I didn't think he would. It wouldn't make a pretty story along the avenue. A man like Gargan has enemies as well as friends. Gargan couldn't stand ridicule." And after a moment's thought, "If it wasn't for the woman I'd start the story myself."

"The woman!" The Commissioner looked steadily at Satan. "I didn't know you had much sentiment. You seem to be doing a lot for her."

"She's going to do a lot for us." Satan nodded. "Gargan abused her the other night. He threw a terrible fear into her. I think he suspects that she warned Greer. I think he's going to try to kill her."

"Kill her! And she's not even being watched; protected?"

"No." Satan was very thoughtful. "We mustn't do that. She's being watched by Gargan. He'll guess I talked to her, or forced the truth out of her. I've promised her the letters back. She'll go a long ways for those letters."

"Satan," the Commissioner leaned forward, "you're not using that woman to trap Gargan!"

"No. I'm letting Gargan use her to trap me."

"She might be killed; murdered."

"She might," Satan agreed. "And Gargan might roast for the killing."

The Commissioner bounced to his feet, looked straight at Satan.

"Hell!" he cried. "It sounds as if you mean it. There are times, Satan, when I don't believe you have a soul."

Satan said very slowly:

"What good would a soul be to a cop?" And when the Commissioner looked very serious, "I don't think any harm will come to the woman. If she traps me for Gargan and I'm killed, he'll be grateful to her; at least, believe in her. If she traps me and I kill Gargan, then he can't harm her."

The Commissioner was puzzled, showed it.

"You'd walk into a trap, knowing it was a trap?"

"Traps," said Satan, "are very interesting. They hold knowledge. Rats aren't the only ones who can get the cheese safely out of a trap."

"But you're only guessing." The Commissioner nodded. "Only hoping he'll use the woman. You can't be sure."

"I'll make sure," said Satan. "I'll make sure today. I'm going to visit Gargan. I'm going to ask him for those two letters, and I'm going to threaten to shoot him to death if he doesn't deliver them within twenty-four hours."

The Commissioner shook his head.

"You can't put that bluff over on Gargan. You can't just shoot a man to death. Gargan won't believe that."

SATAN GOT up very slowly from his chair, walked toward the window, swung suddenly. His face was very close to the Commissioner's. The Commissioner jarred stiffly straight, bent slightly backwards. There was little different about Satan's face; his thin lips were not even twisted. It was his eyes. They hadn't narrowed, hadn't simply glared. Nothing consciously different about them. It was something back in them. Something far back in them as Satan spoke. He said:

"The woman has a kid, Commissioner. Would *you* believe I'd do it?"

"I—" For a moment the Commissioner was lost for an answer. Then, "It's not I. It's Gargan who counts. Will he believe it?"

"That's right—it's not what you believe. It's not even what Gargan believes. It's—" Satan turned his head, let his eyes rest on a corner of the room, high up near the ceiling. "It's whether I believe it or not, when the time comes—the time for Gargan to die."

Satan went slowly toward the door. The Commissioner followed, clutched his arm, held it, said:

"I wouldn't want it like that, Satan. No, I wouldn't." And setting his chin, "Yes, I guess Gargan will believe it. Believes it already so much that all the influence that has been brought to bear to have you removed from the Force has suddenly been dropped. They're not pressing me now. You know what that means."

"Sure!" Satan agreed. "It means that Gargan thinks I'll kill him. Gargan's first thought is that he wants to live."

"It means," said the Commissioner, "that Gargan has made other arrangements for you. There can be only one other arrangement in Gargan's life, and that is death. He intends to kill you."

Satan nodded, smiled almost pleasantly.

"I hope you're right, Commissioner."

Then he turned the knob, and opening the door, passed quickly out of the Commissioner's private office. He was going to see Dan Gargan—at once.

CHAPTER VIII

A MACHINE OF DEATH

DAN GARGAN, ALONE in his private office above the Café Wellington, smoked cigarette after cigarette. Physically, the crash down those stairs had not bothered him after the following morning; but mentally it had bothered him a great deal. He felt that he would only have to speak to Maxie Rosen about that attack to furnish the Other Man with the proper reason for tossing Satan off the Force. But he had not even mentioned it to Maxie. Somehow he couldn't. Dan Gargan crashed down the stairs by a common dick! He could kill Satan for that. He would kill him for that.

He would kill him! And that was what had been on his mind. At first it was a wildly impossible dream. Breaking into Satan's room; sticking a gun against his stomach; waking him up and letting him know who it was before he took the dose! But he had cooled off a bit since then. His plans now called for sticking the gun right into the center of Satan's back and letting him have it.

One thing he knew—one thing he was sure of. Satan was going to die. And Dan Gargan was the man who was going to kill him.

The phone rang. He lifted it from its cradle, started to talk—and stopped. A voice, a very low voice, said:

"It's Detective Satan Hall, and he's on his way up."

Gargan's first impulse was to snatch his gun from his shoulder holster. His second impulse was to rush to the door and turn the key. But he did neither of those things. He straightened his gun slightly in the holster, let his coat hang open a bit and was ready to say "Come in!" when the knock came on the door.

But no knock came. The door simply opened and Detective Satan Hall walked in.

"Hello, Dan!" he said slowly. "I'm not here officially. Take your hand off that phone."

Dan Gargan's fingers loosened. He had not realized until that moment that his hand gripped the phone. Now his fingers tightened again. He said:

"So it's another social call." Gargan looked up. His mouth was twisted; his grin was a sneer. "I let things slide the other night, Hall. I didn't want to embarrass a lady. This time you've walked into it. I've got the same rights as any citizen the Commissioner keeps yapping about to the papers. Busted your way in for a shakedown! It'll be your word against mine and a couple of witnesses I have listening."

"Witnesses?" Satan looked surprised.

"Sure! Sure! Right here in the room." Gargan laughed. "Your sight is bad, Satan. But your ears will be all right when you hear them tell it on the witness stand, if you're still on the Force then."

"So that's how it is." Satan's green eyes widened. This organization held all the cards. He wondered who the witnesses would be. No doubt other respectable people with a past, who would perjure themselves to hide that past.

"That," said Gargan, with a smile, "is just how it is. We'll all listen to what you have to say, after I make my call."

Satan said:

"We'll talk first; witnesses later. Take your hand off that phone." And when Gargan's grin broadened, "Take it off—now."

Dan Gargan leaned slightly down on the desk, started to lift the phone—and it happened. He knew before it happened. Not that he saw the hand move, for he didn't until it struck him. But something flashed first in Satan's eyes.

PALM UPWARD, Satan slapped Gargan across the cheek.

Gargan's body not only shot erect by the force of that blow. It hurtled to one side.

Then his body stopped, shot suddenly erect as Satan's right palm caught him on the other side of the face. Just two cracks that seemed to be one, so quickly did Gargan's body move and so quickly did those open hands strike.

Gargan didn't think of his gun then; he thought of only one thing. A thing he had heard and forgotten, and was just a jumble in his mind now. Satan's stunt! Satan's most feared stunt. Satan was slapping him down. The same method he had used so often to force a man into a draw or force him off the Avenue.

Just a last thought in Gargan's mind; a flash that he and Satan were alone. Then the heel of Satan's right hand shoved out; didn't strike him exactly; at least, it was more a push than a blow. But it brought blood to Gargan's lips, hurled him back into the big leather chair and left him there.

Someone spoke. Gargan knew that, for he heard the words. But it wasn't Satan, for his thin lips were set grimly. His green eyes gleamed. Yet plainly Gargan heard the words repeated over and over.

"I'll kill you for that. I'll kill you for that!" And Dan Gargan didn't know that the words were his and that they came from his bleeding mouth, until he saw Satan's lips move and heard Satan answer him. Satan was saying:

"You've got a gun, Gargan. You've used it often enough. You're mighty proud of your quickness with it. We're alone, my hands are empty. You could tell your own story of how it happened— you and those respectable witnesses. Why not make use of the gun?"

Gargan's head was clear now; very clear. He could see Satan's hands spread out there—white on the dark surface of the desk. He knew it would be a simple matter for him to draw and shoot before any man he had ever met could get his hands off that table. Any man he had ever met! He didn't like that thought. Didn't like it at all.

Gargan didn't reach for a gun. Instead, he shook his head in a dazed way, put a hand to his bleeding mouth; pretended to clear his head. Not pretended in order to lead Satan into a trap, but to keep himself out of a trap. When he spoke, his voice was surly.

"You know I don't carry a gun," he said.

"You have a license." Satan's eyes held Gargan's. "But it's just a license to carry a gun. It takes guts to use it when you're not sure." And walking around the desk and sitting on the edge of it, "I didn't expect anything different. Bentz was shot in the back of the head; the Greek mowed down with the children. Only the children were shot in—in—"

Satan leaned forward, his lips twisted. A sudden mask was drawn down over his face. A satanic mask; a mask of evil—quiet, cool, foreboding sort of evil. He said:

"We won't talk about that now, Gargan. I don't think I came here to kill you tonight."

Gargan straightened in his chair. Threats of quick and awful vengeance hung on his lips, but he didn't speak them. Words simply formed far back in his head. The indifference in Satan's voice seemed far more deadly than if curses had shot from between his teeth. Somehow the word "kill" got Gargan. It was as if Satan had said, "I didn't come to kill you, but I might." Gargan only said:

"If you know so much," and the word "copper" that he wanted to use stuck in his throat and stayed there. "If you know so much, why not make the pinch and see which one of us stands the higher?"

SATAN SMILED and shook his head. "This visit is unofficial, Gargan. I've just taken the night off to bring you a message. You see, it's rather personal, and I want to be sure I'm not making an excuse to kill you." Satan looked at Gargan a long time now, very steadily. "It's about Mrs. Elsie Stone and blackmail."

"Yeah?" Gargan was more composed. But he wasn't sure of his ground; wasn't sure of it at all. He didn't say any more.

"That's right. We think Mrs. Stone might do something desperate. We think it might have something to do with letters."

"Letters, eh?" There were a lot of other things Gargan wanted to say; couldn't understand why he didn't say them. But he didn't just the same.

"That's it." Satan's voice still held a calm indifference. "You may have trouble in getting them from the Other Man, so I'll give you forty-eight hours to deliver them to Mrs. Stone. After that—"

"After that—" Gargan encouraged.

Satan came to his feet, turned his back on Gargan, and walked slowly to the door. It was a broad back, a tempting back with both of Satan's long arms swinging at his sides; both his hands with the long strong fingers white and empty. Yet Gargan never moved; never even reached toward an armpit. He didn't know why then; didn't know why afterwards. He was sitting in the same position when Satan turned at the door, swung so viciously that Gargan half rose to his feet.

There was nothing calm in Satan's voice now; nothing calm in his words, nor his twisting lips, nor his hateful green eyes. Everything of evil was in that face; in his words as he spoke.

"You had your chance, Gargan—a damn fine chance at my back and I wanted you to take it. So have it your way. Fail to return those letters, and I'll take another night off. I'll make another unofficial visit. That's right, Gargan. It will be murder."

The door opened and closed. Satan was gone.

Gargan cursed. There was a single movement of his right hand and a gun was there; a gun held in a hand that did not tremble; a trigger that was carefully, assuredly gripped by a steady finger.

Dan Gargan came to his feet. Anger, hate, a sudden determination distorted his face. His steps were steady as he crossed the room. His gun was half raised. He was again the deadly killer; the feared power that gripped the city. Yes, he knew then. Knew exactly what he was going to do; knew it the very moment his left hand gripped the knob of that door. He was going to fling the door open and empty his gun; empty it into the body of Satan Hall. He didn't have a bit of doubt of that; not a bit when his hand gripped that knob.

But as his fingers twisted and turned that knob, Gargan changed. Not his distorted features; not even his steady hand and the gun it held. Just something inside of him changed. He told himself it had nothing to do with Satan, with his appearance, with his eyes, with the deadly threat in his voice. But it had; he knew it had.

Yet, truth is truth. A man had made a threat to kill him. A man had slapped him around. And that man had turned his back on the deadly Gargan; turned his back, and lived.

It wasn't fear with Gargan. It was just uncertainty. He was deadly; absolutely sure with a gun. Yet Satan had turned his back.

DAN GARGAN dropped the knob as if it were red hot. He hesitated, spun the key in the lock and walked to his desk. He thought of the woman. She had talked then. But she knew nothing except what Greer had told her. But what had Greer told her?

Dan Gargan snapped up the phone.

"Send Chopper Regan up," was all he said.

Five minutes later Chopper Regan entered the room. He was a small bald little man, neatly but quietly dressed. His eyes were dull blue, with a film over them. He listened to what Gargan had to say, nodded once, stroked his chin and looked down at his newly polished shoes. He said, without emotion:

"This Satan dick is bad. Guys never had any luck with him. I'd charge ten grand, only neither cops nor crooks have any liking for him. He wouldn't be missed much by either of them." He hesitated, watched Gargan, finally spoke. "Five grand is the price, and if there's a come-back I'll take the rap alone. I'm figuring, of course, on the way you said. The Terrace Garden Bar."

Dan Gargan got up from the desk and paced the room. He could do the job himself and sink the money in his own pocket.

But the Other Man didn't want it that way. He wanted him free and easy; not mixed up in a cop killing at this time.

"All right, Regan," he finally agreed, sat down at the desk again and went over the details; the exact details of the death of Satan Hall.

Regan listened but didn't talk much. Occasionally he made a suggestion, but mostly he just nodded. Killing men for a price was his business, and he looked on it as a business. Just as the executioner at the death house would. When Gargan had finished talking, Chopper said:

"Thursday night then. You'll draw him through the bar at the Terrace Gardens." And when Gargan made some observation, "You don't have to worry. He walks in the door, turns to come down between the bar and the booths, and I open up. Yep, that's right. A Tommy gun. I'm not fancy enough to dump him over with a rod. They say he's sure death. I'll chop him down and walk out the side door and be back in Philly before they figure just what nailed him to the floor." Gargan nodded. Regan said:

"That's all, Dan. Just the question on money. I'll want that now."

Dan Gargan watched Regan count the bills carefully and push them into his pocket. He watched him come slowly to his feet, jerk up his trousers slightly, walk to the door, open it and go out.

CHAPTER IX

"IT'S MURDER!"

MAXIE ROSEN LOOKED steadily at Dan Gargan across the width of Gargan's private office, and said:

"The greatest things in life, the greatest works of art, are founded on simplicity. This scheme of yours seems rather too elaborate, Gargan."

Gargan said, "Don't put the dictionary on me, Maxie. I don't like it. This isn't life. This is death. It's the blow-off. You never let me believe that you thought Satan a pushover. Others have planned to kill him again and again. Dark alleys, vacant houses, death cars. And what happens? Satan still struts his stuff along the Avenue. There will be nothing secret about this. It's open and above board. Satan may be quick with a gun. He may be a killer. But, like the rest of them, he's just a dumb cop. This time he's been too smart. The woman was too anxious to help

"Just how," said Maxie, "did you get Elsie Stone to tell you that Satan talked with her?"

"I knew he went back into the house,"

"But how did she happen to tell you so much—that Satan forced her to tell about the letters?"

Gargan laughed.

"It isn't your line, Maxie; it's mine. I guess her husband's a soft guy. I walked right in on her, busted her straight in the mouth and threatened to wring her neck." Gargan paused a moment. "And I damn near did. She's a two-timing little tart. She talked her head off to Satan. She lied, but I knew it. She's not so dumb, either; promised to tell Satan things if he got the letters. See the point, Maxie? You've got to understand women."

"And just what is understanding women?"

"Understanding them is not trusting them," Gargan said. "Not any of them. This dame figures she's playing it safe. She'll trap Satan to his death for those letters. She'll trap me for Satan for those letters. That's right! She told me. Satan wants to nail me as she passes over the money; catch me with the goods. She told me that."

"Is that why you have the letters, Dan? You're not thinking of cashing in; selling her the letters?"

"Me?" Dan Gargan straightened. "Do you think I'm a rat? It's like this. The woman will make the call for Satan to come to the Gold Room of the Terrace Gardens. He's to enter by the bar." Gargan snapped his lips. "Chopper Regan will be there, and—" Gargan leaned forward and explained his plan in detail.

"But suppose the woman is on the level with you and tells Satan what you tell her to?"

Gargan shrugged his shoulders.

"I'll know what she tells him. The payoff is to be at the Terrace Gardens, and the payoff is to be Satan's life for those letters. I have them right in my pocket."

"And after Satan's dead," there was hardly a question in Maxie Rosen's voice, "what of the letters? What of the woman then?"

GARGAN SAID, "She knows too much to live. You said that yourself."

"I have talked to her," said Maxie Rosen. "And she doesn't know much about me."

"No." Gargan set his eyes on Rosen. "But she knows too much about me. Greer told her. Greer!" He repeated. "I never thought he had the stuff. Razor Young and Lock—just like that!" He snapped his fingers. "They had the drop on him too; they must have had. I thought you knew men, Maxie."

"I didn't know Greer." And after a pause, "Frank Wheeler could do the Satan job and no one would—"

For a split second, Chopper Regan looked into Satan's eyes and saw death.

"Frank Wheeler, eh?" Gargan shook a finger at Maxie. The lad who nearly got my job as front man for the boss. He's been sneering around here for months. Slow thinking, slow acting. Tell the Other Man to call him off, Maxie, or he'll find him dead."

"Tush, tush." Maxie made queer clucking noises in his throat. "There is just one menace; one single man. No long trials, no expensive lawyers, no high class alibis can help against him. That's right, Gargan. I mean Satan Hall."

"Well—" Gargan lifted the phone, "go sit in the closet there, Maxie. Leave the door slightly open. The dame's downstairs. You can hear what she says." And into the phone, "Okay, Molly. Send Mrs. Stone up now."

Maxie Rosen got slowly to his feet, went to the closet and looked inside. He pushed a few heavy ledgers back with his feet, regarded the space it left, took a small straight chair from the corner of the office, and placing it in the closet, sat down and partly closed the door.

Elsie Stone entered that room. Gargan looked up, said:

"Come here. Stand by the desk." And when she moved across the room and stood before him, "For Cripe's sake fix up that pan of yours. You look like you're going to a funeral."

The woman said, "I can't stand much more of it. I can't! I can't!"

"Hell!" Gargan let his lips curl. "You haven't stood anything yet, sister." And his voice lowering, growing almost soft, "I have had you watched. I'm going to trust you. I think you're on the level."

"I'll do anything to get back those letters. Anything!"

"That's right." Gargan nodded, put his hand inside his coat, pulled out a couple of letters. "Not yet!" He knocked away her outstretched arm; her eager fingers. "You understand what you're doing?"

"I understand." Her voice was mechanical. "I'm to trap a man to his death; a police officer to his death."

Gargan looked at her, slightly startled. Was he wrong about the woman? She sounded as if she meant it; actually meant it. He rubbed his chin. He'd go through with it anyway. If she wasn't a double-crossing dame, he'd have to change his plans. He said:

"Right! I had you at the Terrace Gardens once before. It is a respectable place. I've got dough in it. They listen to me. Now— you're to telephone Satan. There are two entrances to the Gold Room; both of them directly off Broadway. One through the bar, the other through the main entrance. The main entrance leads down a long hall. There's a lounge at the end of the hall, then the dining room. But anyone entering that lounge has to pass between heavy drapes. Be sure Satan comes that way. There will be a man on either side of those drapes."

"I see," the woman said in a listless voice. "It's murder."

"It's business!" Gargan snapped. "Business for you and business for me. You and fifty other people will be my alibi, and you'll have those letters before the cops reach the place. It's worth it, isn't it?" Gargan leaned forward, studied her. "Worth it for the kid."

"For the baby," she said slowly. "But what of thousands of other babies?"

GARGAN FROWNED.

"What the hell are you talking about? Now, look here. You and me are friends; a couple of pals. We'll be eating and drinking and dancing. Play the part. Paint up that sad pan of yours. And see that Satan comes!"

"He'll come. He'll come all right." Elsie Stone looked through and beyond Gargan. "I saw his face when he spoke of you. He'll come!"

"That's right. That's right!" Gargan encouraged her. And when she turned to leave, he got up, walked quickly from behind the desk and took her by the arm. "Don't forget all the instructions I gave you. You're to call him from booth seven, downstairs. That's in the back and out of the way. The time he must come is ten-thirty, exactly. We want him to show up before the theatre crowd drops in." And when the woman nodded, "And remember! The main entrance. Not by way of the bar. Be positive about that. Not by way of the bar!"

"By the main entrance and the drapes," the woman said half aloud. "Not by way of the bar. I'll be sure of that." And turning at the door, "The letters! You must have them with you."

"I'll have them," Gargan said easily.

"You must!" The woman's head raised now. "I'm desperate, Gargan; more than desperate. I'm bringing a man to his death for those letters. I can't stand any more. You'll show me those letters in the cab before we enter the Gold Room. Don't nod, don't lie, don't forget to bring them. I'll break if you do. I'll stand screaming before the Terrace Gardens."

Gargan stared at her a long time. Her eyes were not listless and dead now. They were bright; bright through a film of moisture. Not bright with the sparkle of youth but bright with the madness of desperation. He said:

"Don't worry. I'll have the letters."

Maxie Rosen came out of the closet as soon as the door closed behind the woman. He shook his head at Gargan.

"The woman's going through with it, Gargan. Is that what you expected?"

"No. No. I gave her the hint; the hint that if Satan came by way of the bar he'd be safe. I thought she'd tell him that. But we'll know. We'll know." And picking up the phone, he said, "Cut me in on booth seven, Molly. That's right! Booth seven."

Gargan sat there with the receiver against his ear as Maxie Rosen talked. Rosen was saying:

"Things are coming along fine, Dan. We found some old papers over in Brooklyn. They date back nearly twenty years. Captain Murray! The Other Man traced his past back for nineteen years without finding a thing. Then we struck pay dirt. He was rookie cop at that time, had a mother dying in Detroit when he sunk his fist into the money. It was a tough job but we got every detail."

"Yeah?" Gargan held his hand over the mouthpiece, said to Rosen, "Going to mail the bad news to the Commissioner and put the skids under this Murray?"

"I hope not. I hope not. History is repeating itself. Captain Murray has financial trouble again. He'll be more valuable to us on the Force than off it. I hope, with that evidence, he may work in with us. He—"

"S—sh! Damn it, be quiet!" Gargan snapped, pointing to the phone. He bent his head, listening to the voices that came over the wire. The conversation was interesting; some of it not understandable. Something about "thousands of babies" again. But he repeated the last words to himself. Satan was speaking.

"Ten-thirty exactly, Mrs. Stone, and I'll come by way of the bar. Yes, I promise. I'll come by way of the bar."

And the woman was saying, "I didn't think I could do it But I think my baby would want it that way; want it for the other babies."

CHAPTER X

THE DANCE OF DEATH

GARGAN SLAMMED DOWN the phone, cursed. He told Maxie Rosen what he had heard.

"The dirty little stool-pigeon. I could knock all her teeth down her throat."

Maxie Rosen laughed. There was relief in that laugh.

"It's what you wanted, Dan. What it had to be for your plans to go through, and you squawk."

Gargan grinned.

"I know women." He lifted the phone, called a number, asked for "Mr. Jerome Curtis." When he got "Mr. Curtis" he said:

"All right, Regan. Just as we planned—ten-thirty, at the bar." And as the phone clicked up, "Things are settled, Maxie. All the boys are ready for action. Soon as Satan Hall is out of the picture we'll grab every milk place in the Bronx first. Distributors, dealers, drivers. Slug, beat, and then dump the milk. Sure! Sure! It's a pushover. Have the Preston Protective Agency ready to sell the saps protection; they're going to need it. Chopper Regan never misses what he shoots at; at least, with a Tommy gun he doesn't."

Maxie Rosen laughed far back in his throat.

"That's right!" He nodded pleasantly. "Chopper Regan never misses what he shoots at."

Both men sat for a long time in silence. Then Rosen said:

"You'll have witnesses tonight, Gargan; plenty of them. The boys know that Satan threatened you. It'll be nosed around that Satan is coming. They'll be there to see you make good."

69

Gargan's head moved up and down slowly.

"I'm sorry, Maxie, that the Other Man insisted on the blast-out. I'd have liked to have been with the woman when Satan walked in. Hell! Any guy could get a self defense plea if Satan went for a rod. I'd knock him over like *that*." Gargan snapped his fingers. And when Maxie just looked at him, "Don't you understand, Maxie? It couldn't be anything but a bluff. A cop couldn't walk in and commit murder."

Maxie Rosen took off his glasses and cleaned them very carefully. Listless, dead eyes regarded Gargan. He said:

"That's right, Gargan. Satan couldn't just walk in and shoot you to death. He couldn't just kill you. But he could kill everything you represent. Represent to yourself; represent to the Other Man. In one minute he could kill every bit of influence you have built up; every bit of influence the Other Man has built up for you since you came to the city."

"What do you mean by that?"

"I mean," Maxie leaned forward, "that Satan couldn't just raise a gun and shoot you to death. But he'd kill you just the same; make you a laughing stock. He'd slap you down, Dan; slap you down before all those people, just as he slapped you down right in your own room here."

Gargan's eyes lighted dangerously. He mumbled the words.

"Who said he did? He'd never dare try that."

Maxie Rosen spoke very calmly.

"I saw the mark, Gargan. Satan's mark! The prints where his fingers struck stood out plainly on your face. Don't glare, Dan. I've been along the Avenue for years. It's worse than death, that slap. He'd slap you right out of the racket, if you took it. Slap you right out of the big money and into the gutter. It isn't murder, as you understand it, Dan. It isn't murder as a jury understands it."

Gargan said, "What the hell! Rosen? You don't think I'd take that from any man. On the first crack I'd knock him over. He'd be inviting death—sure death."

Maxie Rosen moved narrow shoulders.

"There's been big guys who said the same thing. One of them was given sixty days last night for rolling a drunk. And he was plenty big once. I'm not trying to advise you, Gargan. I'm simply telling you."

Dan Gargan laughed. "I'd pin him to the floor before he ever raised a hand."

"Fine!" Rosen leaned against the desk and gripped Gargan's wrist. "We need you, Gargan; need you badly. Be prepared to make good on that. If things go wrong, open fire the moment Satan enters the Gold Room. Remember! We have his threat to kill you. But don't wait; don't give him the chance to put the mark on you."

"Nothing will go wrong tonight." Gargan's words were emphatic; his voice assured. Chopper Regan never missed what he shot at. "See you at the Gold Room."

THE GOLD Room of the Terrace Gardens was doing a good business; a very good business for that time of night. Even the owner, Nathan Gross, who had come through the prohibition era without closing his doors, was disturbed. He knew Dan Gargan and took him and Elsie Stone to one of the choice tables on the edge of the dance floor. He also knew Maxie Rosen, and it did not make him feel any better when Mr. Rosen chose a table far back from the others, and close to the door which was behind the screen and led to Gross' private office and the side street.

Nathan Gross was in on the know. Things travel quickly along Broadway, and Nathan had heard that Gargan had "taken it" from Satan. Just what was behind things he didn't fully understand, but he knew that Gargan was a big shot—fast becoming the biggest in the city—and that Satan Hall had no respect for time or place.

Nathan knew that the *place* was his. He hoped that the *time* was not. He knew exactly what happened to men who did not fully appreciate Dan Gargan. He knew also what happened to men who did not appreciate Satan Hall. But he shrugged his shoulders. Not indifferently, but resignedly. Nathan Gross had come through a hard school.

Dan Gargan ordered another bottle of wine, looked over at Elsie Stone and said:

"Twenty-five minutes after ten. We dance the next one, sweetheart. And then, what do you think?"

"I don't know. I don't know." She watched him with uncertain brown eyes. "Satan Hall will come through the main entrance."

"I wasn't thinking about Satan." Gargan sipped the champagne. "I was thinking about you. He'll come through the bar entrance and there's a man there with a machine gun." And as Elsie Stone's face suddenly drained of blood, "Right, lady! You sent him straight to his death." And leaning far across the table, "Don't talk. Don't say anything, or I'll let you have it smack in the mouth right here in the dining room. Sit down!" This as she half rose to her feet. "If you want a scene here I'll give you one. They'll have some respect here for Dan Gargan."

The woman dropped back into the chair. She didn't speak. She couldn't speak. She wanted to cry out, but what good would that do? She didn't have a chance there; didn't have a chance anywhere with Dan Gargan. She knew that. Everyone feared him. Everyone but Satan Hall. And in another minute Satan would be dead. And she was sending him to his death. She didn't think of the letters then. Dan Gargan had showed them to her in the cab. He had them on him now.

"Ten-thirty!" Gargan said as the music started. "Our last dance, Mrs. Stool-pigeon." He came around the table and jerked her roughly to her feet, crushed her tightly to him. "The dance of death!" he went on, as he swung her out on the floor, her feet following his mechanically, unconsciously. "Satan's dance of death, and yours."

He talked through the dance. But the woman didn't know what he was saying. She wasn't thinking of herself then; she wasn't thinking of Satan Hall. She was thinking of her baby. She could scream, of course; attract attention. Surely there were some honest people there! But the letters were still in Gargan's pocket and—there was her baby.

As if he read her thoughts, Gargan said, and his voice was hard and cold, as he pulled her tighter to him:

"You weren't thinking of making a break, were you? You couldn't get away with it. But if you did—if you did," he looked down into her face, forcing her chin up, "well, there are the letters. I'll return them, as I promised. Pin them on the baby's chest; pin them there with a knife, if you want to make a scene."

Dan Gargan pressed his hand into her back so hard that she should have cried out with pain, but nothing but a wheezing gasping sound came from her throat.

"Ten-thirty," Gargan said. "If Satan's on time, he's dead now. The music will drown out the Tommy gun. Slugs will play a tattoo up and down his body as he thinks of who sent him through that bar. Well, why don't you say something?"

The music stopped. The woman tried to jerk herself free. She looked straight toward the swing doors of the bar; the doors behind which Satan must lay dead. Those doors were opening. Someone was bringing the message then; bringing the message that Gargan waited to hear.

The doors swung wide. Gargan dropped the woman's wrist. Elsie Stone raised her hand to her mouth to smother the scream; the scream that never came.

CHAPTER XI

THE BLOW-OFF

THE LONG BAR of the Terrace Gardens, with its row of booths along the opposite wall, had few customers Thursday night. Shortly before ten o'clock Chopper Regan attracted no attention when he sauntered in and leaned against the bar. His coat was open, his hands were empty, his soft felt hat hid the baldness of his head and the wisp of hair that decorated it. He laid two white hands upon the bar, called for a whisky sour and drank it slowly.

Once or twice he spoke to the bartender. His conversation was mainly of food, and his busy day. It was at the bartender's suggestion that he turned to a booth about halfway between the entrance to the hall which led to the Gold Room and the Broadway entrance to the bar.

He ordered oysters, a minute steak, French fried potatoes, and, refusing ale, decided upon a bottled brand. Chopper Regan was not of a trusting nature.

He pulled a newspaper from his pocket, folded it carefully and laid it beside him as he ate. Once or twice he looked toward the entrance to the bar, changed the direction of the newspaper slightly and again looked toward the door. If someone had been watching him in particular, that person would have noticed that Chopper Regan did not again change the position of that newspaper. He must have been greatly interested in the reading matter, as he apparently read it over and over.

He finished his steak, wiped his mouth with his napkin and

dropped the napkin carelessly upon his knees. It was then that the brisk young man with the long suitcase entered. He was just passing the table when Regan looked up, said in apparent surprise:

"Charlie Griffin! Of all people."

Chopper Regan half rose in his seat to grip the newcomer's hand, but he was careful to keep the newspaper in the same position upon the table.

The newcomer laid down his suitcase, said something that sounded like "Curtis," and as Regan dropped back in his seat, leaned over to talk to him. No one saw the suitcase slide beneath the long seat upon which Regan sat. None saw Regan's left hand raise that suitcase to the seat beside him, open it with deft quick fingers, lift the object from within and draw it part way across his knees.

"You didn't touch it; not lay a hand on it?" Regan spoke to the man from whom he had never turned his head.

"Just as you packed it." The man nodded, felt the suitcase, moved by Regan's feet, brush against his toes and lifted it from the floor.

Regan glanced down at the watch upon his wrist. Then the thing in his hand moved upward. So sure and so deft were Regan's movements that a man watching closely could not have told if the long nose of the Tommy gun slipped up into the folded newspaper or if the paper slid down over that steel nose.

Griffin's body, quite unnecessarily it would seem, for the napkin now covered the drum of the gun, guarded Regan's movements from anybody at that bar. But Regan was a careful man. He spoke to the young man whose leaning body shielded him.

"When he comes in, beat it. I'll let him reach the beginning of the bar before I blast. It isn't a face I'd be likely not to know. You hold the side door open. Be quick or I'll trip on your heels. I'll have the rattler with me."

"Hell," said the young man. "You're not going to drag the gun along? There's no way to connect you up with that machine gun."

"I know. I know." Regan nodded. "But it's worth dough." And with a dry laugh as the young man started to object, "Forget it, Charlie. There ain't once chance in a hundred anyone will bother my 'out,' but I only play sure things. The old Tommy wouldn't be a bad thing to have in my hand if some college boy here has enough liquor aboard to make him decide to play the hero act."

A MAN stepped back from the bar almost directly in the way of the innocent looking newspaper and the deadly nose of the weapon it covered.

The man by the table cursed. Chopper Regan said as the man swayed back to the bar again:

"If that lad gets playful he'll be in for a surprise." And with a shrug of his shoulders, "It don't matter much. If Satan Hall leans that way, that mug is sure to get it anyway. George at the wheel?"

"That's right!" said the man, and then, "Suppose Satan don't come through that door!"

"He's got to." Regan grinned. "Dan Gargan paid five grand right on the nose for this job this way. Gargan ain't a man to spend his money foolishly. If I—" The newspaper raised slightly. Regan almost hissed the words through his teeth. "Watch it, boy. The door! On your way. It's Satan Hall."

The young man moved quickly back, turned and went toward the rear. He knew there wasn't going to be much time. But he didn't run. He wouldn't do that until he heard the rat-tat, the sudden staccato notes of the Tommy gun.

He turned once and saw Satan. The broad shoulders, the long arms, the empty hands. Yes, he saw all that, but he didn't notice it or even remember it. It was the face he looked at. The face of a killer who was moving in long even strides toward the Broadway end of the bar and toward sudden and violent death.

To Chopper Regan the job was an easy one. He didn't care how fast a man was with a gun. Men that he blasted out didn't have a chance at a gun once the Tommy gun started spouting.

After that? Well, men full of slugs didn't use guns. Dead men never did.

Satan wouldn't be different than any other man. He'd reach the line; the imaginary line there at the bar. Then his huge body would jar and twist and pitch to the floor, just as the bodies of many others had. Regan knew that; never for a moment doubted that.

And Satan reached the line.

Things happened almost at once. Things that Chopper Regan never was able to explain. The first was—their eyes met, his and Satan's, over a distance of perhaps twelve feet. Regan saw the deadly green light in Satan's eyes; cold, cruel, vicious. For a split second, Chopper Regan looked back behind Satan's eyes and saw death—his death. And in that split second he knew fear. And in that fear the nose of the Tommy gun moved. The newspaper slipped down and Regan's fear turned suddenly to terror.

A black object seemed to jump into Satan's right hand. Regan could have sworn that that right hand never moved from Satan's side, yet it must have, because Satan Hall was going to shoot him to death.

Chopper Regan, who never missed what he shot at, tightened a finger upon the trigger of that Tommy gun; tightened it as a single shot rang out. But Regan didn't get to tighten that finger enough; not quite enough. He was dead before he could.

A tiny hole appeared in Regan's forehead. It was a round hole, that was widening and turning red; turning red just before the Tommy gun tumbled to the floor and Chopper Regan pitched forward across the table.

SATAN WAS still moving as Regan fell across that table. To a white coated figure at the rear of the room who had suddenly turned and started toward the door to the Gold Room, Satan spoke.

"A man just died," he said simply without breaking his stride. "If you want to be another, one, try entering that room."

The white coated man fell back, cowered close to the wall.

He saw both of Satan's hands, knew that they held no guns; but the fear was there just the same. He had trouble getting his words out.

"I didn't know. I don't know anything about it. I don't know who the dead man is. I don't know why he was here."

"I do." Satan's lips were very straight. "He was here to let me know that Dan Gargan is inside and that he is not expecting me."

Satan Hall threw open both of the wide swing doors and entered the Gold Room; entered it just as the music stopped and just as Dan Gargan, almost in the center of the dance floor, stopped, half released the woman, and faced Satan Hall.

Things had gone wrong; terribly wrong. Gargan knew that. He knew also that, despite Satan's threat to kill, Satan couldn't jerk out a gun and shoot him to death. His lips curved into a sneer as he looked at Satan; a sneer that suddenly trembled upon his lips.

Dan Gargan knew then, as Satan walked across that floor toward him, that Maxie was right. He was facing his whole future; saw the past that he had built up tumbling. Satan Hall was going to slap him down; slap him down publicly just as he had privately.

Those in on the know dropped back through fear. Those not in on the know dropped back through instinct. Only the woman didn't give ground. Elsie Stone stood there frozen to the floor, her left hand against her chest, her right clutched tightly at her side. It wasn't fear that held her so. It was something else; a nameless something. Perhaps just death.

Satan didn't speak. He wouldn't speak. Gargan didn't speak. He couldn't speak. He wanted to say something; tried to say something. But a dry tongue clung to drier lips.

Satan's hands were empty and Satan was almost upon him. Gargan had a gun that he could draw and shoot with a lightning-like speed. Satan's hands were empty.

What had Rosen said? To shoot before Satan reached him;

to shoot before those hands came up. And Gargan did it. His right hand shot beneath his left armpit. A gun jarred into it just as he saw the flash of Satan's hand. Just a hand that went up and down, and now held something black.

Gargan fired; wildly, blindly, not with his usual deadly precision.

One, two, three times Gargan's finger closed upon the trigger while Satan's hand was flashing. Satan jarred, half turned, and yellow-blue flame roared from his gun.

A WOMAN screamed; a man knocked over a table. Nathan Gross shouted something, but he didn't step out on the dance floor. Just the three figures held the floor. The slightly bent form of Satan, the little erect form of Elsie Stone, and Dan Gargan, who dropped his gun to his side, clicked his heels together like a soldier on parade and pitched forward on his face.

Few people, in the confusion, saw Satan kneel beside the dead man, run long strong fingers inside his coat, transfer something oblong and white from the dead man's pocket to his own.

The police were there when Satan came to his feet, jerked a handkerchief from his pocket, and, folding it hurriedly, tucked it inside his shirt close against the bullet hole beneath his left armpit. Then he moved toward the swaying woman, caught her with his right arm and led her to a chair beside the table.

"I trapped you! I trapped you!" Elsie Stone was saying over and over. "Gargan fooled me. I didn't know."

"But I knew." Satan nodded. "And I've got the letters, as I promised. Gargan would suspect you'd warn me; might even have listened in on your call. And that's what I wanted. To know the trap and let him spring it. But it's all right now. Your trouble is over. You served the law tonight; the letters are yours. Burn them and—" Satan paused, turned his head, looked up.

"Well, Inspector?" he said to the man standing beside him.

"Not well at all, Satan!" Inspector Falsom was saying. "You killed the man in the bar too. Yes, too. That man," he jerked a thumb back over his shoulder, "is Dan Gargan, and he's dead.

You killed him and there will be hell to pay. Gargan was a big shot. He had a lot of friends."

Satan looked squarely at the inspector, grinned evilly, said very slowly:

"Yes, I killed him. I came to question him about the death of the Greek and the two children. So that cleans up the killing of those kids. Don't worry about Gargan. As you say, he's dead—and dead men have no friends."

Elsie Stone was leaning across the table, clutching both of Satan's hands. Her eyes were wet, her body was trembling.

"To think," she said, "I could see a man shot to death and be glad. Satan—Mr. Hall, I can never repay you. What shall I do to show my gratitude?" She broke then, was sobbing, leaning forward on the table. But she wasn't conspicuous because of that. Other women were doing the same thing.

Satan said, "Go back where you started before the blackmail began. It's just a bad dream that's over. Lead a healthy, normal life."

The woman still held both of Satan's hands. He was looking directly at her and that was why he didn't see the lawyer.

Maxie Rosen came quietly to his feet and passed through the little door behind the screen; the little door that led to Nathan Gross' private office and the street.

Maxie Rosen sighed as he pulled down the brim of his hat and turned up his coat collar. The Other Man would be needing a new "front" now.

CHAPTER XII

COP-KILLER

IT WAS SHORTLY before noon on that narrow business street in Brooklyn. Just at the dull time when the housewives had finished their shopping and gone home to prepare lunch for the children who were not yet dismissed from school.

The two detectives who crouched low in the hallway of the deserted tenement kept their eyes glued on the dirty fly-stained window of the delicatessen store across the street. Their voices low, sounded strangely loud to them in the dank mustiness.

The older man said:

"There will only be a couple of hoods. We'll follow them into the store as soon as they leave the car. The orders are shoot to kill. It's a pushover for us, Clayton. I'll let you go ahead of me. There may be a jump in rank for you."

The younger man's face brightened; he was enthusiastic.

"Thanks. That's swell, Mack. I could use a bit more dough— the new kid, you know. Is it just a stick up?"

"Search me." Mack moved shoulders expressively. "But I think it's a racket.

"They're going to shake down the delicatessen stores in Brooklyn—popping this guy off as a sample. The Gargan gang forming again. You know, Dan Gargan that Detective Satan Hall killed. There's guys that say Gargan really had little to do with this new mob. That he was just a front to work for the man behind him. I met Satan Hall once. He's poison."

"I heard that," the younger man agreed. "It must be tough,

81

though, to have to go it alone. On the police force, yet not really a part of it. I guess the cops hate him about as much as the crooks."

"They don't understand him," Mack started, stopped and laughed, "I guess I don't understand him either. Maybe no man could like him. He's a killer, Boy, just a killer. We've sort of looked on him as the Black Knight of the Department. Well, Gargan pulled the gun first—and Gargan's dead."

"And Satan?"

"Laughed at the police surgeon when he dressed the wound, and never came in again for another dressing. Yep, you hate his guts when you meet him. But you admire those same guts when you hear what he's done or read about it in the papers."

For a few minutes they discussed things in general. The older man speaking of a generation ago. The Haymarket shoot-up. The Rosenthal murder; others.

"It wasn't so different, in a way. Influence, pull, intimidation." Mack mentioned a dozen well known murders that were never solved. "In half those cases the old-timers can tell you the actual killer, but they can't make it stick before twelve men. Today, it's a more modern warfare. Machine guns. Take Chopper Regan— came on from Philly to kill Satan and Satan knocked him off before he ever got a chance. They say the worst of them now is Ford—Johnny Ford. A dozen deaths smack at his door. No evidence to prove him guilty; plenty to prove him innocent."

The young man cursed softly.

"Hell!" said the younger man. "It wouldn't seem like murder to walk up and shoot such rats through the back."

"That's Satan's stuff—only not in the back." And raising his head, "This tip looks like a bast. How's the missus and the baby?"

The young man scratched his head.

"Fine. I was just thinking about 'em. I was to bring home something for the baby's cough, but I can't remember what it was."

"Sorry I can't help you. Boy. I'm not up on things like that now." He laughed. "I drop out in the evening and go a scuttle of suds with my kids now." He shook his graying head. "It only seems like yesterday when—when— Hell! There they are. Get them!"

THE CAR had slowed almost to a stop. Two men threw open its rear door and were on the street running toward the delicatessen store, firing shots through the window before they even reached the sidewalk. The death car jerked ahead, jumped down the street and turned the corner.

The young detective Clayton, was in the lead; his gun in his hand, raised when Mack called to him.

"They're on the kill, Boy. Let them have it before they get in!" And as Clayton raised his gun, "Look out—look out! A trap! And it's Johnny Ford!" The old policeman's voice was high and tense.

Clayton turned his head for a moment; turned it just as the sharp staccato notes of the machine gun started a rapid tat-tat. He turned it in time to see the face of the man who stood directly in the doorway of the empty shop beside the delicatessen store, his legs spread far apart; lips tight, and the spouting gun jerking in his hands. Turned it in time to see the quick flashes that merged at once with the strong glare of the sun. And he saw Mack too. Saw his jarring body twisting and jumping in the air before he went down.

But that was all he saw, for his own body too was twisting, turning, moving without the use of his own legs. He didn't see Mack then; didn't see anything but the blurred whiteness of the killer's face.

At the very moment the spraying lead pounded him to the pavement he had a thought; a single thought. He suddenly remembered the name of the medicine he was to bring home. And he also knew he would never reach that home. He shouted something. He thought it was the name of the medicine, but it wasn't. It was a man's name.

Clear and loud in the lull of that machine gun Clayton

shouted the single name; the name of the man who was killing him. Shouted just the two words: "Johnny Ford."

A car rushed down the street. Two men left the delicatessen store, climbed quickly in the open door. They pulled the man with the machine gun in after them. The car was quickly gathering speed. It fairly bounded down the street.

For almost a full minute there was a dead silence. Then a siren screeched around the corner. People ran into the street. There was life—and death.

A few minutes later school was out. Children stood around and gazed down at the twisted bodies of the dead; the dead servants of the city. Inside the delicatessen store someone had thrown a soiled sheet over another huddled body, the former owner of the shop.

Unseen by the crowd, unseen by the police, a little girl of ten crawled from under a pushcart a few minutes after the shooting. She stood there dazed and frightened, then turned and ran screaming down the street straight into the arms of a stout policeman who for many years had watched the children at the school crossing.

THE FAT policeman had left the private office of the Commissioner of Police, and had taken the child with him. The Commissioner turned to Detective Satan Hall.

"Funny," he said. "That kid was afraid of everyone but you. She'll grow up to know better, Satan." The Commissioner laughed dryly.

An editorial writer in a leading evening paper had called Satan, "The Man Nobody Likes." But the Commissioner liked him. Not because of his deadly appearance and more deadly accuracy with a gun. Not because of his great help to the Department. In fact there were times when he wished that Satan would be less the killer and more the watchful, waiting, patient detective. The Commissioner just liked him for himself—for the man he was.

The Commissioner said, "That's a wise cop, Satan. An old

timer. He didn't shout what the child told him to the first reporter nor even to the first superior officer he met. He came straight to me. Things went wrong—terribly wrong. I was tipped off to that kill by a stool pigeon, but never suspected it was important enough to be covered so thoroughly. It was either an important job or a trap for those cops."

Satan stirred restlessly, said, "I've got to get back to my job. The child said it was Johnny Ford. What do you intend to do about that?"

"She said the dead detective called out Ford's name before he died. She wasn't able to identify Ford's picture, for he had his head buried down on his chest, his hat over his eyes."

Satan said in a dull voice, "Johnny Ford is close to Frank Wheeler. And Frank Wheeler is the logical man to fill Dan Gargan's shoes—the new Front for the Other Man." He leaned forward, "There's a chain there, Commissioner; a chain we've used more than once in other cases. Put the hooks into Ford and he'll squeal on Wheeler. Put the hooks into Wheeler and he'll squeal on Maxie Rosen. Put the hooks into Maxie Rosen and he'll tell us who the Other Man is. Find the Other Man, and the city is freed of its greatest menace. By far its greatest menace. This new power of the Other Man is fast absorbing all other powers."

The Commissioner said, "In that chain every link is a weak one. Johnny Ford will show up with an alibi that can't be questioned. You know that as well as I do."

"He might," Satan's words were low, "show up in the morgue with a bullet in his head." And after a moment, "Would I need an alibi for that—an alibi from some influential person?"

"God in Heaven, Satan! That would be murder." And when Satan just let his lips part and his teeth show, "I'm not denying the finality of it. But it would be vengeance—not justice. Those cops didn't have a chance! It was just a slaughter."

"That's right. It was slaughter. I didn't know either of the cops well, but Mack was on the force for a great many years. Clayton had a wife and kid."

"They'll be taken care of, of course," the commissioner said.

"Sure—the living will be taken care of, but what of the dead? What of Mack and Clayton?"

THE COMMISSIONER tapped his desk, studied Satan, and after two attempts to speak, changed the trend of the conversation entirely.

"Look here, Satan," he said. "Things are breaking rather fast—surprisingly fast. Here we have a situation in which an unknown man—unknown even to the men who serve him—has not only planned, but is actually succeeding in taking over every racket in our city. The newspapers print screaming headlines and scathing editorials that law and order in the city has disappeared. The judicial, the District Attorney's office, and, yes, the police department itself."

"Not the police department," denied Satan. "The police can only make arrests. Crooked and influential lawyers, politically controlled judges whose very existence in office depends on the racketeers whom they are paid to send to jail are the cause of continued and increasing crime. Witnesses are intimidated, bought off, driven out of the State or killed. And perhaps the greatest menace of all—the uncanny knowledge of this Other Man who forces the representative and apparently honest influential citizen to perjure himself by alibiing a wanted man. Wanted for anything up to murder. This Other Man must be well known; must have lived in the city a long time and been familiar with the law and the lawless. He's even gotten to such men as Glenwood E. Nostrom."

"That was the Gargan case." The Commissioner nodded. "You killed Gargan, Satan; Gargan, the Front, who carried out the orders of the Other Man. I thought then that Gargan's death would give us time to locate this unknown terror before a new Front; a new physical leader for the underworld to fear and obey was built up to represent him."

"Has this new Front appeared?"

The Commissioner shrugged his shoulders.

"Not an actual leader yet. At least no one like Gargan has appeared; flouting the taw, blowing of his protection, laughing at the police and even escaping punishment for a murder which we knew about—which you said you saw."

Satan nodded emphatically. "But Glenwood E. Nostrom was willing to go on the witness stand and swear that Gargan was with him at the time of the murders."

"That's right, Satan. You couldn't beat that alibi. There are few men in the city and fewer in politics more respected than Nostrom. What this Other Man could have found in his past to force him to do that, I don't know. Unless you were mistaken about seeing Gargan, Satan."

Satan Hall grinned nastily.

"What about Johnny Ford? They were cops, Commissioner, and no matter how the boys look on me. I'm a cop too." Satan jumped suddenly back to the talk the Commissioner had avoided.

"Patience," the Commissioner said as the fingers of his hands pounded against each other, and the twisting of his face showed everything but patience. "This Brooklyn killing puts a different aspect on things, Satan. I thought the Other Man was going to clean up, take over the Bronx first—the delicatessen stores there. I've sent men over to Brooklyn, the Other Man's organization must have quit the Bronx after the delicatessen owners met, banded together and with my assurance of protection, refused to bow to the racketeers' demands."

Satan rubbed a hand up over his head.

"It's a grand racket. Can't you do anything. Commissioner? Do anything before this Other Man takes over the entire city and the police obey his orders? Why, every meat market in the Bronx has knuckled down, and the racketeers' fee is collected openly. Damn it, Commissioner! If the man who collects this money demanded police protection so that he would not be robbed while he went from market to market, I dare say you'd give him that protection."

THE COMMISSIONER'S lips were grim, but he did not avoid the question.

"I'd have to, Satan. He'd be entitled to it. You understand how cleverly and efficiently it's done. Many of the big chain stores pay for legitimate protection to some of our best known detective agencies. The Other Man is working the same game. Owners are threatened by so called racketeers. They don't pay. Their place is bombed or the owner is killed just as the owner in Brooklyn was killed today. Then the Preston Protective Agency goes to work. They have been in business a long time. They offer their services. Their price is high. But their protection is sure. Not a meat market that bears their little oblong bit of steel with the Preston name upon it has been molested."

"Because," said Satan, "the Preston Agency is controlled by the Other Man."

"Prove it." The Commissioner's eyes narrowed. "We can't do that. No store that bears the Preston seal has ever been bothered. They only have to collect—not protect. The Other Man gives orders and a Preston protected place of business is never threatened; never wrecked."

"There is no doubt about that." Satan was emphatic. "Every racketeer knows that the Other Man is behind Preston—" He paused. "I wonder, Commissioner, if Preston actually is the Other Man."

The Commissioner started, then shook his head doubtfully.

"I don't know," he finally spoke, "I thought of that too. But Preston has been in the private detective business for quite a few years. He would have thought of this sooner."

"It takes time to think up a thing as big as this. Don't forget Preston is a detective—has many working for him. In the course of the years he must have learned many things. He might easily have planned it years ago, and just lately felt in a position to go through with it. But I think I know who the new Front is—Frank Wheeler."

"Wheeler—Smooth Frank Wheeler." The Commissioner thought a long time. "A bad man, Satan. A more dangerous man than Gargan. Gargan was a blustering, conceited gunman who swaggered about the city, threatening almost openly. His plans were not hard to follow. He worked faster, organized faster, caused fear to come faster, but would never dig that fear in as deep as Wheeler could. They say—and other tortures he committed bear it out—that Wheeler cut a living child almost to pieces to discover the hiding place of her father; a hiding place that she did not know." And after a moment as he shook his head, "That's why I ask for patience, Satan. I think the new leader, the new Front, will be my greatest coup against the Other Man."

"Who?" Satan looked puzzled.

"The man," the Commissioner said slowly, "who crossed his arms on a dark street in the Seventies one night and killed Razor Young, the machine gunner, and Jerry Lock, murderer. Eddie Greer."

"Hell—" Satan looked surprised. "Why, I killed those men."

The Commissioner nodded.

"I know that, and you know that. But die Other Man doesn't know that. Nor does the lawyer, Maxie Rosen, whom you believe carries the messages from the Other Man, know that. They all think Greer did it. Greer hid out. Word soon reached him that he is considered quite a man in the racket to wipe out Young and Lock. He's strutting the Avenue posing as a bad guy to fool with—and he's beginning to believe it himself."

THE COMMISSIONER leaned forward.

"That's my coup, Satan, my ace card. Greer was selling me information. That's why Gargan wanted him killed. Now he's a big shot. He has a chance to be the Front man. I put the idea into his head, and he feels certain he'll get it. Satan, he can discover the Other Man for me."

Satan bobbed his head up and down slowly.

"I hope it turns out as you plan. Commissioner. And it might if Eddie pulls off the trick. Frank Wheeler is clever. Maxie Rosen is shrewd, and until he overstepped the line a few years ago, had one of the most brilliant legal brains in the city. As for the Other Man—he must be a genius of crime. No matter what they believe Eddie Greer did one night, he'll always be a small-time chiseler in a big racket. And these men will finally know it. Everything points to Frank Wheeler for the new Front."

The Commissioner pursed his lips, said:

"This time you're wrong, Satan. Eddie Greer is to be the new Front man. It's in the bag. He told me so himself." And as Satan moved toward the door, "Where are you going? Over to Brooklyn?"

Satan shook his head.

"I'm going back to my job. Maybe I never should have left it—even to come here."

"A waste of time that, Satan. Don't worry about Johnny Ford. I'll get to the inside and see if he's prepared an alibi."

"No, no." Satan shook his head very slowly, and the Commissioner jarred slightly erect as he saw that burning hate in Satan's eyes. "I won't worry about Johnny Ford, cop-killer. But I wonder, would he worry about me if he knew the truth."

"Truth, truth—what truth?"

Satan's green eyes widened, and the hate was still there. He said simply:

"What truth? Why that I'll shoot him to death the first time I meet him face to face."

The Commissioner started to protest, words forming on his lips. But before he could speak, Satan Hall was gone.

CHAPTER XIII

SMOOTH FRANK WHEELER

SMOOTH FRANK WHEELER was a heavy-set man in his late thirties. His face was placid and his lips had a whimsical twist at the end. He parted his hair in the center, smoked large black cigars; the smoke of which he inhaled deeply.

"Smooth" had been the title hung on him some years before. He was a big man in the racket now, and although he secretly liked the moniker, objected to being openly addressed by it. He felt that only common gangsters bore such ridiculous nicknames.

He let smoke settle in his lungs for a moment then blew great clouds toward the ceiling. When he spoke to the man opposite him in that room above the Café Wellington his voice was low; not exactly soft, rather with a purr to it—just smooth perhaps.

"It's like this, Maxie." He never took his steady soft brown eyes off Maxie Rosen. "There's an unknown man running this racket. His idea is to control all rackets and although I laughed when he first sat down to play, I see now that he knows the game. But he's got to have a Front. Someone for the boys to see and trust and believe in. Dan Gargan was all right while he lived. But he was a blustering, strutting gun-slinging guy, and his number was up the moment he started making faces at Satan Hall." He leaned forward across the flat desk now; the desk he hoped to occupy and give orders over shortly. He said:

"I could shoot all around Gargan, yet I wouldn't have pulled a gun on Satan Hall, even if his hands did hang empty at his sides. That's his trick—Satan's trick. It makes murder look like self defense Satan gets away with it because he's a cop—and he's still a cop despite this master mind of yours; this unknown power that you call the Other Man. Satan's the Commissioner's pet and the Other Man can't reach the Commissioner."

Maxie Rosen bent shoulders, leaned further forward as he dragged up a chair and sat down. His eyes, sharp and quick, had been and were still studying Frank Wheeler, trying to look down inside of him. Maxie could read men. What he thought as he looked into those soft brown eyes of Wheeler's was more what he knew than what he saw. It sent his shoulders up slightly to make the knobby appearance of them more pronounced. Frank Wheeler was hard and cruel. The men he used were like that, too. But Frank Wheeler was a natural. He wasn't hard only because that helped him rule other men just as hard. And he wasn't cruel because cruelty was feared. Wheeler was just naturally cruel because he liked to see other people suffer. And if the truth be told, that was what Maxie wanted and appreciated and exactly what the Other Man needed.

Maxie spoke finally.

"And if the need arose just how would you eliminate the greatest menace to the Other Man—to his plans—Detective Satan Hall."

"I would shoot him to death," said Frank Wheeler quietly. "And I would shoot him through the back." And when Maxie started to make an objection, Frank Wheeler raised his hand, said, "And I wouldn't shoot until that opportunity presented itself."

"In the meantime?" Maxie wanted to know.

"In the meantime," Wheeler said, "I wouldn't take any of his guff. I've been around a long time. I don't have to."

THERE WAS a long pause after this and Wheeler finally got off what was on his mind. "Dan Gargan is dead. This Unknown Man doesn't make an appearance. The boys have got to have a visible leader. One visible leader—not two."

"Turn around and let us get a slant at that pan of yours."

"Not two, eh?" Maxie rubbed slender quick fingers along his sharp chin. "You mean—"

"I mean Eddie Greer." Frank Wheeler's lips snapped and if the softness went out of his voice, the smoothness remained— a low sort of ominous smoothness. "Eddie Greer laps up the merry mucilage. I think he sniffs coke. He's yellow at heart. Gargan suspected him of selling information to the police. Anyway, Eddie was treading on Gargan's toes. That's why Gargan planned his death. That's why Razor Young and Jerry Lock were sent to kill him."

"Perhaps—perhaps," Maxie agreed grudgingly. "But don't forget that Eddie Greer simply crossed his arms and shot both

Young and Lock to death. Nothing yellow about that. You knew both those boys. None better for a job."

Wheeler shook his head; his brown eyes were puzzled.

"I never understood that," he said. "And I never understood why Greer hid out until after Gargan was killed, if he was so fast, so tough. I've always felt that Young and Lock were over-confident that night; too sure of the cringing Greer. They didn't expect it."

"No one expects death," Rosen said.

"I always expect death." Great clouds of smoke rolled down on the desk and caromed swiftly toward the window. "That's why I've been so many years along the Avenue. But we only have one question, Maxie. I control a lot of territory—a lot of boys. I'm willing to take orders from a guy like the Other Man. He's got brains. But I've got to be the lad who takes Gargan's place—the lad who runs things. Don't shake your head. I mean it. I—I—" A tap on the door stopped him.

Frank Wheeler raised his head, looked toward the door, said, "Come in."

A rat-faced, thin unpleasant looking man slid in, shut the door behind him.

Wheeler spoke impatiently. "Well. Let's have it, Stutt. Did it go right? Go on—yap. You know Maxie Rosen. The Other Man's agent."

"It went off like a shop full of clocks." Stutt rubbed the back of his hand across his mouth. "The two boys who were in Fred's car—you know, Fred from Pittsburgh—hopped right out of the bus. Fred drove on, turning the corner. He give me the signal where I was parked down the street. Them cops thought sure Fred's would be the getaway car and he'd park just around the corner, but he drove on like—"

"Sure, sure—" Frank Wheeler lifted the cigar from his mouth. "We know that. Did the cops fall for the play? Did they run out?"

Stutt licked at his lips, his little eyes burnt; burnt with the fire of false courage. The criminal's ally; the criminal courage—dope.

"They run a bit—rods in their hands. The boys dashed right toward the store; ran for the guy who was to get it. The cops jumped from the hallway across the street, guns out. Hell, it was a laugh. Johnny Ford just stepped out of that vacant store you had a lad rent a month ago and opened up with the Tommy gun. Were them cops surprised! They staggered all over the street before they fell."

"And the boys inside in the delicatessen?"

"Shot the owner of the dump half a dozen times in the chest. Walked out easy, and I picked them up. Everything is Jake."

WHEN STUTT left Frank Wheeler stuck his cigar in his mouth, let his lips twist slightly as he looked at Maxie Rosen.

"How do you like that job?" he said. "The owner of that delicatessen had three kids. I'm pretty sure one of the cops went in for raising a family. I never got that end of it, Maxie. Why a guy with kids? The papers will raise hell about it."

Maxie said, "That's what the Other Man wants them to do—sob stuff, editorials condemning the police protection; pictures of the families. It's psychology, Frank. I had a stoolie give the tip-off to the Commissioner. That's why the cops were waiting."

"But hell," Frank Wheeler was puzzled, "I ran it according to schedule. That guy only had a small shop. It was in Brooklyn. We haven't lined up to collect over there. This makes it a damned good start, I know. But now half the cops in the city will be guarding the delicatessen stores in Brooklyn."

"And that," said Maxie, "is where the psychology comes in. You see, we were all set to take over the delicatessen business in the Bronx. That Dutchman, Otto Shirmer, went straight to the Commissioner of Police when the first small shop was threatened. The delicatessen owners organized. The Commissioner addressed their meeting. But it was that damned Dutchman who held them together. They won't put up one cent for protection. Preston has had his men up there."

"I know. I know. And we laid off them."

"That's right." Maxie nodded. "We laid off them and now

the Commissioner will think we've opened up on the Brooklyn stores." Maxie spread his hands far apart. "You said, Frank, that if the Dutchman were out of it, the boys in the Bronx would pay up. So, take Johnny Ford and the two lads who were with him in Brooklyn up there tonight—and get the Dutchman."

Frank Wheeler rubbed his hands.

"Johnny will blow a hole in his stomach big enough for the Delicatessen Organization to walk through—even carrying wreaths. I'll superintend the job myself. That was damned good thinking, Maxie."

Maxie looked shrewdly at Frank Wheeler.

"It's not my thinking," he said slowly. "It's just the thoughts of another coming through my mouth—the Other Man." And before Frank Wheeler could say anything, "Otto Shirmer has to die. As a matter of form and good policy, Chester Preston from the Preston Detective Agency will visit him before you do. Offer him the same protection the meat market owners took after a few of their places blew up. Remember that, Frank. There is nothing secret about Chester Preston. He's running a legitimate protective and detective agency licensed by the State."

"But won't it look bad his coming in just before like that?"

"Bad for other organized groups of merchants who don't want to pay. They'll remember Preston's visit just before the blow-off. And Preston will have an alibi better than even the Other Man could provide him with. He'll be with a Deputy Police Commissioner discussing the danger in the Bronx; telling him that he has been trying to sell the protection of his agency to the stores, and blowing a bit about all he did for the meat markets when he tacked up his little tin sign—Protected By the Chester Preston Detective Agency."

"It's big—it's big!" Frank Wheeler nodded his approval. "Every delicatessen in the Bronx will sign up tomorrow when the Dutchman takes it." And as Maxie got up to go, "Just a minute, Maxie. About the leader—the Front—the visible head for the Other Man. I'm entitled to that job now and I want it."

MAXIE ROSEN caught the threat in Wheeler's voice.

"That is in the hands of the Other Man," Maxie said. And before Wheeler could put the question that Maxie felt rather than saw forming on his lips, "I don't get much chance to see him lately."

Frank Wheeler said, "Get a chance to see him—soon." He waited a long time, but Maxie didn't speak. "I'll want you to tell me tomorrow night. If you don't—"

"If I don't?" Maxie Rosen stiffened.

"If you don't—well, the Other Man knows that his best alibi witness is Glenwood E. Nostrom. And he knows that I can bust wide open the chances of his ever using Glenwood E. Nostrom again."

Maxie Rosen permitted himself a smile. He appreciated the cool, heartless, almost soulless cruelty of Frank Wheeler. He appreciated it because he felt it himself. Maxie Rosen had started off as a criminal lawyer; had risen to be a big one. Knew all there was to know about crime in its many phases. But the Bar Association and the city officials had switched his profession around. From a criminal lawyer he had become a lawyer criminal. If they no longer permitted Maxie Rosen to practice law, they had not been able to prevent him from practicing crime. But he said:

"If I were you I wouldn't bust up that influence with or over Glenwood E. Nostrom. You see, Frank, if things go wrong Nostrom will be your alibi tonight."

Smooth Frank Wheeler's eyes brightened.

"Things won't go wrong tonight, Maxie," he said. "I'll be outside Shirmer's store, well back in the car. I want the boys to know that their *new leader* goes on the job with them."

Maxie Rosen spoke very seriously.

"If it weren't for this man, Otto Shirmer, those few bombs that were tossed around would have turned the trick long ago. Don't forget, Frank—this Dutchman has guts."

"I won't forget." Wheeler's lips curled. "Johnny Ford will scatter those guts around a bit with a Tommy gun."

Frank Wheeler got up, walked toward the door. "It will make a good impression on the Dutchman's friends when they look at his body. I'll get Ford to run the rattler over him, too." Wheeler grinned broadly. "You know, for the psychology you were talking about. The other delicatessen store owners will feel every one of those slugs as if they'd entered their own bodies; dream of it at night after they get a good look. And if they want it that way and don't pay off we'll make their dreams come true."

Frank Wheeler's head went back and he laughed. "It might make a good song, eh, Maxie? I'll bet you never suspected a touch of sentiment in me."

Maxie Rosen's eyes widened. It struck him suddenly that Frank Wheeler's laugh was real; not feigned. Here was a man who enjoyed dealing out death. An opponent perhaps worthy of Satan Hall. Yes, Maxie thought that the Other Man had at last found a leader.

But Maxie didn't say anything about those thoughts as Smooth Frank Wheeler walked slowly from the room.

CHAPTER XIV

THE BIG KNOCK-OVER

OTTO SHIRMER WAS not very tall. He was thick-set and heavy and his mustaches were rather long and yellow at the ends. He had arrived in America a great many years ago, worked hard and opened his first delicatessen store in the Bronx. He had a son who was now a doctor and a daughter who attended an expensive girls' school in Washington. He had been an American citizen even before his first child was born.

He had not made his money in stocks, bonds or the rise in real estate years back. He had made it and saved it right out of his business; his delicatessen shop. It wasn't a big establishment but it was a good one. People got what they paid for and came back and paid for more and had been doing it for over a generation.

Now he stood behind his counter letting his eyes drop to the evening paper below it. He talked as he read. His words addressed both to the white-coated man beside him and to the broad white shoulders of the man who with his back to Shirmer moved little cakes slowly about on a low shelf.

"It's organization," Otto Shirmer was saying as he read. "I tell these men, these friends and business rivals, that if one man pays nothing all men pay nothing. Then blooey—rackets go bust. Look now, these gunmen go to Brooklyn. I had a brother in Brooklyn, but he don't do well after the times are not so good. He is married and in business in Chicago and would be doing well only he pays so much money every week for protection."

Otto Shirmer paused, read a bit more, and without raising

his head again spoke in his thick voice. "Look now'. They kill two men—two police detectives and the—"

He stopped, looked up and faced the dark, hook-nosed, hard-eyed stranger who walked slowly forward and laid both his arms flat on the counter beside the scales. He let his lips slip back. His nose wrinkled with his narrowing eyes and the ridges appeared in his forehead. That facial contortion was a smile. Otto Shirmer recognized it as such after perhaps ten seconds.

By that time the man was talking, letting his words roll out easily, pleasantly; almost confidentially yet with a touch of something else in them. Certainly not a threat, perhaps not a warning, but a drawling foreboding sound that struck the unsensitive ears of Otto Shirmer with an unnamed, unconscious feeling of impending danger.

"Mr. Shirmer," the man was saying. "I've been reading about you in the papers. How you and you alone defied the racket and others, many others in your business, followed you."

Otto Shirmer smiled.

"Not me. Not me." Rolling eyes, moving shoulders, outspread hands disclaimed all credit. "It was the Police Commissioner—his promise of protection. He came and addressed our meeting himself—and such a busy man too."

The stranger nodded.

"He is busy. Very busy indeed to promise you all that protection; a protection it would be a physical impossibility to give. Why, there must be more delicatessen stores in the City of New York than there are policemen. What about the other stores—the markets up here—they were very wise indeed."

OTTO SHIRMER stiffened, glanced down at the evening paper, realized that the revolver he kept was on the little shelf covered by that paper. His hands were on the counter, visible to the man who faced him. But Otto Shirmer looked straight into those gray-pink eyes; steady mean eyes; eyes that were used to a penetrating stare; that had even practiced such a directness over the years.

"You're not a reporter." Otto Shirmer raised his voice when he spoke. There was the slightest quiver to it. The man in the white coat alongside Shirmer looked at the stranger. The man with his back to the counter didn't turn. He kept his head down, still arranging cakes, at least his elbows moved back and forth.

"No." The stranger opened his right hand and without changing the position of his arms on the counter flipped a card before the delicatessen owner. "No, I'm not a reporter. The name is Preston—Chester Preston—the Protective Agency. Oh, I know, I know. Some of my men have been here—and had no luck." The mask of a smile appeared on his face again while the pleasant good-natured face of Otto Shirmer turned to a frown.

"Well—" Shirmer's voice was loud now; shrill. "I saw your men—three of them. I told them I didn't want to buy any protection—wouldn't buy any—that I pay taxes for that."

"That's all right," Chester Preston said easily. "I don't often go out on jobs myself and try to drum up trade. But in your case I felt it was different. You showed nerve, real nerve. You know what happened to the markets before we protected them. And you know they're safe now." And when Shirmer tried to break in, "It's just our agency's reputation. Tack our little metal warning on your door and these racketeers will leave you alone as if you were the plague. We never let a client down. We follow a case until the crook is punished. We'll spend a hundred thousand dollars just to get one man—an example to others. That's why they never bother places we cover."

Shirmer said, "I told your salesmen and I tell you—I won't spend one cent."

Chester Preston laughed.

"Courageous and wise both, eh? And what's more, with an eye to business. You won't have to spend a cent, Mr. Shirmer. We'll give you protection and put up our house notice free. There, don't thank me. It's good business with us. Your name will have influence with the other delicatessen owners. They'll see you're worried—and become our clients."

"They'll see I'm yellow, you mean," Shirmer bristled. "I've heard about you, Mr. Chester Preston; heard about you and your agency and—"

"And," interrupted Chester Preston, "you were warned not to engage the services of our company, eh? By whom? The Commissioner? Interfering with honest business." Chester Preston stopped, shook his head. "After all, Mr. Shirmer, I only came here to offer assistance. A couple of my men are soliciting business in other delicatessen shops now. They're telling the owners that I have come to see you."

"So what?" Since there was no threat, Otto Shirmer grew almost sarcastic—that is, as sarcastic as he could be.

"So they may understand that you had your chance of safety and didn't take it." Chester Preston paused a long moment. "If anything should happen to you, they'd understand it was because you didn't take my advice and—"

"And?"

"And they'd take it afterward—if anything happened to you." Chester Preston took his arms off the counter and stood erect. "Well, I've heard rumors. I've gone out of my way to help you. I have offered you our service without charge." He raised his voice slightly now. "Your two men will be witnesses to that if you get hurt going home some night. Well—yes or no?"

"No," said Otto Shirmer emphatically, and added, lowering his voice, "If anything happens—I may let you know afterwards."

Chester Preston shook his head.

"They're bad boys up this way. I think they're the same ones who operated in Brooklyn today. I'm afraid there won't be any afterwards, Mr. Shirmer, for you. Sorry, but I'll want the Commissioner to know I did my best. Good night."

CHESTER PRESTON waited nearly a full minute after his final words before he turned and went whistling onto the street.

The assistant beside Otto Shirmer leaned against the counter and tried to peer over his boss's shoulder at the evening paper. He saw that Otto Shirmer had moved it slightly and now a flat black automatic lay close to Shirmer's right hand. The third man in the store was still bent diligently over the rear counter, his back to Shirmer; his back to the door.

"Did you ever use one of them things—them guns?" the tall, thin salesman asked.

"Them?" Shirmer seemed doubtful for a moment and then, "Yes, or maybe no. I don't think I exactly used it." He didn't attempt to explain that sentence and his helper didn't ask for an explanation. He said simply:

"It's almost closing time. It's raining—no more business tonight."

Otto Shirmer said, "Some day, Alfred, you will be in business for yourself. The five minutes before closing time until the five minutes after closing time is the reason of my success. When I first started into business my rival across the street beat me to closing every night. Five times out of six he was right and kidded me about it over our beer afterwards. But the sixth time. Ach, then I would get one, two, three, maybe six customers all at once. No, often the difference between closing for good and staying open is simply the extra few minutes that— What did I tell you?"

Two men had entered the store. They were well but quietly dressed. The taller of the two men was laughing. But it was the shorter man who spoke.

"Mr. Shirmer, and we just made it." He began to give an order rapidly reading it from an envelope in the palm of his hand. "You deserve trade—" He looked up when he finished. "I've been reading about you in the papers. You are Mr. Shirmer, aren't you?"

"That's right." Otto Shirmer straightened again. He hadn't thought of business when he made that impassioned speech to his fellow delicatessen owners. But now—the uptown paper had published his picture, the great city dailies carried the story about him and people were coming to buy at his shop.

"He's the fat Dutchman all right." The taller of the two men bobbed his head. "Say, suppose some of these rats—you did call them rats, didn't you?—walked into your store now? What would you do?"

"I've got a gun." Shirmer grinned at them. "They wouldn't like that."

"And you've got two men here with you. Strong men, maybe?" The taller man was still chuckling. "So you've got a gun. Now ain't that nice. Well, Otto, you shot your mouth off all over your face to a lot of delie guys. Reach for the ceiling, wise guy. It's a blast-out."

Otto Shirmer's eyes popped, the two guns had jumped so quickly into the men's hands. Black, menacing, deadly looking weapons, no different than his own, perhaps; no different if they had been lying under the counter by the newspaper. But now pleasant faces had become hard; smiling lips, quivering snarls. Two pairs of friendly eyes had narrowed to slits, cruel mean slits; deadly slits.

Otto Shirmer's hands never felt for that gun beneath the counter. They rose above his head, trembling arms that he could not control, shaking fingers that seemed numb and dead. Alfred's hands, too, went into the air.

"That's right." The taller man looked at the broad shoulders that still stayed bent over the counter, the black hair above the whiteness of the coat. He half raised his gun, half tightened his finger upon the trigger when his companion spoke.

"Nix on that stuff. This is a one-man blast." He turned his head, called toward the door. "Okay, Johnny, come in and do your stuff." His shoulders raised slightly. "The Boss wants it to be messy," he added.

A MAN swung in the door, closed it behind him, moved his coat a bit and almost indifferently lifted a machine gun. He said in a low voice just as a car drew up almost beneath the light on the street:

"Are all these guys for it—the three of them?"

"That's the show, Johnny. Get to the end of the counter. It's to be rough. It ain't especially for them. It's a show for the other delicatessen owners. It's got to look real messy." The smaller man stepped forward and, putting his gun almost against the back of the white-coated figure who had not spoken nor moved, said:

"This guy might be a dick. Only a couple of cops by the corner. It don't seem natural. Well, fellow, turn around and let us get a slant at that pan of yours while a guy can still recognize it."

The broad shoulders of the white-coated figure moved slowly, a black head with short straight hair began to turn.

The small stocky man drew his gun back close to his own body, pushed his chin up, raised the gun so as to cover the white-coated man's face when he turned.

"Yeah," he thought, "when he does turn. If he ever does, turn around. But hell, who'd be in a hurry for a wipe-out like that?"

"Make it snappy, guy," he said aloud. "Come on—snappy." His gun was steady, his finger upon the trigger, half tightened; ready.

The white-coated figure made it snappy. His slow moving body spun quickly. For a split second the gunman saw a horrible contorted face, pointed V-like features, burning green eyes, white hands, long fingers; fingers that held something; something that flashed. Yellow-blue flamed as the gun in the whirling figure's left hand exploded almost in the short man's face, and it was no longer a face.

The horror of it! The ghastly, terrible and sudden death settled over that little shop like a deadly gas! Just the single cry; a cry from the taller of the gunmen. A cry that all heard. Just a name—just three words. They were:

"Hall—Satan Hall!"

But the tall man was the first to recover. At least the first to go into action. He fired. Fired wildly, blindly, shrieked in terror as those green eyes settled on him; shrieked just once before a single bullet tore into his forehead, crashed him back, killed him a full second before he fell to the floor.

Johnny Ford, the feared, the nerveless murderer. The man

who killed and laughed and cleaned his machine gun to kill again stood paralyzed for a single moment. He had seen one man's head shot away; another pound with a sickening thud to the hard tile floor. He had tried to lift his machine gun, caught it against the side of the counter, then ducked quickly behind the protecting end of that counter.

Satan Hall spoke, his voice sharp.

"On the floor, Shirmer; you, too, Alfred." And as they dropped to their knees and stayed there, Satan fired over their heads toward the front of the store.

Johnny Ford had misjudged his distance. He jumped to his feet as the bullet thudded into his slightly protruding left shoulder; was out in the center of the shop, running toward the door. The door he had so indifferently kicked closed behind him.

He reached it as Satan leaned over the counter again, and spoke. His voice was low, soft, yet it ran up and down Johnny Ford's spine as if it were a piece of ice.

"Johnny," Satan said, "that cop, Clayton—he had a kid."

Johnny Ford knew the truth; knew that he was never going to live to open that door. There had been no warning from Satan for him to drop his machine gun. No sharp order to throw up his hands. Nothing. Well, nothing but the voice; the cold voice of death.

JOHNNY FORD swung. His machine gun was spewing lead before he started to turn. If it was fear or hope that the deadly staccato notes of the Tommy gun would create confusion, Johnny Ford couldn't say. Perhaps he didn't even know. But he was facing Satan when the first bullet pounded into his chest; was trying to raise the gun when the second caught him.

In a misty hazy way he saw Satan leaning over that counter, shooting at an angle. But shooting slowly, deliberately. And Johnny got the machine gun up again; got it up even with that counter; even with Satan's chest and shoulders.

After that there was a single roar; the clatter of steel upon tile and the crumbled body of the gunman. The machine gunner who killed them and smiled. The machine gunner who never took a chance; never gave anyone a chance. Satan vaulted the counter, walked toward the door, stepped carelessly over the smaller man and knelt by Johnny's side.

He didn't know then, and he didn't know afterwards what made him look up. Maybe it was living close to death. Maybe it was the feel of death. But he did look up; did look through that glass door across the width of sidewalk. And he looked straight into the eyes of the man who was leaning over the lowered glass in the rear door of a big car.

There was light there—a good light—and Satan recognized the man beneath it distinctly. It was a face he knew well. It was the face of Smooth Frank Wheeler. But it wasn't simply the face of Wheeler that he saw. It was the thing before that face. The thing held steady on the edge of that car window. A thing that he knew and recognized. It was the long, black nose of the most deadly small weapon in the world; the black nose of a German Luger.

Satan didn't know if he could have raised his gun and shot in time. Frank Wheeler was deadly with a gun. And Frank Wheeler did not have to jerk and fire. He had rested his gun upon that window frame, and drawn a bed straight at Satan.

No, Satan didn't know what the results might have been. All his thoughts had taken place in the fraction of a second; all the events taken place as he raised his eyes. For as he first saw Wheeler and that gun, and jerked up his own, he saw something else. The blue of a uniform as a cop hurled himself between Satan and that gun and jumped toward the step of the long black car.

There was a single explosion while the cop was in midair. Then a hurtling body of blue, the roar of a motor, a dead police-man on the sidewalk, and a gun in Satan's hand; a gun that he could not use.

People were there now. Two harness officers and a squad car

that must have turned the corner as the big car shot from the curb.

Satan was leaning against the wall and slowly dialing the private number of the Police Commissioner on the wall phone when the police entered the shop.

"It's him—it's him!" Otto Shirmer was yelling excitedly while he pointed to the broad white shoulders of Detective Satan Hall. "He's been here day and night. Sometimes in the chair behind the counter, sometimes just standing and waiting—waiting. Only the Commissioner and myself knew. Even Alfred didn't know. Three days, three nights—always he just waits—for this." And in a voice that was meant for a whisper but rolled out like a drum in the small shop, "For death."

The sergeant walked to the pay phone, stretched a hand toward Satan's shoulder. Satan was saying into the mouthpiece:

"I don't care if my voice does sound as if I liked it. What? No, I didn't find it unpleasant." And after a pause and a gruff noise on Satan's part which the sergeant nearest him felt might possibly be a chuckle, "Of course I'm not hurt. It's just like you said about Brooklyn—what the papers said about Brooklyn. It was a slaughter. You take care of the widows and orphans. I've taken care of the two cops who died."

THERE WAS more after that. An elation in Satan's voice which he could not control when he told the Commissioner of seeing and recognizing the man who directed-the attempted kill. Of his conviction that the man was the new Front for the Other Man. Well, they'd roast Frank Wheeler this time. No doubt of Satan's identification. He had looked right into the man's eyes— into the nozzle of death—and saw Frank Wheeler kill a cop.

Satan Hall clicked up the receiver. He picked up a doughnut and took a bite of it as he walked towards the door. The shop was very quiet. The usual police activities had not begun. Hardened men were slightly stunned. Perhaps none of them liked Satan; but all of them respected him, openly or inwardly, consciously or unconsciously. But there was something about the man that none of them could understand.

A young rookie had turned away from the dead, practically headless gunman and was sucking in air by the door, his face gray. Even the others avoided the ghastly, horrible sight upon the floor. Only Satan stared unconcernedly at the bodies.

"Your work?" the lieutenant gulped, made an arc with his hand that seemed to take in the entire shop as well as the three bodies.

"That's right." Satan nodded. "That lad there," his voice never changed nor his eyes never wavered as he looked at the body, "was probably in the Brooklyn killing with the others. He took it rather hard."

Lieutenant Moore rocked back on his heels, clumped forward again, licked at his lips before he spoke.

"That lad there is going to be rather hard to identify unless there are fingerprints down at the department."

Satan swallowed the last of the doughnut, brushed the sugar from his fingers, said slowly:

"There'll be prints all right. I didn't get much of a look at his face, when he had a face. But I think he's Jerome Fargo. Rather fancied himself with a gun. I never could see where he got that reputation." And jerking the lieutenant's hand away with a quick, almost vicious move of his shoulder, "I've got to report to the Commissioner. It's just like you see it. They came to kill Shirmer—and they didn't make good."

"I see that," said the lieutenant stiffly. "But one of my boys— dead outside."

"That's right. That's right." Satan seemed to be thinking aloud. "There are some great boys on the Force—fine men. I'm reporting to the Commissioner the name of his killer—then I'll go and get him."

"Like that?" The lieutenant pointed back toward the gruesome sight.

"Like that?" Satan echoed his words, stroked his pointed chin with those long, strong fingers that gave a false impression of frailness. "Well, he'd be a man to place his shots in a lad's back. Good night. See Mr. Shirmer home safely, Lieutenant, though I don't think he's likely to be bothered again."

When Satan was gone the lieutenant said, addressing no one in particular, but letting his eyes jump from body to body:

"No, I don't think they'll be bothering Mr. Shirmer again for a long time—a very long time to come."

CHAPTER XV

MURDERER'S ALIBI

SATAN HALL WAS rubbing his hands when he walked into the Commissioner's private office the evening following the shooting at Otto Shirmer's delicatessen store in the Bronx.

"Chief," he said, walking right to the Commissioner's desk and laying his hands flat on it, "I have been trying to get in touch with you all day. I told you it was Smooth Frank Wheeler who shot the cop to death. I'd have hunted Wheeler up last night, but you were afraid I'd kill him."

"Or he'd kill you."

Satan laughed. It was rather a pleasant laugh. The Commissioner looked at him for a long time, tossed over an evening paper.

Satan picked it up and stared at the picture of himself.

"Don't you understand what that'll mean to you, Satan? This Other Man and his followers—they don't fear me. They don't fear the law. They don't fear the judges nor twelve men on a jury.

"They recognize you as a single menace; perhaps the only menace to their plans. They'll have something to shoot at now." He turned the paper, looked at that diabolic face, shivered slightly.

Satan said, "They get pictures somehow. But it doesn't matter. Those who know my face don't want to see it again."

"The editorials are rather morbid, but not unfavorable, Satan. These editors and reporters know their business; know their crime news. They're stating ten to one you'll be dead within the week."

Satan's lips parted, green eyes grew more oblique.

"I've saved some money," he said slowly. "Ten to one seems like good odds. Did they print any pictures of the scene at Shirmer's shop after the blast?"

"A couple of the tabloids did." The Commissioner nodded. "It was horrible. Lieutenant Moore said it made him sick."

Satan's green eyes softened slightly, his thin red lips didn't seem quite so hard. But he said:

"That's funny, it gave me an appetite." And after a long moment of silence, "But about Smooth Frank Wheeler. You've got him? Does he know the Other Man? Does he know who he is? Did he talk?"

The Commissioner got up and walked toward the window. His back was to Satan when he spoke.

"No," he said. "Wheeler didn't talk; won't say anything."

"No?" Green eyes widened. "You're not going soft with a lad like Wheeler? He's smooth. He's slick."

The Commissioner looked embarrassed. A light dawned in Satan's green eyes. He said:

"You—you haven't found him—picked him up yet. Is that it?"

The Commissioner nodded. "That's right. We haven't picked him up yet."

The Commissioner watched Satan's face. His eyes were riveted on the emotions it displayed. Surprise, doubt, uncertainty—he stepped back as Satan moved toward him.

"You're not going to drag Wheeler in. That's it, isn't it?" Satan said abruptly.

"That's it," the Commissioner answered hoarsely. "We're not going to drag him in." And quickly as the face before him twisted, lips curved at the corner. "We haven't got the evidence, Satan!"

"Evidence! Evidence! I was there. I saw him. I looked straight into his face and saw him—and he saw me. What more evidence do you want?" Satan snarled.

THE COMMISSIONER raised a hand, laid it on Satan's shoulder, shrugged as Satan shook the hand off.

"It's the same story, Satan. The same story. Frank Wheeler has an alibi for the hours between nine and twelve. You saw him at five minutes after eleven. He couldn't be two places at once. He was with someone whose testimony would carry far more weight with a jury than yours—than that of ten men like you."

"The alibi—the man he was with? It was—"

"It was Glenwood E. Nostrom. Yes, I know, I know. But what can you do?"

"But," Satan was slightly stunned, "this wasn't like the Gargan shooting when Nostrom swore to you that Gargan was with him. It was different then. I was running down the street—too late to save the murdered man. I saw Gargan plain enough, but—but this time I looked right into Frank Wheeler's face!"

"Yes, yes, I know. But what can you do? What can I do? Nostrom is a big figure in financial circles—well known in public life. His messages of assurance to business men have often been quoted in the papers. His picture is prominently and often featured. His speeches have restored the confidence of the people. And it is well known that he is crime's worst enemy; the first in all movements for civic betterment."

Satan said again, "I was there, Commissioner. I was there and I saw him."

"And Nostrom says Frank Wheeler spent the entire evening with him. Now which will a jury believe? The detective who has openly threatened to get Frank Wheeler, or the avowed and known public man whose every action; every word for a generation has been for the public good. The man who has given thousands to the hospitals, thousands more for worthy charities, tens of thousands for—"

"Hell!" said Satan. "I'm not interested in his virtues. I'm

not interested in any man's virtues—only his vices. I tell you Wheeler has to roast. He killed a cop."

The Commissioner shook his head, said slowly:

"If he were acquitted we could never try him for the same crime again. I know and believe in you, Satan. The District Attorney doesn't. There is nothing to do but wait."

"Wait—wait! For what? Until the entire city is taken over by this Other Man? What is it that Frank Wheeler or this Other Man can hold over the head of Glenwood E. Nostrom? What could be in his past that would force him to perjure himself; to protect with his name men who are turned loose in the city to kill? Gargan caused two children to be murdered that night when the machine gun fire took place. Tonight a cop was murdered. What could have come over a man like Nostrom. What can he have done? He even—"

"He even protected you, Satan, when some years back they wanted to remove you from the Force. 'Legal murder' the papers called it then—before our criminals made it a war against the law."

"The law!" Satan said viciously. "You have told me that I am the law. Frank Wheeler is wanted for murder. If the law knew the truth they would execute him. I am the law. I know the truth." He turned suddenly and walked toward the door.

The Commissioner's slender little body moved quickly. Strong wiry fingers bit into Satan's arm. He spoke rapidly.

"Are you mad? You can't kill him, Satan!" he cried. "They'll fear you more and more now, Satan. You, a single man in seven million, to stand in the way of a great power. You'll play right into their hands. You go after Frank Wheeler and you'll never live to—to—" He stopped under the glare in Satan's eyes, said stiffly:

"You are taking orders from me. You can't just make it a wild orgy of death. Many cops have died in the line of their duty; cops whom I have sent to their deaths wishing I might go myself.

Now, Frank Wheeler is but one man; one cog in a great wheel of destruction."

FOR PERHAPS five minutes the Commissioner talked. They must wait. The death of certain leaders of the Other Man gave them time, of course. But it was the Other Man they must get; must, finally get. They must get the Other Man or in the end surrender the city to a great criminal body. No, the thing was not fantastic. It had been done before, years ago, when a single man would grow to great power through political connections. Satan scratched his chin, thought, finally said:

"If there is something in Nostrom's past so terrible that he permits his name, his honor, his soul to be used, then why can't we discover it as well as these men?"

The Commissioner shook his head. He said:

"We may, but I doubt it. You see, Satan, I have had the best trained minds searching his past for weeks. To me as well as to the public his slate is clean. So clean that it astounded me, for I know so much not to the credit of our best citizens. No, it is something this Other Man must have discovered by chance. Nostrom's life seems an open book. I have talked with him, Satan. You'd hardly recognize him—he's a changed man."

"Yeah?" Satan was interested, leaned forward. "What did he say?"

"He said that you must have been mistaken—that he could not be mistaken. There was fear in his face; horror in his eyes. You'd feel sorry for him."

"Me!" Satan's voice rang loud. "Did he feel sorry for those kids? Did he feel sorry for that cop?"

"They were dead before he knew what he was called upon to do. I'm sure of that. And he's a broken man. A great brain is breaking under a great strain." The Commissioner paused, then said abruptly:

"I knew his wife before she died. Knew his daughter when she was a child."

"Did you talk to the daughter? Is she married? Does she live with him?"

"Lynda is single. She's little more than a child. She must be twenty-two or three now. I didn't talk to her. She's ill now."

"Sick to her stomach, no doubt," Satan said sarcastically. "Well, you've fought to keep me on the Force, Commissioner. It's been hard for you. I'm ready to resign."

"To quit?"

"To quit, if you like that word better. When the crooks take over the city—take over the Police Department—I'm not included in the bill of sale."

The Commissioner looked at Satan a long time.

"Would you leave me at a time like this—when I need you the most?" he said finally.

"For what?" Satan asked.

"Wait until twelve o'clock tonight." The Commissioner smiled now. "The clouds are not all black, Satan. Eddie Greer is to take Gargan's place; to be the new Front for the Other Man. He takes over the job tonight. He wants to see you in his office at the Café Wellington at twelve o'clock midnight. You're to go right up."

"Eddie Greer, eh? And what does he want to see me about?"

"He wants to thank you for killing the two men who would have taken his life. And he wants to thank you, and me through you, for not letting anybody know that it was not he. Eddie Greer, who shot Razor Young and Jerry Lock to death."

"Thank me with words?"

"Words—yes; words that may send Wheeler to the electric chair for another crime. It doesn't make much difference just what crime Frank Wheeler dies for."

"Not so long as he dies." Satan frowned. "I don't like it, Commissioner. Eddie's a rat—always was. He always will be."

"But," said the Commissioner, "Eddie is afraid of Frank

Wheeler. If he's the rat you say he is he'd turn up Frank Wheeler, not for us, but for himself."

Satan nodded gravely. But his thoughts were not with the Commissioner or with Eddie Greer or even Frank Wheeler at the time. He was thinking of someone else. He looked at his watch, said:

"Twelve o'clock. I'll be there. Eddie Greer is shrewd. He may need me tonight if things go wrong. If Frank Wheeler should decide to take the play away from Eddie by—by force."

"It would be odd," the Commissioner said, "if you should arrest Frank Wheeler for the murder of Eddie Greer."

"It would be very odd," said Satan, "and very stupid if I should arrest Frank Wheeler for anything." He looked again at his watch, and said:

"I'm going to have a talk with Glenwood E. Nostrom tonight. Nothing for you to worry about, Commissioner."

"All right, all right, but be careful." The Commissioner held Satan's wrist. "And I am worried, Satan—greatly worried. Be careful how you handle Nostrom."

CHAPTER XVI

THE BIGGEST DOUBLE-CROSS IN HISTORY

MAXIE ROSEN SAT strangely stiff in one of the booths of the nearly deserted dining room of the Wellington. He looked straight at the tall, muscular man across from him. He studied the man's face and eyes. They were shifty eyes; mean eyes, incapable of a direct stare. He looked at the "pouches" beneath them, the thick lips with the twist at the end. Yet he detected no sign that the man had been drinking. It was as if the man read Maxie's last thoughts when he spoke.

"I know I was hitting up the bottle." The man leaned broad shoulders eagerly forward. "But I'm off the stuff." He balanced a glass in his hand, let the whisky roll about, and watched the oil that clung to the smooth inside surface of the glass. "Petering off slowly, Maxie. I haven't any worries now—nothing to bother me. Don't need liquor."

"And what," said Maxie slowly, "did you have to bother you before?"

"Well—Gargan. Dan Gargan. I knew he wanted me knocked over. I knew he was putting wrong ideas into your head. I ain't a fellow who generally takes things that way. I'd have squeezed lead in his chest if it hadn't been that I was thinking of you and the Other Man." And when Maxie didn't speak, "Hell, Maxie, you didn't expect me to take the dose that night near Central Park West. I didn't have any choice in the matter. It was me or them. I just crossed my arms and gave Young and Lock the dose,

118

I'm the logical man for the job—I should be the Front for the Other Man."

"That," said Maxie, "is just one man's opinion. Now, listen, Eddie. Why do you suppose Gargan wanted to kill you? Think."

Eddie Greer straightened, cleared his throat, his eyes were steadier now.

"Because he got word through to the Other Man that I was doing a double-cross; that the Commissioner of Police was paying me. Well, that's where the double-cross came in. Gargan got me to play the Commissioner, tip him to small stuff that meant nothing so I could work in on the police end and trap Satan Hall. See, Maxie? Then Gargan fooled the Other Man— and maybe got orders through you to stiffen me."

"So that's how it is." Maxie Rosen came very close to smiling. But he didn't smile. He frowned. After all, it was Eddie Greer sitting there before him, and Eddie had crossed two guns and shot to death a couple of the finest gunmen in the city—or so Maxie believed.

"That," said Eddie Greer, "is just how it is." He sat back now and stuck his thumbs in the armholes of his vest, the black of two flat automatics showing plainly. The confident Eddie Greer of tonight and the sniffling, frightened, drunken Eddie Greer of the night of the killing were two different men. Eddie Greer, whom they had always looked on as a small-time chiseler, was a popular man today. News spread quickly. Eddie Greer had shot two men to death—two feared killers, both with their guns in their hands. Eddie Greer had not only killed them, but he was walking the streets a free man. A killer with influence is a dangerous man. Maxie knew that—and knew too that none of that influence had come from him.

Eddie talked easily flow as he warmed up to his subject.

"I'm a natural for the Front job. This Wheeler's a punk. He sat in a car and let Satan blow the head right off Jerome Fargo in Shirmer's delicatessen. Listen, Maxie, I've got an 'in' with the Commissioner. He thinks I'm working for him. My first

*"I want to talk to you,
Nostrom," Satan said
from the doorway.*

act as the new Front will be to trap Satan for you; trap him to his death."

"The new Front," said Maxie. "I'm afraid you're a little premature, Eddie. Wheeler wants that job and the Other Man—"

MAXIE DIDN'T finish his sentence. He jarred suddenly back. Eddie Greer had leaned across that table, pounded a finger against Maxie's chest. Something was in his eyes now that Maxie had never seen before. A viciousness, a violence; the killer that must have been in Eddie Greer when he killed those two men. Maxie's right hand slipped beneath the table, rested upon a tiny button. His eyes dropped from Greer's eyes to his hands, white and empty upon the table.

"I'm not asking you for the job." Eddie almost whispered the words. "I'm telling you I'll take it. You stalled me this morning. Now you got the naming of the Front. Well, I'm that Front."

Maxie Rosen still held his finger on the button, but he did not press it. His lips parted slightly; his teeth showed. It was a full ten seconds before he spoke.

"You want to know now? You want an answer—yes or no? Is that it, Eddie?"

"I want an answer and it's got to be 'yes.'"

"It's 'no.'" Maxie suddenly came out of his listlessness as he pounded his hand upon the table. "You've tried to dictate to the wrong person this time, Eddie. Tried to dictate to the man behind me, who, if he knew the truth, would have you wiped out like a dirty mark. I know what happens to men who rat out on the Other Man. You've got an hour of life, Eddie, then I talk."

Maxie watched to see Eddie Greer tremble and crumble and slide down in the seat across from him. He watched his hands, too. Then his eyes raised to Eddie's face and Maxie Rosen was surprised—perhaps even stunned; stunned for the first time in his life. Eddie Greer was grinning at him.

"You talk like a book, Maxie," he said.

"A book—" Maxie paused. Words didn't jump quickly from his mouth; quick sure words that he always had ready. He finally said:

"You want to be the Front. You threaten the Other Man. Let us understand things, Eddie. You think you can harm the organization. You think—you think you know something."

Maxie Rosen stopped talking, poured himself a drink from the soda bottle, sipped it slowly. He shook his head, saw the grin on Eddie's face grow broader, remembered why they had had him in the racket at all; why the Commissioner had used him. It was because Eddie Greer was shrewd. Eddie Greer knew things. Eddie Greer had a brain that he could use for something besides soaking up alcohol when he wanted to. Maxie knew he'd have to go carefully—very carefully.

"You're quite a guy, Eddie—quite a guy," he said. "More to you than most of them think. I can't say that the Other Man has definitely decided against you—not quite definitely."

"Perhaps," said Eddie Greer very slowly, "he left the decision to you. You see, it's around the Avenue—news you spread yourself—that the Other Man's Front would be named tonight, about this time. The boys are waiting to hear. I gave them to understand it would be me." Eddie glanced at the phone on the edge of the table. "They'll be ready to fall in line when I lift that phone and tell them the truth."

"So—" Maxie rubbed his chin. "You were that sure."

"Yeah," said Eddie Greer as he gripped the receiver. "I was that sure."

Maxie laid a hand over Eddie's, held the French phone down in its cradle.

"What made you so sure, Eddie?" he asked softly.

"Because," Eddie said just as slowly and just as low, though there was no softness in his voice, "next to you, Maxie, I'm going to be closest to the Other Man."

"What do you mean?" Maxie Rosen asked coldly.

"I mean," said Eddie Greer, "that I know who the Other Man is. And I know he'd rather have a friend know his identity than any enemy—than Satan Hall, for instance."

MAXIE ROSEN'S face went white, then blotches of red showed in it. After that a yellow—a white, creamy sort of yellow. His voice was dull, low.

"You couldn't know that, Eddie—you couldn't know that. I don't even know myself." And even as he denied Eddie's knowledge he knew the truth. Just one thing would make Eddie Greer act as he was acting—defy the quick death. Yes, somehow Eddie Greer knew the truth.

"How did—how could you find out?" Maxie asked.

"I followed you," said Eddie.

"The cops have followed me; everybody has followed me at times. But no one could possibly see me meet the Other Man."

"Oh, you were clever enough about it," Eddie admitted indifferently. "And you fooled everyone—everyone but me. You see, Maxie, there were times when fast decisions were needed and you had to get in touch with the Other Man and get back again in a hurry. It was one of those times that I found out." Eddie was chuckling now, feeling pretty good. He poured himself another drink. "Just a toast to the new Front," he said.

Maxie Rosen was calmer now. His face had cleared somewhat. Only blotches remained here and there on his cheeks. But he tugged at his collar when he spoke.

"You lie, Eddie," he said. "You never could have seen me meet him—never."

"Seen you meet him?" Eddie hesitated. "I've seen you with him many times. So you don't know who the Other Man is. Well, I'll do you a good turn too, Maxie. I'll tell you who he is."

Maxie looked up, reached a hand to Eddie's mouth when he would have spoken, then, leaning forward, put his face close to Eddie Greer's face. Two words only were whispered by Eddie Greer; whispered so low that they would have hardly penetrated the eardrum of another man. Yet to Maxie Rosen they rang out loud and clear. His eyes flashed about the room as if there might be someone else to hear them.

"Well, Maxie," asked Eddie, "has the Other Man got a new Front?"

"Yes, yes—" Maxie's body went through a setting up exercise. When he spoke again his voice was almost cheerful. "I guess you win, Eddie. And I guess you're the man for the job. A man with brains; a man who isn't a fool for shooting, but can kill as you kill, when the occasion warrants it." He stretched a hand across the table. "Let us start right, Eddie."

Eddie looked at Maxie, then he took his hand.

"On the level, Maxie?" he said doubtfully. "You think we'll hit it off? You don't mind my being in on the know?"

Maxie held Eddie Greer's hand tightly.

"I guess I'm glad you know, Eddie; glad someone can share the burden and the responsibilities with me. There are times when I need a man like you."

"And I go up and take charge? Gargan's old office—upstairs?"

"That's right. There's lots to go over. I'll come up later."

"And Wheeler—what about Wheeler?" Eddie Greer frowned. Some of the elation had gone out of his voice, "What of him?"

"Oh, he's a valuable enough man," Maxie said lightly. "Needs someone to handle him—give him orders. A great guy when he's using another man's brains. He made a mess of things last night, Eddie. We might—" Maxie stopped, rubbed his chin. "He's got friends—good boys in a pinch; boys who might make trouble. So we'll give him another chance, Eddie, if you think you can handle him. I'll tell him he'll have to jump, and it's up to you if he makes good or not."

EDDIE GREER buttoned his coat over his expanding chest. Both men turned and looked at the figure coming down that room. They recognized him, too. Smooth Frank. Wheeler was swinging easily toward that table.

"See you upstairs." Maxie half pushed, half directed Eddie Greer from that booth. "There'll be a lot to arrange. Here—" He put his hand quickly into his pocket, handed Eddie a bunch of keys, said:

"Bernie Snyder outside at the bar will know what they're for. He knows a new Front moves in tonight." And as the heavy legs of Wheeler bore him rapidly toward the table, Maxie lowered his voice. "Not a word to anyone, Eddie. Not a word of what you told me."

"Not a word to anyone," Eddie whispered hoarsely, "if things break right for me."

Eddie Greer half sneered as he returned the cold nod of Frank Wheeler. Eddie Greer swaggered as he left the dining room, turned right and crashed through the swing door to the bar. He spotted Bernie at the end of the bar, lunged across the room, tossed the keys on the polished wood. His voice boomed when he spoke.

"I'll be taking over the room upstairs, Bernie. From now on I'll run this joint."

"Yeah?" Bernie looked at the keys, looked at Eddie Greer's flushed face, his excited eyes; looked once again at the keys, then walked quickly from behind the bar. "Glad to have you with us, Mr. Greer." And Eddie knew it was the first time that Bernie had attached the handle "Mr." to him. "I was afraid it might turn out to be someone else. Glad you were *willing* to take things over."

Willing? Eddie Greer wondered about that word as he followed Bernie up those stairs.

He stood flat-footed in the center of that fine office, looking over the big chairs, the great polished desk, the door at the rear that led to the little hallway and the balcony that overlooked: the dance floor below. And the door to the side right in the center of that tiny hall that lead to narrow stairs and to the street; a private entrance—a private get-away. More than one body had gone out that little door.

He felt big; important. He looked at the shelves of books, the pictures above them, said:

"Gargan was a tramp. Look at that mess there. We'll change some of that. Bernie—get some real art in."

"Real art—yes, Mr. Greer."

Eddie let his eyes wander about that room. Indeed he felt like a patron of the arts. He stared long at a picture of a girl. It was a photograph, not a painting, but Greer didn't know that.

"Gargan came out of the gutter, Bernie."

"Yes, sir—the gutter."

"That's junk, that dame's picture. Where did he get that?" Greer demanded. "You'll have to get rid of that."

"That? I don't think I'd get rid of that, Mr. Greer." And before Greer could crash in on him, "That's Mr. Wheeler's—a dame he knew. He's nuts about her."

"What happened to her?" Eddie asked.

"She sang in a spot in Philly. Some guy liked or didn't like her—I forget which. He stuck a knife in her. She's dead."

"I don't blame him." Greer glared at the picture, turned to the desk. "The phone, Bernie, Gargan's private one—where is it?"

Bernie opened a drawer of the desk, took out a phone. Eddie dropped into a chair behind it

"Okay, Bernie. And, Bernie—bring up a couple of bottles. You know the stuff."

"I know." Bernie nodded solemnly as he left the room. He knew Eddie Greer too, and: his weakness for liquor. But he shrugged his shoulders philosophically. He had been a long time in the racket. A clever man can get lots of things besides trouble out of a drunk. Bernie Snyder felt that he was a clever man.

As the door closed behind Bernie, Eddie Greer lifted the phone. He dialed his number quickly, waited, said:

"It's Eddie, Commissioner. I'm the Front. That's right. Oh, I know it can't last, but I'm the only one who knows the Other Man. Yeah, I know who he is… It'll take him time to arrange things for my out. It's eleven bells now. Tell Satan to bring one hundred grand in cash with him when he comes at twelve. One hundred thousand dollars. Yeah, cash on the line, and I'll give him the name of the Other Man."

The Commissioner's voice came back over the wire:

"Are you mad, man? Where could Satan get one hundred thousand dollars tonight, or at any time?"

Eddie Greer watched, the door, licked at his lips, finally spoke.

"He can get it from Glenwood E. Nostrom—and I want it by twelve tonight. Don't try to call me again. Good night."

Five minutes later Eddie took the whisky from Bernie, nodded when he saw both bottles were open, told Bernie to leave.

He poured himself a large drink, swallowed it straight. It was good stuff. He was throwing over everything for one hundred grand; throwing over millions, perhaps, as the Front for the greatest criminal body that had ever been formed in the City of New York; in the whole United States for that matter. Still, one hundred grand was a lot of jack. One hundred thousand dollars, cash on the line.

And when things broke—when the Other Man talked all

over his face it would raise the-roof clean off the City Hall. But Eddie Greer would be on a fast ship far from the vengeance of the knob and of the law. A double-cross, eh? They had suspected him of a double-cross. Well, this would be the biggest double-cross in the history of the rackets.

Eddie Greer poured himself another drink.

CHAPTER XVII

AN OPEN GRAVE

GLENWOOD E. NOSTROM staggered, gripped the stone balustrade beside the long wide steps to his house, straightened, then swayed there upon those steps, leaning heavily upon his cane. He had always been a strong man, enjoyed the best of health and felt that youth was not measured so much in years as it was in physical fitness and mental attitude. For the first time in his life he was realizing that he was no longer young, and for the first time in his life no longer able to face and handle a situation that other men might have flunked.

Smooth Frank Wheeler clutched his arm, motioned to the man on the sidewalk to mount those steps and take Mr. Nostrom's other arm. Wheeler looked once at the car by the curb, then said to the heavily breathing Nostrom:

"I wouldn't take it like that, Mr. Nostrom. You didn't come up through a hard school like I did. You've been used to giving orders and having those orders obeyed. It's really hard to find that there is at least one man bigger than you are—the Other Man. You obey his orders and all will be well. You should thank me for taking you for that ride. All I told you in the car was for your own good."

Frank Wheeler paused before he spoke again, then he said:

"You don't feel like calling up the Commissioner now and telling him you were wrong about this alibi for me? You don't feel like seeing Detective Satan Hall? You don't feel like refusing me that little favor of an alibi for the little delicatessen job?"

Frank Wheeler laughed lightly. "I'm your friend, Mr. Nostrom. I can assure you I wasn't there when the cop died. That should be enough for a friend to know, shouldn't it?" A sudden hard viciousness crept into Wheeler's voice. His mouth twisted nastily. "You don't feel like calling the Commissioner now?"

"No, no," Nostrom said dully. "I don't feel like that now. I'll do it later. You may feel perfectly assured that I will raise my right hand and swear falsely before God and man that you were with me last night."

"For close to two hours before the shooting and for over an hour after it—remember that."

"For two hours before the shooting—and for over an hour after it," Nostrom repeated like a man who was hypnotized.

"That's the ticket." Frank Wheeler slapped Nostrom on the back. "But remember, one false move, one mistake, careless or otherwise, and things happen exactly as I told you."

"I understand," Nostrom said in a far-away voice. "And this man here on the step—this man you say is to be my secretary and constant companion—he is to watch me?"

"Nonsense." Wheeler chuckled pleasantly. "You'll attend to business just as you always attend to it. He could not prevent you from lifting a phone in your own office or in your own home and calling the Commissioner of Police if you wished to. This man is here to protect you, a bodyguard. For your convenience we'll call him your secretary. He's here in your interest, not ours. But if the police should try to force or cajole, threaten or plead to make you change your mind and talk, why he'll be with you to remind you—to protect you from yourself."

Nostrom stiffened slightly. "No one," he said, "would think of trying to threaten me."

"No? Well, let us hope not. Only a fool or devil would try such a thing, I'll admit. And I'm favoring the devil. The devil says he saw me when the cop was killed last night. You threw the lie in his teeth. You're a real big guy, Mr. Nostrom—none bigger. But Satan Hall don't think of power as you and I and right-thinking men do. He thinks of power only as small hunks of lead coming out of the nose of a gun." Wheeler snapped his fingers. "Lads don't appreciate him as I do. He'd knock you around just like he would any bum on the street. He won't like my alibi, and he's the man to come and tell you so."

"You mean—"

"I mean Detective Satan Hall, if I know men; and that man in particular, he'll come and see you. If he threatens, Fred here will protect you."

"You mean," Nostrom started, "that it's a net—a murder trap? That this man here is to shoot Satan Hall to death in my house?"

Wheeler grinned.

"There's such a possibility, Mr. Nostrom. Talk nice. Give Satan the speech I made up for you and everything will be jake. You see, Fred is from Pittsburgh. Satan Hall won't know him. If Satan gets killed in your house, you'll only have to swear he attempted violence and Fred was protecting you. Everything is figured out. After the shooting Fred suddenly changes; at least to the police and the newspapers he does. He is no longer a secretary, but a detective; a detective employed by the Chester Preston Agency. Nice, eh?"

"Nice? Nice! Before God, Wheeler, I will not permit anything like that."

"Let us hope," said Wheeler, and his voice was hard and smooth, "such a situation will not arise. That's up to you. But if it does not happen, you're in the same position you were, and must still act as the Other Man directs." Frank Wheeler stuck a finger hard into Glenwood Nostrom's chest. "But if Satan dies here, your troubles are removed with his body—we will not ask you to help us again. Think that over. Good night."

AND AS Nostrom turned toward his door, leaned heavily against it, pressed a finger unconsciously against the bell, Frank Wheeler whispered to the man from Pittsburgh:

"Nostrum is one of the most respected men in the city. His word will carry even a kill. Preston's is a licensed detective agency, and there will be fifty grand laid smack on the line for you after you get Satan Hall."

Fred made clicking sounds with his tongue. "For fifty grand I'd do it without any friends or protection," he said.

The door opened, the two men passed into the lighted hall. Frank Wheeler went whistling down the steps and climbed into the big car that waited at the curb.

"You can go to bed, Cummings," Nostrom said almost gruffly to the butler. "The other servants have retired'? Good! No, nothing—nothing. I'll be busy with this—" His words choked as he looked at the big man who, having followed him in, stood beside him—"this secretary from the office."

"Very good, sir." The butler looked troubled as he started toward the stairs. He had been with Mr. Nostrom a great many years. To him Mr. Nostrom looked very bad indeed. And he had taken to drinking heavily lately.

Inside the library Fred sprawled easily into a big chair beside the flat desk. He looked at Nostrom, who almost fell into the chair across from him. He squinted his eyes and wondered what Nostrom's thoughts were. But Glenwood E. Nostrom was having trouble following them himself.

It was a nightmare—an unbelievable nightmare. The Nostroms had stood for something in the city for years. Not for money, though the family had always had plenty of that. They had stood for square honest dealing-honor. His father, his grandfather, and his father before him had all been honorable men. With a gulp Nostrom realized that he too had once been an honorable man.

His eyes raised to the huge blank back of the picture directly above the fireplace—the picture he had turned to the wall. That seemed like years ago instead of only a few days. Well, it was years to him. A few days ago he had been young and strong, and now he was an old man.

He looked at the back of that picture again. He had loved his wife very much. He had missed her terribly. Now—yes, he was glad that she was dead.

His dull eyes rested on the man, Fred, across the desk from him. A hard, vicious face, Nostrom wondered if he could buy him. But Wheeler had said the man was from Pittsburgh. Of course he wouldn't know anything or Wheeler would not have brought him to the house. Wheeler was a shrewd man, would suspect attempted bribery. Yet, there was no harm in frying. If he could only clear his head—do something—not just sit there like that and—

BOTH MEN jarred erect as a door slammed out in the hall. The butler's voice came loud, excited. The "secretary's" hand shot suddenly beneath his left armpit. He fell back slightly in the shadows of the huge chair as the library door burst open and Satan Hall hurled his big body into that room.

"I want to talk to you, Nostrom," Satan said, leaning forward there in the doorway. "And I don't want your butler hollering out windows for help. Tell him I wish to see you alone."

Glenwood Nostrom was almost himself for a moment. People didn't walk in on him like that.

"It's quite all right, Cummings," Nostrom said. "You may retire and close the door."

But the butler had no opportunity to close the door. It crashed shut on his receding heels. Satan spun the key, looked straight at Nostrom beneath the light. Nostrom spoke; he had to.

"Just what did you wish to say to me?" Nostrom didn't understand fully why his words shook slightly or why, for the moment, he was glad the "secretary" was there with him. He had never faced a man like this. Fury in green eyes, devilish cruelty to thin red lips, and a dominant, deadly, unfailing determination to that set V-shaped chin. One thing was certain in Nostrom's mind. If Satan Hall wanted something it would not be through any fault of his own that he did not get it.

Satan Hall said, "I want to know why you're making a dirty liar out of me before everybody, and a dirty liar out of yourself. I want to know why you are protecting and shielding a murderer—the killer of a cop—and why you once before protected a killer of little children. I want to know what rottenness in your past life has suddenly made your present one less foul and your future a—a—"

Satan paused as he stepped-forward and put his left hand on the desk. For the first time his eyes spotted the man in the chair beside the desk. He jerked his thumb toward the man and said to Nostrom:

"What's this monkey doing here?"

"He's my secretary and—"

"Toss him out." Satan didn't wait for Nostrom to finish. "I said I wanted to talk to you alone."

The "secretary's" hands were on his knees, both visible and white. He had heard about Satan Hall, but he only half believed the stories he had heard about him. But he had never expected an entrance like that. A common dick forcing his way into the house of one of the most influential men in the city—and the menace in that evil face slightly shocked him.

Nostrom turned his eyes toward the "secretary." He didn't know what to say. He felt so repulsed by Satan that, for the moment, he was almost glad to have the gunman there.

The "secretary" sat as though hypnotized by Satan's eyes. He didn't look at Nostrom even when the white-faced man turned to him. It came to him suddenly that all the stories he had heard about Satan Hall were not silly at all. He was stunned by the realization. Yes, he had thought he'd show these New York boys how real guys from Pittsburgh handled a flatfoot who wanted to be rough.

Now, Fred from Pittsburgh realized that he wasn't simply looking at a cop. He was looking at a killer, just the same as he would look at any killer in the underworld. Fred was not a young man—young as they go in the racket. He knew the value of influence; had always counted on influence, but he knew that influence would not do him a bit of good if he were dead.

HE FINALLY did speak, and he hoped that his voice did not tremble as Nostrom's had. He said:

"I stay with Mr. Nostrom, and I hear what Mr. Nostrom hears." But he couldn't help adding, though he didn't mean to, "That's my job."

Nostrom was talking. The little hope of ever accomplishing his purpose could be shattered to pieces by this man, Satan Hall. So Nostrom arose to the occasion, talked well and clearly.

"I didn't know it was public, Mr. Hall, that you were at the scene of those two—two crimes. I have been told that for your owe satisfaction, and perhaps in your own way for the good of the city, you are willing to swear a man's life away." And hastily, when Satan's green eyes came off the "secretary's" and fastened on Nostrum's sunken orbs, "Of course, I did not believe that I believe that in your zeal for the public good you have been mistaken in your identification. In fact, since the man you would accuse was with me makes me sure that you were mistaken, honestly mistaken and—"

Satan leaned forward.

"You're a big man, Nostrom, have a lot of influence. There are nineteen thousand cops who would realize that influence and not say what I'm going to say to you now. But I'm going to say it. You lie in your throat. You lie in your heart. You lie down in your cowardly soul. And you do it all to protect murderers because you want to protect yourself from something in your past that has crept up on you. Do you know why I tell you this—why I'm not afraid of your influence?"

"Why?" Nostrom gasped. He had a strange feeling. He hoped it wasn't fear. This man before him feared nothing!

Satan said, "I'm not afraid of your influence because you won't be alive to use it against me."

Glenwood Nostrom straightened. Fred came half out of his chair; the words just burst from his lips.

"That's a threat," he said. "A threat," he repeated slowly. It suddenly struck him that Satan had given him a very good reason for shooting him in the back—if Satan would only turn that back and walk toward the door.

Satan turned very slowly and looked at Fred. He bent his head forward and peered straight into those filmy blue eyes; into them and behind them. Satan's head raised. His lips curled cruelly when he spoke.

"So you're a secretary; the man who stays with Nostrom and hears everything. Is that right?"

"That's right," said Fred, and sensing something he couldn't understand, but remembering Frank Wheeler's instructions that if possible to get the Commissioner on the phone before the shooting, "I think, Mr. Nostrom, it would be advisable to get the Police Commissioner and tell him just what one of his coppers is threatening you with." His hand reached for the phone on the desk.

Satan said, "Take your hand off that phone!" And when the Pittsburgh thug's hand remained tightly gripping the instrument, "So you want to stay with Mr. Nostrom and hear everything?"

The "secretary" had not taken his hand from the phone. Instead he had started to lift it from its cradle. Satan stood very still. That was better. That was more in line with what Fred was used to. He forgot he was the "secretary" now. His own lips curved; his words came through the corner of his mouth:

"I'm going to stay and I'm going to hear—"

HIS MEAN eyes widened. The "secretary's" hand left the phone. He screeched something at Nostrom, hesitated whether to go for his gun or protect his head. But it didn't matter. He couldn't have accomplished either. Satan's hand went under his coat; then out and up, and finally down. All in a single movement, like an athlete well trained and long practiced in a simple physical exercise.

Satan's hand, that was white, now held something black; something black that cut through the air with terrific force. There was a dull thud as steel hit bone; a cry from Fred's lips that died almost the moment it started. And the Pittsburgh killer sank slowly as if to return to his seat on the chair. He never reached that chair—just scraped it in falling and lay in a huddled mass upon the floor.

"Fifty-fifty," said Satan. "You're going to stay, but you're not going to hear."

Nostrom had seen that blow. He had heard the thud; recognized the viciousness of it. Then he was on his feet, clutching Satan's shoulders, shaking him, crying out:

"You don't know what you've done. You've ruined every hope, every—" And with another glance down at that blood-soaked head, "God help me! You've murdered him!"

Satan threw up his right hand, knocked Nostrom from him, back into the chair.

"Hell," said Satan. "What's a murder or two with a friend like you to swear that he climbed to the top of the bookcases and jumped off on his head." And, looking down at the man, "He'll live—I'm afraid. You've picked fine company. Nostrom, I'm putting you on the level with the rats you're running with. I knew when I got a good look at him that he wasn't your secretary."

Nostrom tried to control his voice; tried to put an earnestness in it—an earnestness that he actually felt. "I'm willing to forget what you said tonight; willing to do nothing about it. I'm willing to explain, to cover even this—this man you struck down. Don't you understand? I won't raise a hand against you. Satan, why do you look at me like that? If you knew it, believed it, I am the man responsible for keeping you on in the department."

"It might be true," Satan nodded gravely. "I can only hope that it isn't. For I'm a man who wouldn't want a man like you to keep me on the force." And, walking to the wall above the mantel, Satan swung the frame round, looked at the painting, said, "Your wife, eh? Ashamed to look at her picture even."

Satan looked across at Nostrom. His head was buried in his hands. He turned back to the mantel, and his eyes fell on a small standing frame. A frame that was face-down on the mantel. He turned it over. The girl was young and pretty in a boyish sort of way; slightly turned up nose; freckles. He took the picture across the room with him. It was Lynda, all right. Glenwood E. Nostrom's daughter.

Satan pulled up a chair, sat down, faced the man, their knees almost touching. Nostrom did not raise his head. Satan asked the question suddenly:

"Was that man there on the floor here to kill me?"

Nostrom's head jerked up suddenly. "Good God—no!" he said. "I wouldn't have let him—"

SATAN GOT up, shook his broad shoulders. Somehow he believed the man—believed that Nostrom didn't know Fred was there for the purpose of killing him. He sat down again.

"Nostrom," he said, "I have never liked many men—admired even fewer. I used to admire you. But I guess you could just give it—not take it. You have money, lots of it. But that's all you ever gave. The rest was a fake; the giving of yourself for the public good, the giving of your influence in politics—in police business. Maybe it was just your conscience bothering you for the terrible thing you once did. Well, others were caught in the same net by this Other Man. Some of them laid down as you did. Others took the dose and refused to be a party to the murders of cops and of little children."

"Stop—stop!" Nostrom cried out. "I did nothing. I knew nothing until after the crime was committed. I could not have prevented it. I could not have saved those children or the police officer—" Nostrom stopped.

"Go on." Satan leaned forward now, knocked Nostrom's hands aside, thrust up his chin, looked deep into his eyes. "The officer who died so nobly saving my life."

"So that's why you're here." Nostrom's eyes brightened. "That's why you've come. To kill me. Well, why do you wait? I cannot protect myself."

Satan's green eyes widened. He said: "So—it's not death then. You're not afraid of death. No, I'm not here because of that cop.

I would have come anyway, but I would have come differently. Not with my insides turning over and over. What made you think I came to kill you?"

"You said—said my influence would not be of any use; that I would be dead."

"Oh—that," Satan said almost indifferently. "I meant suicide. At the end you'd kill yourself, of course. Others have. I managed to save a woman with a baby from suicide. She had the gun in her hand."

"That might be the best way. But no, I can't—not yet," Nostrom said.

"Can't, eh? Not yet." Satan leaned forward eagerly. Nostrom was practically admitting everything that Satan had guessed. Satan spoke quickly. "Listen, Nostrom." He clutched the man's wrists and unconsciously let his strong fingers bite into the bone. "You say those children would have died anyway. And the cop, too. Maybe they would. But there will be other murders, and you will be used to save the murderers by false alibis. Don't you see? Don't you understand! These may be murders that wouldn't have been committed if they couldn't count on a big name like yours. And some day they'll slip. The witness to murder won't be Detective Hall, a common cop, with an ax to grind. It may be someone big, or it may be several people. Then you'll be guilty too. Is it worth it? Will this thing they found in your past put you in the electric chair?"

Nostrom sat stiffly erect; his dull eyes brightened, a feverish sort of brightness.

"Electric chair! Me? What are you talking about. I have no— no—" He jumped to his feet, snapped back in the chair again from Satan's grip. His eyes became dull again. "I tell you," he said. "Wheeler was here with me—he could not have committed the crime."

Satan stared at the man. He thought of the men the Commissioner had going back into the past of Glenwood E. Nostrom and unearthing nothing; nothing but deeds of kindness, of generosity, even of chances Nostrom had taken of wrecking his own fortune; his own business in a political move that he thought was right. Satan looked at the photograph in his hand, held it so Nostrom could see it.

"She's not dead like your wife, who will never know the truth," Satan said. He watched the look of horror rise in Nostrom's eyes. "Nostrom! I'm going to tell this girl the truth about her father. I'm going to find her and tell her the rotten truth. She's a Nostrom just as you are. She won't be fooled. She'll read it in your eyes. A murderer who shrinks at the actual deed, but protects the murderer with the Nostrom name."

NOSTROM DIDN'T speak. Although the room was cool, great beads of perspiration broke out on his forehead; grew larger. Saliva appeared on his lips; made tiny bubbles.

And Satan suddenly knew the truth; knew why they could find nothing in Nostrom's past. Knew why a good man, a big man, an honest man could do the things he was doing. Could even protect brutal murderers.

Satan was on his feet. "So that's it—it's your daughter, Lynda." He shook the man now; shook him by both shoulders. He didn't like the look in his eyes. The coming of something. The breaking through of that tiny thread in the brain—the line of balance that separates a normal man from an insane one. He struck Nostrom sharply across the face, saw the beads of perspiration disappear and tiny rivulets flow down over his mouth.

"They got Lynda, eh? They've got her. That's it, isn't it, Nostrom?" And when Nostrom still didn't speak, "Tell me— tell me just when it was you saw her last."

The feverish light went out of Nostrom's eyes; at least the light of madness disappeared. But they did not grow dull and lifeless. They were still bright. Nostrom's mouth opened, his lips moved; his words were very low, almost like a person who was trained to "speak to the deaf, who could read the lips. But Satan bent forward and caught every word. Nostrom said:

"I saw her tonight—just an hour ago. I saw her face. They

took me to see her. She was lying there in an open grave, alone in the night."

Satan gasped, had hard work speaking himself. When he spoke it was one single word:

"Dead?"

"Dead?" echoed Nostrom. "No, she was still alive."

CHAPTER XVIII

THE GIRL IN THE GRAVE

SATAN STEPPED BACK and regarded the haggard, tired face of Glenwood E. Nostrom there in the library of the Nostrom home. He didn't give a glance, even a thought to the man from Pittsburgh, who was huddled in a silent heap upon the floor. Satan thought of one thing only: how badly he had misjudged Nostrom.

Of course, it was plain now. There could be nothing in Nostrom's past life so bad that he would protect murderers to keep it secret. No, not even if it ruined his future; not even if it brought disgrace to the honored Nostrom name. Just one thing had caused Nostrom to perjure himself and be an alibi for ruthless murderers. And that one thing was his daughter, Lynda, whom the Other Man had taken from him and now held prisoner.

Nostrom had said that the last time he saw that girl was tonight, that she was lying in an open grave—and that she was alive.

"How did you see her? What do you mean, Mr. Nostrom?"

Nostrom said, like a man who talked words yet did not know he spoke them, "They took her from me. Just lifted her off the public street. She wrote me a letter and I knew the truth. First it was Gargan I had to swear was with me. Tonight—well, I refused to go further with the thing. I told Wheeler that I would deny that he was here with me. That he would die in the elec-

tric chair for the death of that policeman; the policeman you
saw him shoot."

"And what did he say? What did he do?" Satan urged.

"He said nothing, but he did something. He took me in his
car, blindfolded me. When he lifted the blindfold from my
eyes I was in a cellar. There was a hole in the center of the floor
where cement had been chopped away. It was like a deep grave."
Nostrom jarred erect, his hand shot out, gripped Satan's sleeve.
His voice was shrill with a crack in it. "It was a grave. Even the
mound of dirt was there. There was a long funnel-like tube
protruding from that dirt. And a man with a shovel who dug.
It seemed very deep. Then I saw her face; Lynda's face, and I
saw—God, it was horrible!"

Nostrom's head went into his hands, Satan looked about the
room. There was no liquor of any kind, no water either, and he
did not wish to call a servant. He did not wish an interruption
that would stop Nostrom talking—cause him to think of what
his speaking might mean.

"Yes," Satan encouraged, "and she was alive?"

"That's right." Nostrom spoke-now without raising his head.
"She was alive. A thick rubber hose ran from that funnel above
to a glass mask over her face. So she breathed. Then-then she
opened her eyes and saw me. Yes, she was alive and still sane."

"And after that?" Satan was not used to such gentleness in
getting information from a man.

"After that the man with the shovel filled up the—the hole
again." Nostrom gulped, he could not say the word "grave" now.
"I watched every bit of dirt pound down—trickle in and cover
the mask. I watched how carefully the man put in the last few
shovelfuls. A little mound of dirt remained beside the hole—up
near her head.

"Frank Wheeler said to me, 'You see, Mr. Nostrom, how careful our grave-digger is to keep the dirt out of that funnel so that
she may breathe and live. Of course, our grave-digger is paid well
for keeping the dirt out of that funnel. But if anything happened

to me he wouldn't get paid and might get careless. That little mound of dirt at the head of your daughter's grave would be far more than sufficient.'"

THERE WAS a long pause after that, then Nostrom said:

"You may understand now, Satan, why I protect murderers. I love my daughter. I want her back," And, watching the green lights in Satan's eyes, the burning green of hate, Nostrom finished slowly:

"Tell me, Satan Hall, have I placed my confidence in the wrong man?"

Satan pulled back, rocked for a moment on his heels.

"What do you mean, 'confidence'? There is nothing personal between us. I represent the citizens of New York. Not one—not you, but all."

"I see," nodded Nostrom. "And I didn't tell you all this, Satan, because I'm a broken, shaken old man. I didn't tell you because you glared through those eyes and struck that man lying there-upon the head. I told you because you entered that door of mine in a way no other honest man in the entire city would dare to do. I did it because I knew that you knew I had only to lift that phone to drive you forever from the force. I thought, 'A man like that is a man worth trusting.'"

There was nothing soft about Satan's words when he said, "What do you want me to do?"

"I want you to wait until my daughter is brought home to me—alive."

"When and under what conditions was she to be returned to you?" Satan asked.

"She was to be returned when—when you were dead. That man there upon the floor intended to kill you tonight. I was to trap you to your death for my daughter's safety. Don't ask me if I would have done it. Before God, I don't know. I love my daughter very much."

And Satan threw the words that were hard to speak:

"It's not a pleasant thing, Mr. Nostrom, but it's truth and you must recognize it as truth. Your daughter cannot and will not ever be returned to you alive by Frank Wheeler. Can't you see that? It would mean his death in the chair, just as your telling the truth now would mean it."

"No, no," Nostrom ran in quickly. "I have given him my word that I will never talk; my word that my daughter will never talk—that Wheeler will be safe."

Satan's head shook. "He would not take that word. When the time comes when you cannot serve him any more, the girl will die—and you will die. Don't ask me how he would kill you. But it would be simple enough—take you out as he took you out tonight and not bring you back."

"What do you want me to do? Go on the stand, swear away the life of my daughter? But you said when the time came that I cannot serve him any longer."

Satan cleared his throat, felt his words stick there, but he said them just the same.

"The time has come now, Mr. Nostrom. The time when you can no longer serve him. I'll arrest Wheeler tonight for the murder of that policeman, and if you alibi him then I'll tell the story you told me here."

"I'll deny it. They won't believe it! They—you can't—I took you for a man!"

"I am not a man," Satan said thickly. "I am the State. I am the Law. If you refuse to alibi Wheeler, your name need not be brought into it at all. I don't ask your help. I simply say 'stay out of it.' They'll believe me if I tell the story, for you'll be asked to produce your girl in court."

"She'll be dead. Won't you help me?"

"What can I do? If I thought there was a chance of her being saved I would do anything."

"At least you can keep her alive. I can keep her alive by asking to see her every time they—they need me."

Satan shook his head.

"It would serve no purpose in the long run," he said brutally. "At present you have only protected a murderer. But if the thing continued, then you would be the cause of murders; murders perhaps so desperate that they would not dare to commit them if they did not count on your name as a protection. No, Mr. Nostrom," he looked at the photograph of the girl again. "Somehow I don't think your daughter would want it that way."

Nostrom said, "She'll die slowly—very slowly. No! No—I'll deny it all!" He reached for the phone. "I'll telephone the Commissioner. I'll—"

AND THE phone rang. Satan snatched it from Nostrom's hand. It was the Commissioner of Police. He said abruptly:

"Listen, Satan, ask Mr. Nostrom if he's got one hundred thousand dollars in cash in his house... I know—I know. It all sounds very odd, but Eddie Greer says he has it, and if you deliver that amount to him at twelve o'clock he'll give you the name of the Other Man. We'll watch outside. We'll have men downstairs when you visit Greer. But you'd better go up alone."

There was more the Commissioner had to say when Nostrom admitted having the money. Then he hung up. Satan dropped the phone and turned to Nostrom.

"Tell me about it." There was a change in Satan's voice; a certain eagerness. "Tell me about Eddie Greer; about that money. There's a chance that this may save your daughter."

Nostrom told him of Eddie Greer.

"Greer rang me up first," he said, "just after my daughter was kidnaped. Then one night he came to see me. I didn't trust him, but I wanted to. He knew that they had taken my daughter, but he didn't know where she was. He didn't want money then. He wanted me to have it where I could lay my hands on it day or night. He wanted my word that I'd place it in his hands the very minute he delivered Lynda to me."

"You have the money? It's here in the house?"

"I have it." Nostrom hesitated and then, "I was afraid to keep it here in the house. Not just the fear of the money being stolen, hut the fear that my servants might be hurt or killed. It's in the house of a friend across the street—in his safe."

"Get it at once," Satan told him. "And give it to me now. Eddie Greer would have delivered your daughter to you for that money if he could. He would have taken her for money." Satan was thinking how Greer had double-crossed Gargan and the Other Man when he blackmailed Mrs. Elsie Stone.

"But my daughter—the money is for her release."

"The money," said Satan slowly, "is to be given to Greer to tell me the name of the Other Man. If he's not lying, such information might save your daughter."

"Might—might! It must! It must!" And when Satan's eyes stared steadily into his, "No, no. I won't—I will not give it to you."

"You must give me that money." Satan leaned forward. "This unknown Other Man is the greatest danger that the city has ever had to face. One man who knows the weakness of many important men in the city just as he knew yours. One man, unknown to us, unknown to the hundreds, perhaps thousands who serve him. But known to Eddie Greer. Eddie Greer, who offers me his name for the one hundred thousand dollars that you have. One hundred thousand dollars that you'd never miss. Your greatest chance to serve the city and the millions of people in it. No one knows better than you what this danger is—what your service would be."

"Serve the city." Glenwood E. Nostrom spoke slowly. "Even you will not deny that up until lately no man ever served his city more. The Commissioner will not deny it, the newspapers, the people will not deny it. Well—" and the strength that had made the Nostroms flashed into his eyes again; into his body. The sudden rising of his chest, the straightening of shoulders that had been bent. "Now," Nostrom continued, "I want that city to serve me. I want you to serve me."

"Just what do you mean?"

"I mean," Nostrom's words rang with a new vigor, "I want you to put my daughter, Lynda, before every other person in the city of New York. I'll want your word on that, Satan. Lynda comes first—after that the law."

SATAN GRINNED, thin lips a longer and thinner red gash, green eyes slanted and narrow.

"Get me the money," he said. "Get it now—for your daughter."

Nostrom looked at Satan a long moment, then, without a word, left the room.

Satan heard the front door close. If Greer had the information he promised or not he did not know. But certainly he could not find out until that money was shown to Greer. But Greer must know the identity of the Other Man. Greer knew that it would not do to play loose with Satan. Others might do it, but not Greer. Besides, Satan had saved Greer's life, and kept silent about it so that the underworld thought that Greer had killed the two gunmen that night. Greer would remember that.

Satan looked at the unconscious man on the floor. The man from Pittsburgh called Fred. There was nothing familiar about that face. Satan knew he must be just an imported gunman who must have been considered tough. They were considered tough when they had a man's back to shoot at. This sort of hood Satan took in his stride. Wheeler was a dangerous man. So was Chester Preston, and even the knotty-shouldered lawyer, Maxie Rosen. He was dangerous because he worked with his head. He took orders to kill, all right, but never executed those orders himself, simply passed them along to others.

But the Other Man. How dangerous was he? Satan didn't know the answer to that. He was most dangerous now because he was unknown, yet must be well known to everyone in the city. A man who was familiar with the underworld; a man who was familiar with the police department; a man who bribed, intimidated, killed. A man who would dare to have cops shot down for the effect it would have on the honest citizens who paid those cops to protect them.

Satan walked to the window, pushed the drapes back, let the shade run up. Then he opened the window and looked out. A narrow strip of walk there. Hard flags leading around to the back of the house, and beyond that a high stone wall. The pavement was ten, perhaps twelve, feet below him, for the walk sloped and he hadn't been looking straight down at first.

He glanced toward the man on the floor, raised the window as far as it would go, then walked over and knelt beside that silent figure. He threw the man's head back and watched the body loosen up and spread out upon the rug. For a moment he wondered if Nostrom was right and his blow had killed the man. But it hadn't, for now as Satan searched him he felt the man's breathing. He didn't expect to find anything, and was not disappointed when he didn't. The search was just routine with him, but a thorough routine.

Satan leaned down and, although the man was broad and heavy, lifted him from that floor as if he had been a small child. He walked to the window with him, had difficulty in getting his feet over the sill. It was a fair drop to the alley below, not so bad if Satan eased him down feet first and let him go. Oh, he wasn't apt to get up and run away, though the thing was possible.

And Satan thought of a number of things at once. This man was hired by Frank Wheeler; hired to shoot him through the back. This man was part of the vast system that the Other Man controlled. This man was part of the system that buried a young girl alive and brought her father to that grave to look at her. And Satan didn't think further. His lips twisted slightly, his hands opened, his arms lowered.

IF SATAN heard the thud of the body he gave no sign, nor did he look out the window before closing it. He simply looked down at his hands, regarded the right one a moment, saw the red on it and, after wetting his handkerchief with his tongue, wiped it clean. Then he walked across the room, picked up the phone, and, sitting on the edge of the desk, called the Commissioner of Police.

"It's okay about that money, Chief, and stay away from the Wellington to-night. I don't want any suspicion, any chance that you or your men are seen before I get there."

"One man police force, eh, Satan?" The Commissioner laughed nervously. "Do you think Greer will actually tell you the name of the Other Man?"

"If he doesn't," said Satan, "I'll have taken a bribe of one hundred thousand dollars." And when the Commissioner wanted to know what he meant, "Just my little joke. Commissioner. What I wanted to tell you was that there's a lad lying out in the alley beside Nostrom's house. Send around for him, but keep it quiet. He was here to kill me. No, I don't think he can tell us anything. How did he get there? Well, he sort of fell out the window."

The phone clicked, the Commissioner still held the receiver to his ear, then realizing that there was little satisfaction in talking to himself, hung up. Most of the time he didn't fully understand Satan, but there were times when he didn't understand him at all. This was one of those times.

For a while the Commissioner sat in silence. Then he got up and removed his dressing gown. After all, he'd better get down to the Wellington. If Eddie Greer lied to Satan—well, there were windows in the Wellington. The Commissioner had not liked the tone of Satan's voice when he said, "fell out the window."

CHAPTER XIX

AN ENGAGEMENT WITH DEATH

MAXIE ROSEN LOOKED from Frank Wheeler toward the retreating figure of Eddie Greer. Finally he adjusted his glasses, said:

"Did you want to see me, Frank?"

"That's right," Frank Wheeler nodded stiffly. "I want to see you." He slid into the dining booth, put hard eyes on the lawyer across the table from him. Frank Wheeler had come for the showdown. He knew that Maxie understood, but he didn't speak right away. He wanted the purpose behind his presence there in the Wellington dining room to sink in.

Maxie Rosen did understand; understood so well that he beat Wheeler to the punch. He talked first, instead of letting Wheeler's silence, protruding chin and steady eyes make Wheeler's position stronger. Maxie said:

"You made a mess of things last night, Frank. I like you, but Johnny Ford and two other good boys are dead. You yourself killed a cop, and Detective Satan Hall spotted your kill. I took care of you, of course, Frank, and Nostrom."

Wheeler's lips set grimly, he said:

"I handled Nostrom myself. He was going soft. I took him out to see his daughter, Lynda."

"That," said Maxie, "was my suggestion—the Other Man's words coming through my mouth. You let him see her in the grave? It quite convinced him, of course."

"I convinced him—yes. But that isn't what I—"

"You want to be the Other Man's visible leader, eh? It was not so easy to convince him about you, Wheeler. It took me two hours. He doesn't like failures. He doesn't understand, as I do, the strength of Satan, the fear Satan creates in all men—even in you, Frank. You see, the Other Man doesn't know fear. You—"

"Me." Frank Wheeler leaned forward. His eyes bulged; his lips curled in an ugly snarl. "I don't fear Satan. I never did; never will. He has no right on the police force; men who are paid by the citizens. He's just a common killer, a murderer like— like—" Frank Wheeler paused. The hand that he had clenched into a fist ready to pound upon the table stayed in the air, the fingers opened. He looked at his hand and smiled. So that was the game, was it? Maxie was clever, damn clever, but Smooth Frank Wheeler didn't have that "Smooth" preceding his name for nothing. He understood. Maxie was trying to put him on the defensive.

"It won't wash, Maxie." Frank Wheeler smiled easily now and his voice was low. "This is the night—and this night is almost over. The cop in the Bronx had it coming to him. Well, I want to run the show for the Other Man. Do I? Yes or no?"

"After last night's fiasco, Frank?"

"After anything." Frank Wheeler's eyes were hard and steady, bat no anger or excitement in them. "The Other Man knew so much why didn't he know, that Satan was planted in that store? But do I get the job of being the visible head of the mob—the Front Man?"

Maxie moistened, his lips nervously. Frank Wheeler was a good man; a damn good man. And he had his own crowd— his own boys. They could be wiped out, of course, but it would take time; It would cause trouble, Certainly, Eddie Greer was the mob man for that job. But Maxie was a cautious man. He simply asked:

"And if you don't get it, Frank, you'll still play with the Other Man, of course?"

"Of course." Frank Wheeler's laugh was like fingernails scraping along a wall. "I'll play a game the Other Man will under-stand. I'll pull out my boys. I'll bust the Chester Preston. Agency end of the racket—blow the Nostrom snatch higher than a kite." And when Maxie Rosen only smiled, Frank! Wheeler chucked his bomb. "And I'll take away from the Other Man his go-between—the man who brings his messages to the Front—to the boys. I'll knock over the man who delivers his orders."

"What—what do you mean?" Maxie's elbows came off the table. He sat very straight.

FRANK WHEELER leaned forward now, slipped his right hand under his left armpit.

"I mean I'll lay a couple of slugs in that go-between's chest."

"Go-between. You—you mean me?"

"Sure, Maxie. I mean you. Right in the chest."

Maxie; stared, at those eyes a long moment. He didn't like what he saw there. He tried to smile as he said:

"When would all this lake place?"

"If by 'all this' you mean your death," Wheeler told him bluntly, "it will take place in my car outside—to which you'll walk when I leave here. Or it will take place right here in the dining room—now. If you feed me a line and I don't know it's a line, it will take place just as soon as I discover the truth. It's too bad, Maxie. I like you—really like you; like that head of yours, the brains in it. But I like myself better. I wouldn't like those brains to be; working against me."

Maxie shook his head sadly. "I wish I'd known how you felt about things sooner, Frank. I'm afraid it is too late." And as he saw Frank's fingers tighten there beneath his coat, "Perhaps I'm wrong;"

"You gave the job to Eddie Greer. That's it, isn't it, Maxie? The Other Man—"

"The Other Man gave me my choice, Frank."

"And your choice was Greer?" snapped Wheeler.

"Would the death of Satan Hall bring my daughter back to me?"

"Greer," Maxie played with a spoon on the table, "threatened me first. Do you think it would be fair to fool him now?"

"What do you mean?" Wheeler's fingers loosened, but his hand stayed where it was.

"I mean," said Maxie, "that I talked you up to the Other Man. You see, he favored Greer because of his shooting of Young and Lock, and he favored Greer because of your mess last night—" And, not liking Frank's reaction to those words, "I mean your failure in the Bronx,"

"That sounds good; But it doesn't help things any, Maxie. Doesn't help you any. If you want to hold a mutual admiration society, why I like you too; like you enough to toss an expensive wreath on your chest."

"Well," said Maxie, "you like my brains. I'm working them now. You threaten to kill me. Greer threatens to kill me. I want to live. Only one of you can be the Front."

"So what?" To Wheeler this talk sounded like a stall for time.

He glanced out into the dining room, looked at the phone at the end of the table against the wall.

"So—" Maxie looked toward the ceiling, followed the smoke from Wheeler's long black cigar, "Eddie Greer is up in the room upstairs now—Gargan's old room. Gargan liked it private. Hardly a sound can come out of that room—and if it did I could arrange that it wouldn't be heard. Then there are the stairs that lead down from that little hall."

"What the hell are you driving at?" Wheeler's eyes were growing wide; very wide indeed, and the cigar ran slowly across his mouth.

"Nothing—nothing." Maxie played with the black ribbon of his glasses. "I was thinking of that room, Frank. It has memories. Other bodies were taken down those stairs. They were found a few days later in the East River and no one at the place here heard a shot."

"They didn't, eh?" Frank Wheeler's cigar started to smoke furiously again. "Not a sound, eh?" He blew a ring, watched it thicken, then twist and widen in the slight draft. "You'd like me to be the Front, eh, Maxie?"

"Under the proper circumstances—yes." Maxie's shoulders shrugged. "I'd rather have you for a friend than an enemy, Frank. And I don't want Eddie Greer for an enemy, either mine or yours—or the Other Man's."

FRANK WHEELER looked intently at Maxie Rosen. He, himself, was a plain spoken man, but he knew many that weren't. Politicians, ward heelers, big timers who liked to talk around things and were surprised when those things happened; surprised, but not displeased. Maxie was that way now. But Frank Wheeler started straight talk. He said:

"Am I to understand that you—"

"You are to understand exactly what is in your mind," Maxie Rosen cut in quickly. "There's the phone. If you really intend to take over the whole racket, then you'll occupy the room upstairs a lot. That makes privacy for me, headquarters for the big boys.

You'll want your laundry man to know where to come. Give him a call."

Frank Wheeler grinned evilly.

"Now you're talking, Maxie, It's lucky I speak English." He lifted the phone, said:

"Molly, get me Rattigan's Game. Hell, you should know where it is." And, after a bit, "That's a good girl, Molly—kiss your hand for me." He waited for a full five minutes, and then to the cracked voice at the other end of the wire he said, "Pull Willie Simes out of that game and trot him to the phone." Another minute. "I don't give a damn what card he's got in the hole. Drag him to the phone!" And to Maxie, "Some of these guys make me sick. That's why they don't get so far in life. When I want a— Oh, Willie? I'll have a package for you at 33 in ten minutes. You'll have to jump with the delivery wagon. Wait a minute."

Frank Wheeler turned to Maxie, who gripped his arm. Maxie whispered:

"Make it ten minutes of twelve, Frank. Eddie will be doing a little drinking." And when Frank scowled Maxie went on, "No, no, Frank. Do it my way. I don't want that damn wagon too long in the street."

Frank Wheeler nodded, said into the mouthpiece:

"Ten minutes of twelve, Willie. What! Cripes, a grand for a short haul like that! No, no—not your garage. I'll tell you where to take the package when you come."

Frank Wheeler banged the phone down, turned to Maxie.

"Some guys think of nothing but money. The future reward for good and faithful service means nothing to them. It burns me up, Maxie." And, with a grin, "Why I could do better at Camp's Funeral Parlors for one-fourth the money. But I'm giving you service, Maxie. The grave we used for the girl will work fine. They won't spot Eddie for years maybe. Why—"

Maxie looked Wheeler straight in the eyes.

"I don't know what you're talking about, Frank," he said seriously and steady. "I don't want to hear any more about such talk. Tell me about tonight."

It took Frank some minutes to find speech. Here he was arranging for the disappearance of a body; a body that had not yet been produced. That was action. That was organization; that was the kind of service Maxie and the Other Man should appreciate and understand. Yet Maxie tried to make a game out of it. Hell, it didn't matter. Frank Wheeler was feeling pretty good. He said:

"I told you Nostrom threw a back somersault about my alibi. The Commissioner had talked with him. Satan had seen me kill that cop, and I had a feeling that Satan might go up and bulldoze Nostrom. What's more, Nostrom isn't able to take it. So I trotted Nostrom out to the house in the Nineties and let him look at his daughter. He saw her buried and all, just as if she'd been there for days and would stay there for days longer, He should have guessed it was a show for him. She'd go mad in a few hours—damned near did in those few minutes. She isn't a bad piece of goods either, if a lad had the time for—"

"We won't go into that," Maxie snapped. "Did it strike Nostrom hard enough for him to trap Satan to his death?"

"Yes, I think it will. But I got a feeling that Satan has kicked out by now." Wheeler moved thick shoulders. "I told Fred to shoot Satan only in the back." Wheeler leaned over confidentially. "That's the only way, Maxie. The only sure way with Satan. It's just plain dope or bravado this shooting-it-out stuff. Look at me. Thirty-seven—old in the racket. That's the way I'll—" He paused.

MAXIE ROSEN had picked up the phone and called a number. A few minutes later he finished his conversation with Glenwood E. Nostrom with these simple words:

"I'll be up to see you right away. It's important; important to you, Mr. Nostrom… Good-by."

"So that's how it is." Frank Wheeler's voice rose slightly. "An alibi if things go wrong here tonight."

"That's how it is." Maxie Rosen nodded. "And an honest alibi. Your guess about it being unnecessary to trap Satan was wrong, Frank. Oh, I didn't ask Nostrom about it. Satan may have been to his house and gone—or he may not have gone there at all." Maxie looked at his watch. "I'll buzz Eddie Greer in his room upstairs, tell him you're coming up to see him; tell him he's to take you on. That you'll knuckle down and take orders from him. He'll like that."

And this time when the phone went down Maxie said:

"You heard what I said–to Eddie. He'll receive you at ten minutes of twelve—not a minute sooner. He's been drinking. His voice was thick. Well, I'll run along. Mustn't keep an influential man like Nostrom waiting. After you have your talk with Eddie, will you need help in the delivery of your laundry?"

"No," said Frank Wheeler. "Eddie Greer may have friends. I'll go it alone. You're not making a mistake in me, Maxie. You can tell the Other Man that."

"I never make mistakes," Maxie said slowly as he slid from the booth and stood leaning over the table: "When we select a Front, we don't want to lose him. Don't you make mistakes."

"Mistakes?" Lines appeared in Wheeler's forehead.

"I mean Satan Hall. He saw you kill that cop. He doesn't like cop-killers."

"What do you mean?"

"I mean," said Maxie Rosen slowly, "that you've kept away from him so far. But if he continues to live you'll have to meet—and if you meet he may not turn his back." Maxie Rosen's smile was superior. Frank Wheeler didn't understand Maxie's parting words nor like them either. Maxie said:

"To paraphrase the immortal bard; Shakespeare, Frank—'Death by any other name would smell as bad—to you.' Good night."

Smooth Frank Wheeler sat a long time smoking in silence. No waiter bothered him. Occasionally he looked at his watch. At thirteen minutes of twelve he came to his feet. Quite a few tables were occupied now. The music was only slightly dulled by the scraping feet. Many of the people nodded to him; some of the girls smiled. There was one girl in particular that Frank fancied. He watched her dance for a moment then moved quickly toward the bar entrance when she started to break from her partner. She drew back as Wheeler hurried on. No, he didn't care how many people saw him. He didn't need an alibi. There wasn't going to be any *body* found tonight.

He turned once to look at the girl again as she swung by. Hell! He'd like to have taken her away from that potbellied sap and shown her a real evening. But the clock over the door showed eleven minutes to twelve. Business was business. The girl would have to wait. Smooth Frank Wheeler had an engagement to shoot a man to death.

CHAPTER XX

A PROMISE OF DEATH

WHEN GLENWOOD E. NOSTROM returned to his library he did not at first notice that the man, Fred, no longer lay upon the floor. When he did Satan's explanation was sharp and crisp.

"He's gone," he said. "A police car will pick him up at once. You couldn't have him here if Wheeler should come back. Just don't bother about it. You've got the money?"

"Yes." Nostrom held the heavy brief case in his hand. "Yes, I've got it."

"Well—" Satan stretched out his hand. "Let me have it."

Nostrom spoke with some difficulty, but there was force behind his words and sudden determination on his face. For a few minutes he was the strong, honest, fearless man who had gained the respect of big men; the biggest men in the city. He said:

"You talked to me of your duty and mine. You talked or at least suggested the unimportance of my daughter's death compared with the millions you serve. This money was brought from the bank to be given to a man for saving my daughter. I understand you want this money to learn the name of the Other Man; learn it to protect these millions of people. I hope you are following me intently, Detective Satan Hall, and understand fully that I am thinking of just one person—my daughter, Lynda—and I am not ashamed of that thought."

"I can understand." Satan was impatient. "I will do everything possible to save your daughter."

"Everything possible, eh?" Dull eyes grew bright; a haggard face raised. "Yes, you must do everything possible, even to offering your life to save hers." And before Satan could put his question, "Would you offer your life for this money which you hope will give you the name of the Other Man?"

"I face death every day for that purpose." Satan spoke with a simple truth. There was nothing of pride in his voice; no thought of conceit.

"Face it. Yes, and I know your word is good, Satan. But you must do more than just face death for this money with which I hoped to buy my daughter's freedom. You must sacrifice your life for it."

"Just what do you mean by that?"

"I mean," said Nostrom seriously, "that I am, unfortunately, mentally unable to attempt to trap you to your death. I mean that you must permit yourself to be trapped, give yourself to these men in return for Lynda's life."

Satan rocked slightly back on his heels, then jarred forward again.

"Are you mad?" he said.

"I am mad enough to refuse you this money if you answer 'no.' You want this money for what you think it will buy these citizens you serve. Are you mad enough to give your life for those citizens?"

Satan said almost brutally: "What you ask is impossible because these men will never permit you to receive your daughter alive. You know far too much now and you would have no reason for keeping such knowledge secret if she were returned."

Nostrom clenched his hands; his voice shook.

"They must keep her alive. They must! I must see her—I must see her alive every time they demand something from me." And as Satan stepped toward him Nostrom stretched out a hand for the large brief case. "No, No! This money is for my daughter's life, not for the death of the man you seek. This Greer may call for it—he will find my daughter."

Satan spoke quickly:

"If Eddie Greer could locate your daughter he would have before now. He would double-cross his own mother for this much cash. Your only chance is through me. Give me that brief case, and whether the money buys the name I want or not I will spare no effort, even to risking my life to save her. But I offer you little hope. If I thought there was a chance, the smallest chance, I would gladly take it."

THE BRIEF case fell to the floor. Both Nostrom's hands sought Satan's shoulders; shook them frantically.

"That's it! That's it! Your word is good, Satan. The Commissioner has told me that. I know that. Even the murderers you hunt know that. If there is a chance, the slightest chance—" Nostrom's eyes were bright burning balls now. "Well, a reasonable chance that the sacrifice of your life will save hers—will you give your life for my daughter?"

"And who," said Satan, "is to be the judge of that reasonable chance?"

"You." Nostrom suddenly shot the word at Satan. "Just your belief that there is a chance."

"Give me the money," Satan said. "You have picked a bad judge, Mr. Nostrom. But if you want my word you can have it."

Glenwood E. Nostrom watched Satan lift the bag from the floor. He said:

"Remember your word to me has nothing to do with the Other Man. It has only to do with this money. Just for one hundred thousand dollars."

"Just for one hundred thousand dollars," Satan repeated, and as he walked toward the door Nostrom clutched him by the arm.

"Your own death for hers. I drove a hard bargain, eh, Satan Hall?"

"No," Satan told him. "I am paid by the people to risk my life for their safety. I am glad that you made it necessary for me to try to save your daughter. You see, you made it impossible for me to serve the millions who pay me—unless I made such a promise."

"But it's death, man! Your death for my daughter's life."

Satan shook his head. "I am convinced that she cannot live if I die. She can only live if I live. It might be possible that we die together, but—" The phone rang. Satan nodded his head for Nostrom to answer it.

A moment Nostrom listened, then he hung up.

"It's the lawyer, Maxie Rosen," he said. "He's coming over to see me at once. He says he wishes to help me. I—I sometimes fear him, but in his day he was a great criminal lawyer."

Satan turned back from the door. Maxie Rosen, the go-between, the man who brought the messages from the Other Man. He was coming there to see Glenwood E. Nostrom. Why? Nostrom was saying:

"Someone got me on the telephone the night my daughter disappeared. He said there must be a go-between. I suggested my lawyers, other lawyers, but the voice on the wire would trust none of them. I don't know how Mr. Rosen's name came up, but the man was suddenly talking as if I suggested him. Anyway, it was I who called Mr. Rosen and asked him to come and see me. He was reluctant to have anything to do with such a case, but I convinced him that I needed him; that a life depended on him. He has acted for me since then, and, naturally, has visited me here."

Satan's lips parted; his eyes narrowed.

"You couldn't have a better go-between. Maxie's very experienced—very," he said. "I would like to hear what he has to say." Satan looked the room over, noticed the long curtains at the end, said, "Those curtains there. What's behind them?"

"The conservatory door." And when Satan put the question Nostrom continued: "Yes, you could listen there. You could slip away and back again if he should be curious." And, with a puzzled frown, "Frankly, he mystifies me, Satan, I'm not sure but he is telling me the truth when he says he simply wishes to serve Justice, and that he hopes that my influence may get him reinstated in the Bar."

SATAN DIDN'T answer that statement with words. The pronounced slant to his eyes and shrug to his shoulders expressed his opinion beyond any doubt.

Then he turned to examine the small conservatory and the narrow hallway beyond it—the locked door which led to the alley. He liked that. It was a quick getaway exit if the conversation did not interest him sufficiently to make him late for his appointment at twelve o'clock at the Café Wellington.

It was exactly fifteen minutes to twelve o'clock when Satan, parting the curtains and looking from darkness into light, saw Maxie Rosen enter that library. Glenwood E. Nostrom, though visibly nervous, greeted him cordially enough.

Maxie Rosen adjusted his glasses, played for a moment with the long black ribbon that was lost some place beneath his jacket, and let his swift, sharp eyes cover that entire room.

Satan saw Maxie start as he glanced at the floor and saw the hardly discernible patch of red on the thick rug. But if Maxie recognized if as blood, he said nothing. Nor did he show visible surprise that Glenwood E. Nostrom was alone—that Fred from Pittsburgh was missing.

He was talking as he took his seat, nervously rubbing his hands together; his voice ingratiatingly soft as he addressed Nostrom.

"I'm not complaining, Mr. Nostrom," he said. "I appreciated your offer of money, and I am sure you appreciated my refusal and the reason for it. My hope—my ambition—to some day plead a case again for a client is my one interest. But you are a big man and I am a small one. It hurts me to say so, yet it is the truth that big men escape the scorn and even the punishment meted to small men. My interest of simply helping you would not be as entirely understood as your interest—your fatherly love and devotion for an only child."

"I am afraid," said Nostrom slowly, "that I do not understand you."

"Of course, of course." Maxie Rosen bent his head for a moment, finally raised it, looked straight at Nostrom and said, "I think perhaps it would be best for you to go right to the police."

"Good God!" said Nostrom. "They'd kill her! This Frank Wheeler would—"

"Stop!" Rosen half came to his feet. "I don't want to know who is behind it. I have been a fool to go as far as I have with you. I ask only that you leave my name out of it. These kidnapers are big, influential men. I've guessed that. What you are thinking about me is true, Mr. Nostrom. I'm afraid."

"Why this sudden change? The police are the last people I was to go to. You agreed with that yourself."

"That was before I learned or, rather guessed who is behind this thing. I brought messages to you that I never should have carried. If you are afraid of the police, why not confide in Detective Satan Hall?"

Nostrom straightened, and so did Satan behind the curtain. It was a surprise, but only a surprise for a moment to Satan, for Maxie cleared that up in his very next words. He asked:

"You haven't confided to anyone, have you, Mr. Nostrom?"

Satan watched Rosen's face change. Hard, cold, cruel, but shrewd eyes were searching the face of Nostrom for the answer to that question; the answer, perhaps, he did not expect to be spoken.

Nostrom gulped, but he said:

"I have confided in no one." And after that single gulp Satan thought Nostrom played the game well. He tried to draw Maxie Rosen out. He said:

"It's strange that you should pick that name—that man. He has every reason to-well, to despise me, Mr. Rosen. For it is in direct contradiction to Detective Hall's statements that these people want me to swear falsely."

IF MAXIE were satisfied or not with Nostrom's statement, Satan could not tell. Satan's fingers twisted at his side, turned up and bit into the palm of his hand. He was sure, as sure as he could be without actually seeing the meeting, that Maxie Rosen was closest to the Other Man. But he wasn't sure that Maxie actually knew the Other Man. Maxie, even more so than most of his kind, could be bought over—had been bought over any number of times in the past. That was one reason his political friends had deserted him in his hour of need.

Why then would a man with such power and knowledge as the Other Man possessed select a man like Maxie Rosen as a go-between? The only one to carry his orders. If it was brains or cleverness or shrewdness, certainly the Other Man could not have found a more brilliant assistant. But what would all that avail him if he knew that for money or simply through fear his most trusted ally would betray him? No, Satan doubted that Maxie knew who the Other Man was, and he wondered if that doubt didn't prove the cleverness of the Other Man.

But Nostrom had asked a question and Maxie was answering it.

"I picked the name of Satan Hall for you to confide in for several reasons. First, he can be trusted absolutely. Second, he could do more to protect you than any man on the police force. Third, and this is also the reason I am withdrawing from all connection with your daughter's—er—disappearance, I was told to bring a message to you. Satan must die that your daughter may live. You must trap him to his death if you wish your daughter to live."

A long pause after that as Maxie watched Nostrom intently. Then Maxie continued:

"Of course I could not be a party to any such horrible suggestion. I am only telling you this so you will understand why I seem to leave you when you need me most. Understand, I hold no brief for Satan Hall. I deplore his methods; he is anything but friendly toward me." Maxie shrugged visibly, dramatically. "But the murder of a police officer. It is too terrible."

Nostrom said very slowly:

"Would the death of Satan Hall bring my daughter back to me?"

Maxie looked about the room; he lowered his voice, said:

"Undoubtedly. But would you consider such a thing?"

Nostrom wasn't listening. His eyes were directed toward the floor, his face was thoughtful. When he spoke his voice was hollow.

"If I could be assured of that—absolutely assured of her safety—" He raised his eyes suddenly to Maxie's. "Could you assure me of that, Mr. Rosen?"

Rosen started, taken off his guard. A remarkable actor, Satan thought. He spoke as if without thinking.

"Of course—of course. Why—why—"

"You know where my daughter is, then?" Nostrom said.

It was as if the words were forced from between Rosen's lips by the piercing, awful, tragic eyes of despair that Nostrom fastened on him. "No, no—" Maxie was saying. "But I could make a guess, Mr. Nostrom—a damn good guess."

The clock struck the hour. Maxie Rosen jumped to his feet.

"I must be going. I really must be going," he said over and over as he almost ran to the library door. "I can't—mustn't be further mixed up in this." At the door he turned, "Mr. Nostrom, I would do anything for you. You know my telephone number. God help me—I can't see that lovely daughter of yours die—die so horribly—so terribly—in such agony."

THE SLIGHTEST beat of feet across the outer hall, the soft closing of the front door and Maxie Rosen was gone. But he left something behind him. Something terrible; something that gripped Nostrom inside, ripped and tore as if the pain were actually physical. Then, as Satan stepped out from behind the curtain,

Glenwood E. Nostrom leaned heavily upon the table, clutched once at his heart and sank slowly to the floor.

Satan Hall was already late for his appointment. Yet it was another five minutes before he had aroused the servants, seen Nostrom recover and helped upstairs to bed, and assured himself that Nostrom was all right.

It was close to ten minutes after twelve when Satan entered his old car, parked around the corner, and started for the Café Wellington. He had one hundred thousand dollars in cash that would buy the name of the Other Man. And he had something else—he had a hate. A new hate that would force from the lips of this Other Man the whereabouts of the girl, Lynda Nostrom.

Satan smiled grimly. Lynda Nostrom, the finding of whom would perhaps save his own life; a life the Other Man had so cleverly planned to take through Glenwood E. Nostrom.

It wasn't long after that that Detective Satan Hall walked through the entrance of the Wellington Bar and struck terror into a half a dozen gentlemen of the night who had been but a minute before bragging loudly of their connection with the right person—the right man—the Other Man. There was hate in Satan's soul and it was reflected in his face.

CHAPTER XXI

READY FOR THE LAUNDRY

EDDIE GREER WAS feeling pretty good in more ways than one. But the liquor helped him along. It was good liquor, damn good liquor. Not the stuff Maxie had dealt out to him before. Sure, that's the way it went. Before Maxie just threw him second rate stuff and a few century notes now and then. The Other Man, who used a guy like Maxie, was entitled to exactly what he got. The other Man! Eddie Greer laughed. He knew why the Other Man used Maxie—had to use him. Yep, he, Eddie Greer, was entitled to what he got. And in the future he'd get it too. He was going to pull off the biggest double-cross the Avenue ever saw, ever heard of. He'd see that Maxie, Wheeler, and, yes—the Other Man, too—got what was coming to them.

Eddie poured himself a double dose of whisky, flopped into a chair and leaned back. Liquor didn't bother him. It was good for him. He lifted the bottle again, glanced at the clock. Ten minutes to twelve. He cursed, set the bottle down on the table.

With a hundred grand he could cruise around the world, drink what he wanted, be pleasantly crocked day and night if he felt like it, and not be afraid of a bullet in the back either.

Smooth Frank Wheeler was coming to talk with him. Eddie hated his guts. He was going to enjoy walking all over Frank. He'd tell him where he got off, then blow the works to Satan Hall for one hundred grand.

Eddie Greer straightened in the chair. There was a knock on the door. He felt a sudden apprehension that had a sobering effect. Smooth Frank Wheeler, the coolest, cruelest murderer who walked the city streets, and yet he tapped before entering a room he was used to bursting right into. Eddie saw that his fingers were trembling, had wished that he had not let Wheeler come up. Quickly he poured himself another stiff drink, drank it hastily. There was nothing for him to fear. Satan would be there any minute. Eddie Greer called out sharply:

"Come in."

The door opened slowly and Smooth Frank Wheeler walked into the room. His face was pleasant, his eyes a mild, almost gentle brown. His lips parted, and he smiled.

"Shake, Eddie," he said. "The Other Man knows his business. If he wants you for a leader—well, you're the tops with me. I know you'd feel the same if it was the other way around."

Eddie Greer came to his feet. His face was not pleasant. This was not the conversation as he had pictured it. He said:

"You do, eh? You do." But he ignored Wheeler's extended hand, grew bolder, more sure of himself. "Then you know who's boss and who you'll take orders from."

"That's right" Frank Wheeler slid into a chair, nodded affably, "You're the boss, Eddie."

Eddie's lips curled into a sneer, Frank Wheeler, too, believed that it was he, Eddie Greer, who had shot Gargan's two gunners to death. So Wheeler was yellow then. People had looked on Eddie Greer differently since that kill—Satan's kill for which Eddie now accepted full credit.

FIVE MINUTES to twelve. Five minutes more and Satan would be there. Well, Eddie would spend those five minutes rubbing Wheeler's face into the dirt and making him like it. He said:

"Maxie's put in a good word for you, Frank. But you mess things up—mess them up a lot. You should be an inside man— errands and things like that. Hell, don't sit there like a dummy. Straighten out that desk. I need a guy who at least can make himself useful."

Eddie Greer looked for the sudden gleam of anger in Wheeler's eyes, and for the moment he thought he had gone too far. Then his fear subsided. For Frank Wheeler, the cruel, feared Frank Wheeler, walked across to the desk, took the handkerchief from his breast pocket, lifted the whisky bottle and wiped away the ring on the highly polished surface. He straightened the huge onyx ink stand, moved the pens, placed both hands flat on the great blotter, eyed it critically. Then he spoke.

"Anything you want, Eddie. You're the big boss. I know how to take orders."

Eddie Greer glared. His whisky-sodden brain didn't figure things correctly. He wasn't hurting Frank Wheeler any. Wheeler was glad to do those things because Eddie was the big boy in the racket now, and Frank wanted—wanted— And then Eddie's eyes lit on the picture—the picture of Wheeler's girl; the girl who had died with a knife in her back.

"Cripes," Eddie Greer said. "That lousy dame there on the wall will have to come down. Where Gargan ever got a picture of that dirty little mug beats me. Grab it down, Frank, and bust it up for the garbage can."

Eddie leered at Frank Wheeler. He had him then. He had him at last! He saw it in Wheeler's eyes. Just a flash, then it was gone and Wheeler was saying:

"I can't take it down, Eddie." And when Eddie scowled, "You know me—superstitious. Bad luck to move that picture."

"Bad luck, you mean bad stomach." Eddie swung, walked toward the picture, grabbed at the thick, rough frame. The right side of the frame came off in Eddie's hand. The picture swayed sideways and so did Eddie Greer.

"See," Wheeler said. "Bad luck."

Eddie cursed, jerked a chair before the picture, climbed upon it, steadied himself with his left hand against the wall. He started to lift the picture with his right hand, stopped, stood so with his face close to the wall, his back to the rest of the room; his back to Frank Wheeler.

Eddie Greer never understood how he knew. But he did know. Did know before Frank Wheeler spoke; before Frank Wheeler said:

"Hold it, Eddie. You know me—my motto— In the back. Always in the back."

Eddie Greer cried out:

"Don't, Frank! I'll make you—give you anything you want! Don't! I—"And then he got it.

Frank Wheeler pressed his finger tightly upon the trigger of his gun. Eddie Greer's hands left the wall. His body swayed, bent backward. He turned very slowly on the chair, put one foot down on the floor. He made no attempt to draw a gun. He cried out for mercy, begged, then threatened, cursed, and finally screamed for Frank not to shoot. Though the pain in his back where the bullet had lodged hurt, Eddie managed to raise his arms in the air.

Frank Wheeler pressed the trigger of his gun again; slowly, carefully. Eddie Greer's right hand dropped to his side, remained there; the whiteness of his hand becoming red as the blood dripped down his arm.

Frank Wheeler said, in a smooth, purring voice:

"I warned you it was bad luck, Eddie." He moved the nose of his gun slowly, drew a head on Eddie's other arm. "I'm going to shoot you to ribbons, Eddie."

"No—no! God, no!" Eddie Greer cried out. "I'll give you everything—anything." Wheeler's gun roared again and Eddie's other arm dropped to his side.

Wheeler's lips set rather tightly; his eyes seemed to twinkle. His gun lowered.

"Give me? I'm taking over your job, Eddie. Can you stand on one leg?"

"The Other Man! The Other Man! I'll tell you who the Other Man is!" Eddie Greer screamed in pain, in fear, in abject terror. I know. He's—"

The telephone on the desk rang. Frank Wheeler looked

toward it, looked back to Eddie Greer just as Eddie's crippled left arm rose, a trembling hand clutched at his chest, tried to cross to his right armpit.

"So that's how it is," Smooth Frank Wheeler said without raising his voice. Then he shot Eddie Greer straight through the center of his face.

WHEELER WATCHED a moment; watched the body twist and fall. Then, walking to the back of the room, opened the door and stepped into the little hallway. He slipped back a tiny bit of wood in a door to his left, called softly, then opened the door. A rat-faced man and two other men entered.

"Ready?" said the rat-faced man.

"Quite ready, Willie. Straight through the door there. You hear anything—from in here?"

"Not a sound," said Willie Simes as he motioned with his hands for the others to follow him, unfolded a blanket and walked across the room. Then he said:

"Eddie Greer, eh? I heard he was getting a little tough."

"Never mind opinions," Frank Wheeler snapped. "That blanket will drip. You should know your business better. Okay, I didn't see the oilcloth." Then he lifted the phone, changed his voice, said gruffly:

"What do you want? Oh—Maxie—wait a minute. The men are here for the laundry."

Smooth Frank Wheeler followed the men and the body with his eyes. When the door in the hall behind clicked closed he said:

"Sure—sure, Maxie. Come up any time and look over the desk. I remember what you said about Satan and I won't move in until tomorrow—or later. What?"

Frank Wheeler turned his head, studied the spot where Eddie Greer had gone down, the blotch of red. Then he said into the mouthpiece:

"A little, but you can move a chair over it. What the hell, Maxie. You can't make ketchup without smashing a few tomatoes."

CHAPTER XXII

DEATH IS INTERRUPTED

SATAN HAD ONLY one thought in mind when he entered the bar of the Café Wellington. Eddie Greer knew who the Other Man was. And Eddie Greer was going to sell him that information. What an insignificant word it seemed compared to all it meant to him, to the city, to the people. The most decisive blow against crime that had been struck. It meant the end of this great network of blackmail, extortion and murder. The end of an organization headed by a man whose influence had actually crept into the police department itself.

Judges, lawyers, politicians, influential business men would, no doubt, topple with the very criminals this Other Man controlled. The arrest of this single man would wreck homes, destroy respected names, cause many self-inflicted deaths by men who could not stand the public shame.

But what did that matter if an entire city of seven million people were saved from the most deadly onslaught against society that had ever been attempted.

Satan didn't stop at the bar. The clock above it showed it was well past twelve—nearly at the half hour mark. Others might believe that Eddie Greer was a dangerous killer. Satan knew better. For Satan had killed those feared murderers that the underworld credited to Eddie Greer.

Satan had mounted those rear stairs in the narrow hall behind the bar too many times to be unfamiliar with them. Now he went straight toward them, paused for a moment at the foot, and peered at the figure there in the dim light.

Bernie Snyder's face was white. His whole body trembled. His lips quivered and his voice had an odd sound in his own ears when he spoke. But he said his piece as he always said it—at least they were the same words that he spoke to others.

"You can't go up there now," he said.

Satan stood before Bernie without speaking a word. He seemed simply annoyed rather than angry. The light was no good, but Bernie saw Satan's eyes plainly. He saw the green of them, read in them what others so often read in them, and he didn't like it. He saw that Satan's right hand was empty, that his left held a dark brown brief case.

Bernie carried a blackjack up his right sleeve, the leather strap of it around his wrist. Just a quick flick of the wrist and an upward and downward movement of his arm. He carried a gun beneath an armpit in a shoulder holster. He thought of neither of these weapons now. Bernie Snyder's lips were dry. When Satan said nothing he said:

"I'm only obeying orders. Detective Hall." Consciously or unconsciously his voice was a hoarse whisper that no one outside that hall could hear.

Satan didn't speak. He swept his right hand up over his chest, then across it and back. Knuckles smacked hard against Bernie's face. Bernie staggered, stretched out a hand, his head hit the wall of that narrow hall. His knees gave, then straightened and he leaned against that wall. He still had the blackjack and the gun, but still had no thought of using them. He just stood and watched the broad back of Satan Hall go rapidly up those stairs.

THE DOOR at the top of the stairs was not locked. Satan didn't knock. He turned the knob, threw the door open, stepped into the room, and heard the door spring shut behind him. The one quick glance he had of that room did not disclose Eddie Greer. It disclosed another figure whose shoulders stood up at each end like knobs and whose glasses rested on the end of a sharp nose.

If Maxie Rosen was surprised he did not show it. Nor did he show any of the signs of fear as had the man downstairs. Maxie Rosen had been a long time in the racket—a big frog in a big puddle.

"A late hour, Satan," he said. "You wished to see me?"

"Where," said Satan, "is Eddie Greer?" Satan was surprised; disappointed. He showed it outside, felt it inside. The biggest, at least the expected biggest moment of his life was a flop. The curtain had been rung down on his show in the middle of the last act.

"Greer?" Rosen's eyes narrowed; ridges appeared in his forehead, on his nose. When those ridges straightened out again his glasses moved slightly higher as if an unseen hand guided, them. "Well, it's about time someone came looking for Eddie Greer. It's been open gossip in certain circles that he killed a couple of men."

"And it's open gossip in another circle that I saw a friend of yours kill a cop last night. I mean Frank Wheeler—Smooth Frank Wheeler," Satan said.

Maxie Rosen rustled some papers on the desk. "I know Frank Wheeler fairly—" He seemed to think a moment, as he took off his glasses and tapped them on the palm of his hand. "Indeed, I might say quite well. Such a thought is impossible—ridiculous!"

Satan walked over to the flat desk, stood before it, placed the brief case that contained a fortune in currency on the floor.

"Maxie," he said, "would this Frank Wheeler you know 'quite well' bury a young girl alive?"

Maxie Rosen was startled this time and showed it plainly. He quickly recovered and his eyes were wary as he said: "Good Lord, Satan! What made you say such a thing—such a horrible thing? Why—it—the very thought of it nauseates me."

"That's too bad." Satan nodded his head up and down, but his eyes never left Rosen's. "You see, the girl is Lynda Nostrom—Glenwood E. Nostrom's daughter. I've got to find her, Maxie. I offered my life for her life—or rather my death for her life. You never knew me to break my word, did you?"

"What the devil are you talking about?" Maxie didn't have to pretend now—he didn't understand.

"You wouldn't want to see me die, would you, Maxie?"

Maxie's brows knitted. He knew Satan. Had known him a long time. Humor was not one of his virtues—or vices, according to how you look at it. But he answered:

"To be perfectly frank, Satan, I'd hardly be interested one way or the other."

"And you wouldn't want to die, would you, Maxie?" Satan's voice was soft now.

"Hardly," Maxie laughed. But his eyes remained hard and his lips set. "Why?"

"Because," said Satan, "if you don't tell me where Lynda Nostrom is I am going to kill you."

MAXIE ROSEN jarred back hard in the swivel chair. His eyes widened; his mouth hung open. He was as nearly off his guard as he had ever been. There was no threat in Satan's voice, nothing melodramatic in his words. Yet, Maxie felt rather than knew that those soft-spoken words of death were more to be feared than the cursing, foul threats of a gunman.

Maxie Rosen had difficulty in speaking.

"You know about the girl; something about the girl, Satan? What?" Maxie was sparring for time, looking toward the phone, the row of pushbuttons on the desk. He dropped his hands to the papers again, began to rearrange them, slipping one hand toward the push-button, the other toward the phone.

"Yes, I know something about—" Satan started, stopped. His right hand moved, black flashed across the desk. Maxie screamed with the sudden pain, put his fingers to his mouth, sucked at the back of them where Satan's gun had crashed.

"I was going to say," Satan continued slowly, and Maxie Rosen had a feeling, a terrible sinking feeling that Satan was holding himself in check—perhaps was having difficulty in holding himself. "Is it surprising that I know when you suggested that Mr. Glenwood E. Nostrom seek my advice, my aid in saving the girl?"

Maxie Rosen laughed. It was a laugh of relief. He hadn't thought that Nostrom would even consider his suggestion, let alone act on it so quickly. Maxie came very slowly to his feet. He placed his glasses back on his nose. He stroked the broad black band of ribbon that hung from those glasses. He had all his usual dignity when he spoke.

"If Mr. Nostrom has consulted you as I suggested, he must have told you of my part in this deplorable and terrible suffering he and his daughter have gone through. He might have told you, also, I refused to take any money. He might have told you that I acted only in his interest. It was stupid of me to go into it. I have withdrawn entirely. And Mr. Nostrom has broken the confidence of a man who endangered his life—his reputation for him." Satan watched Rosen with his piercing green eyes.

"Nostrom didn't have to tell me anything," he said. "You heard what I said, Maxie. Where's the girl?"

Maxie Rosen turned and faced him. His eyes brightened. He played a part he had played many times before in court. Frankness, honesty seemed to shine in his face, his eyes, and in his voice as he spoke.

"I don't know, Satan. I don't know. I wish to God I did. I—"

Instinctively Maxie raised his arm to ward off the blow. Maxie's arm was beaten down and the gun thudded upon his head. He dropped to his knees.

Then Satan was standing over him. That gun was raised again, the barrel was twisted around, the sight was above him, ready to strike again.

Satan was saying, "Where is the girl, Maxie? I know the truth. A young girl lying in an open grave, perhaps dead now; perhaps slowly going mad because you won't talk. Think, Maxie, will I hesitate to save that girl?"

"I don't know. I don't know," Maxie cried again. Then he shrieked, shrieked for help. Then he remembered with what satisfaction he had told Frank Wheeler that the room was sound-proof.

The blow came, the twisting gun, the cutting sight, the awful pain of it and blood upon his face; in his eyes, running over his mouth.

EVEN AS his head fell forward a hand jerked it up. Satan's hand. Not the hand that held the gun. That hand was above him ready to strike again. Maxie looked into that distorted face. He had warned others about Satan, yet thought himself safe from this. Person, place or time meant nothing to this man. Just before that gun started down, Satan said:

"Think, Maxie, think!" And then the very words that Maxie had used at Nostrom's house, "Just make that damn good guess you spoke about."

So Satan knew! But it was not Satan's knowledge that affected Maxie then, made him decide to talk. That was only an excuse he made to himself afterward. It was burning hate in green eyes, the flaying gun, and Maxie cried out:

"I'll tell! I'll tell!"

After that the whistling air from the gun, and the slightest burn as the sight chipped at Maxie's cheek in passing. But the gun was up at once, and burning green still shone back behind Satan's eyes.

"Talk," Satan was saying. "And if you lie I'll know it—and let you know I know it."

Maxie Rosen almost sputtered the words, so anxious was he to get them out.

"She is in a house up—up on—"

Maxie stopped. Satan twisted around suddenly. The door had burst open.

The Commissioner of Police and his two aids, Inspector Redman and Captain Carey, were in the room.

"Satan!" the Commissioner cried as he almost threw his small body across the room and clutched at Satan's arm. "What is this? What's going on here?"

Satan turned, walked slowly to the flat desk and leaned upon it. It was some time before he faced the Commissioner. He watched Maxie Rosen stagger to his feet, run a handkerchief up over his forehead that was smeared with red. Maxie was saying:

"I want this man arrested. He broke into this room here. I was Gargan's lawyer, at least I handled his estate. I was going over some of Gargan's papers and—and—I'll break him for this."

Satan stepped forward. He seemed very tired, very worn. He said in a faraway voice:

"No, you don't want to make trouble for me, Maxie." He looked straight at the lawyer and shook his heal. "You and I both talking at once would blow the manholes off every sewer in the city—every rotten, dirty sewer, Maxie." His green eyes stayed on Rosen. "I'm not making any charge, if you don't. I guess I lost my head."

The Commissioner looked from one man to the other. The atmosphere seemed less tense. His eyes widened, though, at Maxie's reply.

"Perhaps I provoked Detective Hall. If I feel differently about it in the morning I may—may— That is all, gentlemen. Good night."

It was Satan who left the room first. The Commissioner and the two officers followed him. To the Commissioner's frantic questions, Satan replied, "I never saw Eddie Greer. He wasn't here then."

"But Maxie Rosen—he's been trying to get you out of the department. I know that. Now, if you had something on him— any charge we could make stick—"

Satan sighed.

"Nothing we could make stick—not on Maxie. He's the closest one to the Other Man." And, with a shake of his head, "You never interfered before when I was in action. And you had to pick tonight to begin. Tonight—tonight." Green eyes regarded the Commissioner. "You probably caused a young girl's death—and mine, too."

"What the devil are you talking about?" the Commissioner asked. They had reached the sidewalk before the Wellington. "Damn it, Satan! You can't run loose like this. I have a good mind to drag you off this case—entirely off it."

"No," said Satan, "you can't do that." His voice was very low. "My life belongs to a girl—a girl in an open grave.

ONLY VENGEANCE

SATAN SAT VERY straight and stiff and looked directly into the sunken eyes of Glenwood E. Nostrom. Nostrom was repeating for the third time:

"You wanted to discover the identity of this Other Man. I gave you one hundred thousand dollars to buy that information. That is correct, isn't it?"

"That is correct." Satan looked around the library. His eyes spotted the tiny stain of red on the rug where he had struck down the gunman from Pittsburgh earlier in the evening.

Nostrom went on. "And you promised me that, win or lose, for that one hundred thousand dollars you would give your life to save the life of my daughter, Lynda."

Satan rubbed his hands along the arms of his chair. Has lips tightened. It wasn't often he was ill at ease. He was now. He was facing a man whose only daughter had been kidnaped by Frank Wheeler; kidnaped so that Nostrom would have to give Wheeler an alibi for the murder of a policeman that Satan had seen Wheeler kill. Yes, and this father had been taken and shown his daughter, buried alive in a cellar; a glass mask over her face, and a tube leading down to it which gave her air.

Satan finally said, "You sent for me to come to your home, Mr. Nostrom, and I am here." He lifted a brief case, tossed it on the fiat desk. "And the money is still there. I did not get my information. I did not find the Other Man."

"But your promise—your life for my daughter Lynda's life.

181

Don't you understand? If I lead you to your death these men will spare her, let her return to me. Wheeler has sworn to that. Maxie Rosen promised me that. Don't you see how hard it is for me to ask you this—demand that you keep your word? I don't want the money. I want my daughter—alive."

Satan stiffened. "I promised to sacrifice my life if there was any possible chance of my saving your daughter. They would not free her now even if you did put me on the spot for them. With what she could tell-with what you can tell—they can't take such a chance. The Other Man is too smart. And if I were dead I could not help your daughter."

"And alive, what can you do?"

Satan shrugged.

"Nothing for her perhaps, since you will not talk. Nothing for justice as our State looks on justice. But I can give you vengeance, Mr. Nostrom."

Nostrom jerked his head erect, looked straight at those green eyes. He put his head into his hands. "What good will vengeance do me? What good would their deaths do me?" And suddenly, "But they cannot kill her—they dare not. They must bring me to her occasionally that I may know she lives. If she dies, then nothing can stop me from talking. They must keep her alive. But if she should go mad! I have thought of carrying a gun with me that I might kill her; kill her in that grave."

Satan stretched out a hand and clutched the trembling man's wrist. It was wet and cold. Satan said:

"I shan't mislead you with false hopes, Mr. Nostrom. You have but to open your mouth and the men who have your daughter, die. You have only to deny that Frank Wheeler was with you the other night and he roasts at Sing Sing. With my knowledge you will be of no further use to this gang of murderers. Anyway, your daughter must die; they won't allow her to live. You might as well talk now. Make her death serve the State as she would wish you to."

"No! No!" the distracted man cried out. "They cannot kill

her! They dare not. I knelt there and looked down at her; knelt there by the pile of dirt on the cellar floor above her head—the pile of dirt that could be poured down the funnel at the top of that tube and—"

NOSTROM STOPPED, his eyes wide with horror, looked at Satan, drew far back in his chair. Green, burning eyes were piercing his sunken ones. Satan's voice shook.

"Nostrom, Nostrom—" Satan stretched a hand across and shook him by the shoulder. "You have told Maxie Rosen that I agreed to meet these men, place myself in their hands for your daughter's life?"

"Yes—yes," Nostrom stared dully at Satan. "I told Wheeler that when he telephoned me. Maxie Rosen is here now. I sent for him. You think he's part of this—this criminal ring?"

"Of course. I know it. And I know that I made an agreement with you to give my life for your daughter if it was possible to save her that way. Mr. Nostrom, this is fact, not conceit. I am the single obstacle today that stands between the Other Man and his entire success. All that he needs from other men can be bought. Either for money or extortion through exposing past wrongs or through terror, such as kidnaping your daughter. Judges, politicians, perhaps even police and city officials—everything can be fixed. Every man of his can be protected except against one thing. That thing I control."

"You control? What?"

"Death. The kind I deal." Satan tapped the gun under his left armpit. "He can't fix that. He hates me. His rats hate me. Frank Wheeler hates me. Maxie Rosen hates me. Yes, they would all like to see your daughter removed from that grave and put me in her place—without the tube for air. I'm banking everything on them taking me to your daughter; to that grave in the cellar you described. Everything depends on that."

"Depends on that? Then you're going?"

"Yes, I'm going. You say you believe they will release your daughter in exchange for my life?"

*"Don't come near
me!" Nostrom said
in a hollow voice.*

"Yes, of course. Of course. There is no doubt—no doubt."
Nostrom came to his feet. "Satan, I didn't think you would! They
will kill you horribly. I can't let you do it! I won't!"

Satan smiled, said, "You would give your life to save your
daughter, wouldn't you, Mr. Nostrom?"

"I don't want to live without her. Yes, I would gladly die."

"You may get your wish," Satan told him grimly. "Since they
will give her life for mine, they might also give me their word to
let me live also if I turned myself over to them as their prisoner
until they have accomplished the control of the city."

"No." Nostrom shook his head. "They wouldn't do that. I
know they wouldn't."

"But I think they will," Satan said.

"You—you seem so sure?" Nostrom answered doubtfully.

"I am sure," Satan told him. "They will give their word to
anything to get me in that cellar unarmed. Why not? What is
a word to them? There is not a bit of doubt, Mr. Nostrom, that

they intend to kill all three of us. There can be no other assurance of life for them."

Nostrom dropped his head in his hands.

"So it's you who fears death. Here—" Satan's Land flashed suddenly in and out. A gun was there. Satan was pressing it into Nostrom's hand despite Nostrom's objection that he never had even shot a gun. "Never mind that. It will give you a chance to help tonight. It's a hundred to one chance, and even those odds depend on you. Listen."

NOSTROM LISTENED for a full ten minutes. He didn't speak until Satan had finished. Then he said:

"I couldn't do it. I couldn't. Anyway there will be men there. I release you from any promise. You are right. The people need you. My death—my daughter's death—may save the city now. Yes, I see my duty. I'll write you a statement—anything—everything."

"A statement of what?" Satan asked. "A statement that would electrocute Frank Wheeler—a mere cog in the wheel. A man who doesn't even know who the Other Man is. A statement that I doubt very much would even convict Maxie Rosen. No, we'll play it all the way. Stake everything on one mad chance."

"I can't. I'm not—"

Satan gripped his hand. Squeezed it with iron muscles.

"I only ask that you be the man you were before your daughter was taken from you. Before you bowed to the will of these murderers. If you can be that man, then there is no other man I would rather trust. After that, it must be life as I have led it. I try to do the best with the cards that are dealt me."

"You're a brave man, Satan Hall."

Satan shook his head. "It is not such a long chance if things break right. If they don't I shall not come. It is possible that they may simply kill you there, but I doubt that. You are Frank Wheeler's only alibi for murder."

"But he made me sign an affidavit to that effect. He would not need my testimony."

"Clever—yes, clever," Satan said. "Still, if they killed you they would leave me here—alive."

"But you have no proof of anything with me dead."

Satan said, "I don't think they'd think about proof with me back here alive. No, I don't think they will kill you there." And dropping his hand from his gun, "You say they wish to act at once?"

Nostrom nodded.

CHAPTER XXIV

A SMOKING GUN

THREE MINUTES LATER Nostrom opened the door to the hall. Maxie Rosen stepped into the room. Directly behind him was Chester Preston of the Preston Detective Agency. He spoke back over his shoulder to men in the hall.

"You have your orders. You know what to do." Then Preston entered the room and closed the door behind him. Maxie Rosen and he stood side by side.

Satan grinned. Maxie Rosen spoke first.

"The last time we met, Detective Hall, things were entirely unpleasant—and I was about to speak words that would have been lies. I have forgotten and forgiven that little incident." He tapped a bandage across his forehead.

"Mr. Preston, eh? The detective." Satan had a sneer in his voice; "And other men in the hall. You flatter me."

Maxie Rosen smiled nastily.

"I made a rule when I practiced at the bar never to under-estimate an opponent. But to business—I have a great sympathy for Mr. Nostrom, a great respect and admiration. I have come here at his request. He wishes me to relay a message to a certain party. He says that you are willing to take the place of someone else."

"In the open grave of his daughter—is that it?" Satan said sharply.

Maxie started, looked at Chester Preston. Preston's sharp features were expressionless. He looked at the mantel above the fireplace as if he were not listening. But Satan watched him. Maxie was talking.

"I think, Detective Hall," he said slowly, "that we will go about this in a business-like manner. No matter what your opinion may be, I have no interest except Mr. Nostrom's interest. Mr. Preston here heads a well-known and respected protective agency of long standing; He is being paid a fee, of course, for his work. But the less he knows the better."

"All right, let me have it," Satan said calmly.

"For a man going to his death you are quite composed."

"Quite," agreed Satan.

"A death," Maxie went on slowly as his lips smacked slightly and his hand went to his head, "which may be most unpleasant and prolonged."

Satan watched Maxie's eyes; watched the way the shrewd lawyer studied his face, trying to read what might be hidden there. Maxie was trying to discover why Satan was willing to go to his death.

"You are keeping your word to Mr. Nostrom, eh?" Maxie lowered his head slightly. Satan was not a man to die so easily, else why had he lived so long. Yet, Maxie knew that Satan's word was good.

Satan said bruskly, "If I had made such a promise to Nostrom I would have kept it. But I didn't. If you have any idea that I am nobly offering myself on the altar of sacrifice that Mr. Nostrom's daughter might live, forget it. I am not such a fool."

"What do you mean?" Maxie Rosen was both surprised and relieved. He couldn't imagine Satan Hall in such a noble, self-sacrificing role. The thing had worried Maxie. It smacked of trickery; trickery that he did not understand.

"I mean," said Satan. "I'm keeping my word to Mr. Nostrom. I know the Other Man wants me out of the way. I know that he fears me. Don't shake your head, Maxie. You fear me too. For the freedom of Mr. Nostrom's daughter, Lynda, I am willing to be the Other Man's prisoner for two weeks—three if he needs that much time."

"And you will take my word that you will not be harmed just as Mr. Nostrom has taken it?" Maxie asked.

"I am afraid," Satan told him, "that I am not as trusting as Mr. Nostrom. But I believe the Other Man will keep me alive because he will fear to kill me."

"And why should he fear you?"

"Because," said Satan, "Nostrom and his daughter will be free. If I am not returned in the time specified, then Mr. Nostrom will act—and you will be the one acted upon. Clear and clever, eh?"

"And impossible." Maxie snapped his lips tightly. "The girl and Nostrom free, and only your promise that you will then give yourself to this Other Man. I know that the Other Man will not agree to this."

Satan shrugged his shoulders.

"Before I leave this house, Mr. Nostrom will have to telephone me that he is safe. We have agreed upon a message. If he telephones me that message, then I'll accompany the men sent for me—"

"Unarmed?" Maxie leaned forward, his eyes for a moment bright, eager through his glasses. He was thinking quickly and his thoughts were not unpleasant. He was thinking, too, that Satan Hall was quite as clever as he had thought. He turned toward Chester Preston. Chester Preston was smiling.

"Unarmed," Satan answered.

"Well," Maxie said. "I will have to get in communication with—with the right party."

Satan pointed at the phone on the desk. Maxie Rosen grinned pleasantly, said:

"I am old fashioned. The French phone with its single instrument confuses me. I will telephone outside, and be back with you at once."

At the door Maxie paused, turned and looked directly at Chester Preston. They returned nods, then Maxie left the room.

MAXIE ROSEN was back. He closed the door, spoke quickly.

"Everything is settled. The Other Man pledges his word."

"Good." Satan seemed so at ease that it worried Maxie.

"Mr. Nostrom leaves now. When he is assured that his daughter is alive and safe he telephones me," Satan said.

Maxie said. "I have nothing whatever to do with that. Mr. Nostrom meets certain people who will have a car at the corner. I understand that these people know nothing of Mr. Nostrom's ultimate destination, so it would be useless to interfere with them. They will simply drive Mr. Nostrom to one point where more men will pick him up in another car if they are certain the first car has not been followed. If they are not so assured it will mean death for his daughter. I understand, Detective Hall, that you will follow the same procedure as soon as you receive Mr. Nostrom's telephone call here?"

"Right." Satan nodded. "One other thing." His right hand crossed his chest. Rosen jumped back. Chester Preston half reached for a gun, hesitated, then his hands shot quickly toward the ceiling. Satan laughed, twisted his gun around, held it toward the silent Nostrom, said:

"Since Mr. Nostrom is threatened with no danger, he goes armed. We insist on that." Nostrom took the gun.

Chester Preston dropped his hands. Again he and Maxie exchanged glances.

"And you will go unarmed?" Maxie asked Satan. "As you agreed?"

"After seeing how my display of firearms distressed both you gentlemen, I will travel unarmed. Your men in the car can easily make sure of that But they must not unarm Mr. Nostrom. I want his assurance on the phone after he gets there that he still has tire gun. His message to me will be. 'Everything is all right.' If I do not receive that message from him, then I don't come and—"

"And what?" Maxie asked. He was alert and suspicious.

"And I will give myself the pleasure of some day shooting both you gentlemen to death."

Maxie Rosen and Chester Preston both laughed, and both their laughs lacked mirth.

But when they left they insisted that Glenwood E. Nostrom accompany them to the street. No words that they could not hear must pass between Nostrom and Satan Hall. At the door Satan gripped Nostrom's arm, felt that arm tremble violently.

Satan's voice was low, tense, but clear to both Chester Preston and Maxie Rosen. He said:

"Remember, Nostrom, *Everything is all right.* And that is to mean that you and your daughter are alive and safe. It is for you to decide that you are safe,"

Satan stood there at the top of the steps and watched the party descend to the sidewalk. He watched the two men who had waited in the hall follow Chester Preston and Maxie Rosen into a car, wait until Glenwood E. Nostrom had gone down the street and turned the corner. Then the car sped from the curb.

Satan remained in that doorway for some minutes. Then he went back into the library, closed the door, and lifted the phone. To the Police Commissioner he said:

"Have every cop notified: to keep an eye on every basement in the city, especially the brownstone fronts. The whole town, for I'm sure the house is in town." And after a pause and a harsh laugh, "If no one hears anything I'll be dead. If I'm alive they'll know it for blocks around."

He slammed down the phone, lit a cigarette and stood with his back to the fireplace.

Who was the Other Man? Satan still didn't know. But he felt that he would know tonight. Dead or alive he would know. He counted on the vanity of the criminal for that. Big or small, every criminal possesses that vanity. Yes, Satan was convinced that the man he hunted would also have that weakness.

He would want to show his face to the man he hated most before he died. And the Other Man certainly must hate Satan.

Satan knew he was playing a long shot attest. Had he sent

Glenwood E. Nostrom to his death? And would he himself shortly follow to that same death?

Satan smoked his second cigarette and: felt that death was very close. He flipped his cigarette into the fireplace. If it was, he had it coming to him.

Satan's wish now was a silent prayer. If he were to die tonight, he wanted it to be with a smoking gun in his right hand—and a dead man on the foot before that smoking gun. And that dead man the Other Man—the Other Murderer.

CHAPTER XXV

THE OTHER MAN IN THE FLESH

FRANK WHEELER OPENED the door and walked into the room. The air was bad and he coughed slightly before he snapped on the lights and looked at the heavy iron shutters across the inside of those windows. Then he looked at the girl, her white face, her burning eyes, her swollen lips. She was lying flat on the floor, her arms outstretched, her hands reaching toward the pail of stale water just beyond her fingers.

She drew back quickly, blinked in the light, leaned against the edge of the large bed, rubbed a hand across her swollen ankle, and let the chain loosen; the chain that was also attached to a huge bolt that had been driven deeply into the thick wood of the baseboard.

She tried to speak. A dry tongue attempted to moisten drier lips. At length words came.

"Water—you promised me water."

She held her hands tightly together, tried desperately not to fling herself along the floor again to the pail that she knew she could not reach.

Frank Wheeler laughed; threw back his head and laughed.

"Now just think of that, sister." He kicked the pail toward her, watched her put the dirty warm water to her lips, gulp it eagerly. "On the level," Frank continued, "I didn't mean to put it out of your reach. That's the only thing I've ever had against the water system. It takes too long to starve people into talking. Now—"

His shoulders shrugged. "Just my luck. There's not a damn thing you can tell me."

Lynda Nostrom looked up at him. She said:

"You deliberately put it out of my reach. You told me so. You said it would give me exercise."

"Did I?" Frank Wheeler shrugged indifferently. And with a mock bow, "Let me assure you it was not intentional. Get up!"

"No!" The girl screamed now, turned and clung to the bedpost. "Not that—not the grave, again. I couldn't stand it again. I tell you I'll go mad. I can't—I won't be any use to you mad."

"You're not any use any more. But it's not the grave. Besides, your grave's occupied." He leaned down and gripped her arm, tried to jerk her to her feet, but she clung to the post screaming.

"No—no! I can't. Not again."

Frank Wheeler straightened. The room was hot. He rubbed a hand across his forehead, kicked out suddenly; viciously. The girl groaned, gasped as the toe of his foot pounded twice against her side. Frank Wheeler didn't speak again. But she came to her feet, staggered slightly and sat on the edge of the bed.

She turned her head and looked straight at him. She said very slowly:

"I'll never forget your face. I'll always remember it—just as it is now."

Wheeler said and his voice was smooth:

"I've tortured men and I've tortured women. It makes no difference to me. You might as well know the truth now. It's a rub-out. You've given me trouble—plenty of it. Death isn't always just passing from one world into another. It can be hard or it can be easy. I'm a man who likes little fuss. You make it easy for me and I'll make it easy for you. There's worse things than lying in that grave with a glass mask over your face and a tube bringing air down into your lungs."

"Worse—what could be worse?" Fear chased fear across her face.

"No tube at all," said Wheeler. "Just you alive there, and dirt above. Air gets through, you know—not much, but some people live for a long time." And the girl cried out and threw herself down on the bed. "There's no use your going into hysterics. You're to have a visitor. A big guy that I want to make an impression on. You see, he wants to see you die. He wants to see your father and Detective Satan Hall die, too. It's the Other Man—he's here to see you three die."

THE GIRL shuddered. She knew about the Other Man. She had heard these men who guarded her speak of him in tones of fear. Wheeler turned, pointed at thick drapes over a door that could be seen behind them.

"He's the big boss," Wheeler went on. "And I'm his right hand. I'm to meet him here tonight." Frank Wheeler spun toward those curtains. Two knocks, then a scraping of fingers. A key scraped in a lock and the door beyond was opening. Then there was a slight movement behind the curtains.

Smooth Frank Wheeler prided himself upon never showing emotion. He didn't show it now. But he prided himself also on never feeling any emotion. He felt it now. It wasn't fear, but a sort of awe. He was to be face to face with the Other Man for the first time. Face to face was a figure of speech only, for Wheeler's instructions from Maxie had been clear. He would not see" the face of the Other Man. He would be but a shadow in the room now. A shadow in the cellar later. A figure in black that must see all and remain unrecognized.

Maxie Rosen had delivered his orders to Wheeler beforehand. Wheeler was to kill three people tonight. The Other Man was to be there to see them die—to know that they were dead. Maxie would have an alibi tonight—a real one. The Other Man would have the alibi he always had. The alibi of a man who did not exist.

Frank Wheeler saw the white fingers extend through the curtain; saw the ring that Maxie had shown him for identification. Then he spoke his piece as Maxie had given it to him.

"Everything has been arranged to your satisfaction," he said and the stiffness of his words and the odd sound of his voice bothered him. "All three will die. Their bodies will disappear."

Frank Wheeler stopped talking, tossed his arm out toward the girl on the bed. Then he walked to the hall door by which he had entered. He followed every instruction, even to not looking back over his shoulder. His hand was on the doorknob when the voice spoke. It was as if the Other Man's mouth was placed against the curtain to disguise the voice. It was a single word.

"And—"

Frank Wheeler swung. He had wanted to make an impression; do everything as he had been told to do it, say everything as he was told to say it. And now he had forgotten. He gulped twice, but spoke quickly.

"And no one in this house will make the slightest effort to discover your identity."

As Frank Wheeler stopped that voice spoke again. It was hollow; unreal But the words were clear.

"Maxie Rosen," it said, "did not have all my messages. He would not have the stomach to deliver it properly. I wish to stand alone above that grave. Satan Hall is to be buried alive and he alone is to see my face; see it and recognize it before he dies. That is why I am here. I want Satan Hall to know me."

Frank Wheeler paused, said, "Certainly. I'll arrange all that." Frank Wheeler had his hand upon the knob, about to open the door and the Other Man spoke once more.

"The man who leads for me will, after tonight, be worth much money. To try and discover my identity through my voice would be useless. To try and identify me through elimination of others will be just as useless. To try and identify me through shrewdness, cleverness, bribery and trickery will only mean your death. I have no suspicions of you. My enemies die as you would wish your enemies to die. Go below and be ready to entertain the father of this charming girl."

THIS TIME Frank Wheeler passed out the door and closed it behind him. He didn't speak again. Everything that the. Other Man had said was in his mind. But it was in his mind also that if he identified the Other Man, the Other Man would not know that he knew until Frank Wheeler saw a chance for personal profit and a personal safety in the disclosure.

Lynda Nostrom watched with fascinated wonder mixed with fear as those curtains parted and the figure came into the room. Tall or short, fat or thin, she couldn't tell. Just a long black cape-like coat held out perhaps by spreading arms. A large black hat pulled well down over the forehead. Coat collar turned high hiding the lower part of his face. He came closer to the bed on which she lay.

Lynda looked up, realized now why that face was hidden entirely except for restless eyes; eyes without color in the dimness. It was the scarf the man wore. His white hand lifted it from about his neck as he drew near and pulled it above his nose. Nothing now but eyes; burning, malignant eyes.

The hollowness had gone out of his voice when he spoke. It sounded natural, human to her, but low and unfamiliar and muffled behind the scarf. The Other Man said:

"So you are the girl. Yes, my dear, I very much wanted to look at you. My whole success in life has been due to women." A slight chuckle. "The keeping away from women. Your father throws aside his honor, everything he holds most dear, in the hope that you might live. A man—a killer of other men," and there was hate now behind that scarf, "offers his life that you may be saved—or pretends to offer it. He thinks himself rather clever. And he trusts your father not to trap him to his death."

"My father won't—my father couldn't do such a thing." The words came through tight lips.

"But he will, my dear. He saw you last lying in a grave." And as the girl's body trembled, "Ah, you remember that. Well, he saw you so, and protected a murderer. Now he will see you so again. He will listen to your screams of agony and send to Satan the message that—"

There was a tap on the door. The Other Man turned his head slightly. As he did the girl acted. Her words and her hands shot forth together.

"I want to see the kind of a face you have!" she cried out, and both her hands gripped at the scarf and pulled it down.

The Other Man's head turned back; wide clear eyes stared into his. He nodded his head and smiled pleasantly at her.

"What do you see, my dear?" he said.

"I see a face." She spoke like a woman in a trance. "A face that I will know again, even if I see it after death."

"Quite right—quite right." Bat his mouth or eyes didn't smile now. "Only in death will you see it again. Any possible chance you had to live is gone now. But you have hurt your right to choose your death. The knock on the door means you are needed below. You are now going to meet your father."

The Other Man moved slowly from the bed, walked toward the curtains. He spoke over his shoulder:

"Mr. Wheeler and some friends of his will be in at once to take you below. Your father will be anxious, of course." Then he passed between the curtains, and they closed after him.

The door to the hall opened. Despite Frank Wheeler's threat the girl screamed and fought. Frank Wheeler cursed as he unlocked the chain from her ankle and watched the two men drag her from the room, and hurl her onto the stairs at the end of the hall.

CHAPTER XXVI

A SHADOW BY THE WALL

NOSTROM'S RIGHT HAND was sunk deep in his jacket pocket as he plunged down those cellar steps. Frank Wheeler from one side watched that hand carefully. The two men who stood on the steps above were gunmen of reliability. They carried guns openly in their hands. They knew that the man they had brought there was armed.

Another figure also watched; a man who sat on an upturned box in the deep shadows just beyond the oblong stretch of dirt in the cement floor. He leaned forward on a cane. His coat collar was turned up. His black slouch hat was pulled well down, and the scarf raised just above his nose, making his breathing difficult in the musty dampness of that cellar far below the street.

Nostrom saw the stocky form of Frank Wheeler. He saw too the dirty door that had once been white which led to the coal bin. But these things he saw only in a hazy way because they forced themselves upon his vision. For Nostrom's eyes sought but one thing and fastened on that one thing—the long hole in that cellar floor; the grave that had contained his daughter's body.

He saw it now, the pile of dirt up by the head of it, that Frank Wheeler had told him on his last visit would be placed in the funnel at the top of the tube; the tube that gave his daughter, Lynda, air.

Nostrom ran to that grave, cried out in agony. There was no funnel there now. There was no tube that led to the glass mask he had seen above his daughter's face! There was no air going down to the bottom of that pit! Just dirt. She was dead! Worse than dead, she might still be living—buried alive.

Glenwood E. Nostrom fell to his knees beside that mound of dirt. His right hand came from his jacket pocket, and a large gun appeared in his hand—Satan's gun.

Frank Wheeler called out a warning. The men on the stairs raised their guns. The Other Man in the rear bent further forward. It was Frank Wheeler who spoke.

"Don't be a fool, Nostrom. We wondered why you wanted a gun. Wondered why Satan insisted you carry one. Why—don't! Don't!"

And now fear rang out in Wheeler's voice. Even the Other Man half came to his feet. Only the two men upon the stairs didn't understand—didn't see any cause for alarm. But Frank Wheeler saw the cause; the Other Man saw the cause. Saw every hope they had of getting Satan shattered. Saw every step that had been so carefully plotted out, destroyed. And Frank Wheeler saw the electric chair, smelled his flesh burning in it. Yes, Glenwood E. Nostrom, his alibi witness, was going to die, and Satan would be on the outside.

None of the men in that room had any fear of personal danger. Nostrom was holding that gun tightly pressed against the side of his own head.

"Satan feared a trap," Nostrom said in a hollow voice. "And I brought the gun. You had to let me keep it or I wouldn't send any message of safety to Satan. I would not have told him he must keep his word and give himself up to you. Don't move closer to me—don't come near me!" He looked at Frank Wheeler, half faced the men upon the stairs. Apparently he did not see the man who sat in the shadows and leaned forward upon his cane; leaned more and more forward until he was coming slowly to his feet.

Nostrom crouched low now, close to the mound of dirt.

"The truth is," he said, "I brought this gun with me to shoot my daughter to death if I feared you did not intend to keep your word. Now she is dead, so I shall kill myself."

FRANK WHEELER watched the Other Man moving slowly in the shadows, his back sliding along the cellar wall, his cane moving in his hand; the heavy grip of it lengthening out as the Other Man's fingers slipped toward the ferule at the end.

A man upon the stairs spoke.

"Hell, Frank. He's in for the dose, ain't he? Why not let him do his own job?"

"Shut up, Stutt," Wheeler fairly snarled as he swung his head and then back to Nostrom. "Your daughter's not dead, Nostrom. Don't you see, man? We kept her there only when you came, that's all. Listen. Wait! Lower your gun. Lynda's safe in that coal bin there. Don't be a fool—look! Watch him, Stutt!" Frank Wheeler went straight to the coal bin. But he kept talking continually as the shadow behind Nostrom moved closer; closer to that grave and to Nostrom.

"Look, damn it, look." Frank Wheeler opened the coal bin door, cursed once, pulled a small flashlight from his pocket and sent a pencil of light into that coal bin. "Look! Look! She's okay."

Nostrom drew his left hand from the mound of dirt which was almost between his knees now, shook his head, raised his left hand to his eyes, peered under it. There was relief on his face. A sort of triumph, too. But he didn't lower the gun. Wheeler watched him carefully. What did that look of triumph mean? Did it mean he intended to kill his daughter, himself too?

A black shadow moved swiftly; a black arm with a white hand on the end of it went up and down. There was a dull thud, a breathless moment for Frank Wheeler as he wondered if Nostrom's gun would go off. A second of dead silence in that room, but for the stifled cry of the girl tied and gagged in a chair. Then Glenwood E. Nostrom fell forward on his face.

The Other Man did not speak. He slipped back to the shadows, placed himself upon that box, pointed once from Nostrom to Nostrom's gun, then once again leaned heavily upon the cane.

Frank Wheeler rubbed his handkerchief across his forehead, dropped his gun back into its shoulder holster. Then he quickly crossed to Nostrom, picked up his gun and motioned to the two men upon the stairs.

"Get him over into the chair there." And when they did, "That's right. Tie him, but leave his hands free. No—a little closer to the table. Sure, so you can plug in the phone and set it on that table. We'll give him a little show with his daughter the star performer. And Stutt, search him. I don't expect he has another gun, but go over him carefully. The damned idiot was actually going to blow his brains all over the place."

Frank Wheeler was the efficient leader now and he wanted the Other Man to know it, recognize it and appreciate it. Things hadn't gone according to schedule, but they would from now on. Why didn't Chester Preston come down and lend a hand? But it was the Other Man's fault. He had agreed to let Nostrom cart that gun. Of course, no one would think for a moment that Glenwood E. Nostrom could be dangerous with a gun, but then who would ever think either that he intended to use it to kill himself? Wheeler grinned. He wished to hell some of his enemies would have such pleasant ideas about using a rod— Satan Hall, for instance.

Nostrom's head was bobbing in the chair. His eyes were opening and dosing. Damn Nostrom! Wheeler raised his hand, slapped it twice against that bobbing head, sent the eyes to blinking more. He'd show the Other Man his stuff now. Show him how quick he'd make Nostrom listen to reason, jerk up that phone and call frantically to Satan.

Nostrom opened his eyes, looked straight into those of his daughter, tried to jump from the chair and fell back again in the grip of the ropes.

Smooth Frank Wheeler went to work with a sneer on his lips, hate in his eyes, and the rotten pleasure of inflicting physical torture on the daughter of the man who had almost made a monkey out of him before the Other Man. Yes, Frank Wheeler wished Nostrom was tough, wished he could take it. It would be a pleasure to cut the girl apart bit by bit. For the first time in his life Wheeler hoped that his work wouldn't be easy—at least too easily accomplished. He smiled as he ripped the gag from her mouth.

CHAPTER XXVII

AN INVITATION TO
BE MURDERED

GLENWOOD E. NOSTROM opened his eyes to see a figure in a long black cloak crossing before him. He saw the slouch hat, the pulled-up muffler, the cane which was the weapon which had struck him down. Nostrom tried to move and found himself bound there in that chair. He saw the figure stop and heard Smooth Frank Wheeler speak to him. "The basement is deep and a single gun-shot would hardly be heard on the street."

The Other Man didn't turn his head toward Frank Wheeler. He raised his arm slightly and talked into the cloak when he spoke.

"If the girl's screams will be heard, gag her again."

Frank Wheeler spoke quickly. "They shouldn't be muffled. We need them for her father!"

The Other Man spoke, his voice still that hollow, unnatural tone:

"I will stand behind her and muffle them myself when it is necessary." He raised his voice and turned partly toward the bound man in the chair. "The expression of her contorted features, the moans of agony from her lips should be quite sufficient. But you have a reputation for giving complete satisfaction, Mr. Frank Wheeler. The stage is set. The show is yours. Do not waste time."

The black figure of the Other Man moved quickly. Nostrom and his daughter faced each other. The girl just inside the coal bin; the father ten feet beyond the open door. Both cried out

Cruel blows flayed Satan's back.

together, both were inarticulate. It was as if they spoke a foreign tongue, which they alone understood. The girl in sudden fear with the knowledge of their deaths she had gained upstairs. The father in sudden relief that she was alive.

Frank Wheeler spoke to Nostrom.

"We are not equipped with any fancy methods of torture here. You and the girl are going to die. It's up to you to choose the method. There's a phone beside you. You're to use it. Call your own house, get Satan Hall and give him the message that is to assure him of your safety. That message is—" Wheeler paused, consulted a small card, then reading aloud slowly, "Everything is all right. Just those words, Nostrom, nothing else. Satan believes that you would not speak them unless you were sure you and your daughter were quite safe. You are going to speak them now."

"Never! Never!" Nostrom set his lips tight; his sunken eyes burned.

"When you speak them," Frank Wheeler continued, "Satan will leave your house, be picked up by a car, searched for weapons, changed to another car and brought here. There's the phone."

"I will never do it—never bring him to his death. Do you

think I am a fool to sacrifice at any price the only chance we have oh life? If we are to die anyway, why should I do as you say?"

Frank Wheeler shrugged, turned to Stutt; took the long sharp knife which Stutt handed him. He ran his finger along the edge.

"We won't waste time, Mr. Nostrom. I shall not describe to you the agony of torture. I'll just say that I'll cut the girl to ribbons before your eyes, then throw her into that grave alive. If you are the kind of father that can take that in the hope of saving your own life, why we'll go to work on you later. What do you say?"

FRANK WHEELER took a step forward, turned suddenly and brought the knife through the air, directly toward the girl's face.

The girl screamed. The Other Man stepped forward, stretched a hand out. The cry died, on the girl's lips. Her upper teeth sank into her lower lip as a stream of blood flowed beside her eye. It was just a scratch. The girl cried:

"Don't do it, Father. Don't phone. I am to die anyway. I—"

The knife moved again. This time the blood came from below the other eye. It was a deep gash this time. Frank Wheeler cursed, turned to Nostrom.

"I'm not as clever as I used to be, Nostrom." He shook his head; laughed shrilly. "A little more practice? Next time—" He leaned down and spoke to Nostrom. The others in the room did not hear Frank Wheeler's words, but Nostrom did. There was a cry, an almost inaudible cry, so deep was it down inside of him. When Nostrom did speak he said:

"Give me the phone! Give me the phone!"

Frank Wheeler straightened, looked toward the girl. Her head was forward on her chest. He looked too in the shadows behind her, the deeper shadows that the black cloaked figure had slipped into. The Other Man's head nodded. Wheeler grinned his appreciation, turned back to Nostrom.

"You disappointed me, Nostrom. But if you've got a weak stomach you did the right thing. Lean assure you I was not fooling. There is not that much of a hurry, you know. If you wish to wait to use the phone I—"

Frank Wheeler laughed; gripped the hand that stretched toward the phone.

"No tricks, Nostrom. No cry for help into the phone. It would save Satan's life, but it would make your daughter's death ten times more lingering and horrible—and your own too."

Frank Wheeler made Glenwood E. Nostrom repeat the single sentence he was to give Satan. Nostrom's voice shook with fear and Wheeler made him repeat it until his voice was steady.

"All right," Wheeler said finally. "Be ready." He lifted the phone, called a number, waited. He saw that the Other Man was looking at the phone—at his fingers that gripped it, Frank Wheeler cursed to himself, half turned his back. His fingers shook.

A voice spoke. It said: "Mr. Nostrom? Mr. Nostrom—Satan Hall speaking."

Frank Wheeler switched the phone to Nostrom's lips. Nostrom said:

"Everything is all right."

Frank Wheeler dropped the phone quickly back in its cradle, wiped the perspiration that had suddenly formed on his forehead. He didn't look at the Other Man as he shook his head. It had gone off fine, he thought.

"Listen, Nostrom," he threatened, "nothing can save you— nothing. Two boys go to meet Satan. If he's armed they quit. If he shoots them or threatens them, they don't know anything. Any fake can't help you. Understand, if they don't bring him you—" Wheeler stopped talking. Why tell Nostrom all that? If it was a fake message that Nostrom sent it was over with now anyway. But why would it be fake? What good would that do them? Wheeler straightened, took hold of himself. Damn it, he was talking himself into a panic. And what could happen no matter how things broke? Just the thought that Satan had taken his word—Frank Wheeler's word—made him suspicious and uneasy.

BUT SATAN hadn't relied on that word. He had relied upon Nostrom, the belief that Nostrom would have let himself be torn to pieces before he betrayed or trapped Satan. Neither Satan nor Nostrom would have thought of Nostrom's daughter being hacked to pieces before her father's eyes. Wheeler felt suddenly better. Nothing to it now except to wait for the coming of Satan.

Frank Wheeler turned to the stairs. His voice was steady— his orders sharp.

"Trot back upstairs, Stutt, and get the rattler. Yeah, the Tommy-gun." And when Stutt looked somewhat surprised, Wheeler laughed. "We just want to be sure Satan's dead if he runs for it."

"Okay," Stutt grinned. "I'll chase him up and down the cellar steps with it."

If a clock had ticked in that cellar for the next ten minutes it would have sounded like a pneumatic drill. Twice Wheeler pounded Nostrom on the head, to stop his breathing so loud. Finally he spoke to the Other Man, that silent black figure in the corner.

"Now that Satan's on his way, why not get rid of these two?" He jerked a thumb over his shoulder at the seven-foot long mound of dirt. "There's plenty of room below and the boys need exercise."

The Other Man said, "No, they cannot die until Satan is dead. It's a protection for you and for others. Satan might not come. He will, of course, but we must take into consideration that he might not."

"You want them to see Satan die?"

"I want to see Satan die." The Other Man moved quickly forward through the open door of the coal bin, toward the stairs, stopped. The phone was ringing. Wheeler lifted it. After a moment he said:

"Yes, sure. Yes—yes." He dropped the phone, could not keep

the elation out of his voice as he turned to that muffled figure, doubly hidden now in the light with his chin well down upon his chest so that nothing showed but his hat above the turned-up collar of his great cloak-like coat.

"They got him." Wheeler almost spat the words out. "Unarmed now and on his way. They found two guns on the dirty rat. Five minutes, ten at the most, and he'll be here."

The Other Man bent even lower so that it was impossible to guess at his actual size.

"Good," he said. "He will dig his own grave with that child's shovel there. And Frank Wheeler will-beat him into it with the sharp steel whip. I will return when Satan arrives."

The Other Man—bent very low—walked slowly up those steps.

Frank Wheeler rubbed at his chin. Certainly, he must know the man. The voice was vaguely familiar. The figure and the face, however, were so well hidden it was impossible to guess. And the walk—a studied, unnatural walk like the voice; a limp first to the right foot, then the left.

Across the room in the coal bin Lynda Nostrom shuddered and stifled a moan. And across town Satan Hall was coming to his death.

CHAPTER XXVIII

SATAN TAKES IT

SATAN HALL GOT out of the car and walked up the worn stone steps of the house. His coat and vest were gone—his shirt was torn. He knew the street, he could guess at the number. He had not been blindfolded. He knew that was because he was not expected to return alive. It was the word "expected" that had brought him here to gamble with death. It was too late to turn back now even if he wished to. Guns stuck against his sides. They had practically undressed him in that car, particular attention being given to looking for a small arm gun and a larger leg gun. And they had not been disappointed—they had found both.

The door quickly opened and Satan was shoved inside. Darkness engulfed him for a moment with the closing of that door. Then he saw light, and in that light Satan Hall looked directly into the face of Chester Preston, head of the Preston Detective Agency.

"So it's to be death? You must be very sure of yourself, Preston."

"Why not?" Preston shrugged his shoulders indifferently. "You've always known the racket—always known I worked for the Other Man. He is here tonight."

"I am quite aware of that," Satan said.

Preston showed surprise. "What do you mean?"

Satan shrugged his shoulders. "I have suspected you of being more than just one man in the racket."

Preston's eyes narrowed. He said, "You mean—"

"I mean—" Satan started, but stopped at sight of the two hard looking gunmen who appeared suddenly.

Preston turned to them. He handed them money. "Here's your dough. Keep your faces closed and beat it. Hold the car down by the corner. I'll have to see to the upper part of the house, then I'll join you." He turned to two other men who came into the hall, said, "All right, Stutt. You and Morgan take him down the stairs to the cellar. And, Stutt, keep that machine gun on him every minute—every second—on the way down and while he's in the cellar."

"Every second." Stutt prodded Satan with the gun.

"That's right, Stutt. The eyes of the big boss will be on you tonight. Maybe you'll guess who he is. Maybe you won't, but after tonight with Satan dead it won't matter. Go ahead. I'll stay above."

Satan looked straight into the eyes of Chester Preston before he felt the nose of the gun in his back and moved down the hall. That was the second time Preston had said he would remain above.

Satan saw Glenwood E. Nostrom and his daughter, Lynda, before he was halfway down those steps. He saw too the gruesome length of dirt with the little mound at the end of it. The mound of dirt that Frank Wheeler had threatened to drop into a funnel and into a young girl's gasping lungs.

Satan's trained eyes took in the coal bin door too, the peculiar window in the back of it that seemed to lead into the house instead of out in the alley. These old houses used hot air furnaces in the old days, and some of them still did.

Satan spoke before Frank Wheeler could. Morgan and Stutt took up their positions at the top of the stairs. The Tommy-gun was held tightly in Stutt's two hands and the nose of it, beyond the round cylinder, slowly followed Satan's every movement. Satan knew that once a finger closed upon that trigger, quick death would follow.

Satan said: "This is quite a reception, Frank—flattering and all that. I have kept my word and come. You should now release Mr. Nostrom and his daughter."

"That's what you think." Frank Wheeler held his heavy forty-five gun tightly in his hand. "You've come for a visit, all right, and you may live for quite a time. We were in a hurry to get you here, but we've got plenty of time, now. We have a regular act for you, Satan."

AND THEN Satan saw him; saw the black cloaked figure slowly descending these stairs. He tried to see a resemblance in that walk to someone, but he could tell nothing. Satan waited for the Other Man to speak. The black figure stopped in the darkness of the staircase wall. Finally Satan spoke.

"Am I to understand that you're not going through with things as promised? You're not going to free Nostrom and his daughter now that you have me?"

The man behind the scarf and beneath the hat laughed. He raised his arm against that scarf when he spoke.

"Quite the contrary," the Other Man said. "Things are going through as planned—exactly as I planned them. There is a grave there, Satan. It is already occupied by a man who was to betray my name to you. Ah, you remember our mutual friend, Eddie Greer. But it's a deep grave, and there will be plenty of room for two. It seems almost unbelievable that you came here, like this. You the single man—the only one in the entire city who interfered with my plans."

"Who are you?" Satan asked.

There was a sound that might have been a laugh.

"I am the Other Man. I am the one who has seen my plans destroyed, my leader killed, my men blasted beyond recognition by your gun. And now my men shall see how you die."

"So that's how it is." Satan backed closer to that grave. "And just how do I die?"

"You will be beaten until every inch of skin is off your back, then buried alive in that grave with the man who would have sold you my name." The Other Man's hand shot beneath his robe, appeared quickly again. Something shot from his fingers, thudded upon the cellar floor at Wheeler's feet, clanked heavily. It was a heavy handled whip with steel thongs, curved like sharp nails at the end.

"Your coat and vest are already removed, Satan Hall." The Other Man shook his head. "No, I wouldn't resist Wheeler if I were you. If you can't take it like the man you're supposed to be; if you don't wish to be broken as the many you have broken, then there's the wall for you to be strapped to. I promise you before you die you shall see my face."

"That," said Satan calmly, "will be a break. I know when I have to take it. I hope you men—all of you here—will know how to take it when your time comes. Which will be so soon that—"

And the whip struck. Satan's whole body jarred. At the second stroke the shirt seemed to be torn from his back, the skin from his bones. He was being struck by a man who hated him; a man he had been determined to send to the electric chair, and that man would have no mercy on him.

Satan faced the Other Man, the girl and the back of Nostrom's head, as he staggered beneath the blows. He would have to go down, of course, but he was a strong man—a very strong man. The Other Man who knew everything would know that. He couldn't fall to the floor too soon; he couldn't be yellow. This Other Man would know as well as Satan knew that he wasn't yellow, and a fall at the wrong time would mean death to Nostrom and the girl too.

CRUEL BLOWS flayed his back. He staggered beneath them. He dug and he flinched beneath the whip, a physical action that he could not control. But no cry came from his lips. Satan strained to see Nostrom's face. Why didn't they turn Nostrom around? But he saw the girl's face; saw the terror in it, heard her cry out for Wheeler to stop.

And then Satan slipped back. His foot struck the pile of dirt. And suddenly he caught the girl's eyes and he laughed. It was a queer sort of laugh. The pain was terrific, tearing into his bones, jarring inside his body. Was he going mad? He didn't know. He didn't care. All hell would soon break loose in that cellar.

Frank Wheeler was flaying now with both hands. He wanted to beat this man to the floor, this devil with the charmed life who stood upon his feet under such punishment. Wheeler was broad, strong, and his body in good condition. He changed the direction of his blows. The thongs bit higher. One twisted about Satan's throat, swung his great body around. And for a moment the blood-stained face of Satan Hall looked into the sweat-streaming face of Frank Wheeler.

Satan—helpless, battered, swaying. Yet as Frank Wheeler looked into those eyes; those furious green eyes, he drew back; stepped back as if in fear; terror. And as if suddenly realizing that nothing could subdue that bleeding, beaten hulk that was Satan Hall, killer cop, Frank Wheeler rushed forward. He swung that cruel steel whip, saw Satan turn, and as the whip struck, fall down; fall flat on his face into the little mound of dirt at the head of that grave.

CHAPTER XXIX

ALL HELL BREAKS LOOSE

FRANK WHEELER RAISED the whip again. And then it happened. That "all hell" that Satan had thought of "broke loose." Frank Wheeler's eyes bulged. His hand with the whip in it hung in the air. Satan wasn't face down upon the floor now. His body was twisted. He was leaning on one elbow—the left elbow. Something in his right hand flashed a yellow-blue flame. Frank Wheeler saw the streak, heard the blast before he actually saw the gun—the great black forty-five in Satan's hand. Then he saw the man with the machine gun sway, twist backward, roll out upon the cellar floor and lay still.

Frank Wheeler wasn't sure of what followed. He knew that a black figure moved upon the stairs. Then he hurled his own body forward, started the whip down.

After that—oblivion.

Only the girl with the staring, horror-stricken eyes knew exactly what Frank Wheeler never knew. She heard a single blast, saw a single flash, saw the body of Frank Wheeler jump into the air, twist grotesquely and drop to the floor. She didn't see anything more after that, for a black figure shot through the opening door of that coal bin, turned swiftly and closed the door. She could see white trembling fingers fumbling with the lock.

After that a second of silence, then a horrible, inhuman laughing voice that cried out:

"Turn and take it—rat!"

Then another crashing, roar of a gun, another horrible satanic laugh, and the sound as if a body rolled down steps—to stop finally on hard cement.

Then someone was grabbing her, tearing at the ropes that held her, pulling her numbed body from the chair and forcing it toward a hole in the wall that was dark, but large; large enough to admit her body.

She cried out, "Satan! Satan—help!"

Naked to the waist, blood now thickening upon his chest and back Satan stood in the center of that cellar floor. He had seen the man, Morgan, tumble down those stairs and had heard the door above close with a bang, and a heavy bolt slip across it.

There was no pain in his great body, at least he felt none. He stood there, legs apart, gun dangling in his hand—a gun from which three bullets only had been fired and three men had died. A gun that had been planted there in the mound of dirt by the frightened, shaking hand of Glenwood E. Nostrom.

Satan didn't think of his own sudden holocaust of death as any act of bravery. But he did marvel at Nostrom's courage in the face of a great fear. For Nostrom had done a brave thing while facing man's greatest enemy—fear. Satan didn't know the meaning of fear himself, but he could recognize it in others, and what's more could understand it in them. Yes, that gun that spewed death in that cellar was the first of the two guns he had given Nostrom.

The girl's cry cleared his head. He dashed toward that coal bin door. The girl was there. The Other Man was there also. All he had done was simply failure so far. Two things he had still to accomplish. The first, to save Lynda Nostrom. The second, his desire, his longing, his passion to find, yes, and perhaps to shoot and kill the Other Man.

Nostrom cried out to be cut loose as Satan flung himself against the door. And Nostrom, despite his fear, thought that he was trying to attract the attention of a madman. For that dirt covered, sweat covered, and blood covered body was ripping hard against wood; strong wood that no man in Satan's condition could possibly knock down, Nostrom thought.

But Satan could and did. For the wood was cracking, breaking and tearing beneath that hurtling red mass of animal-like fury.

Glenwood E. Nostrom turned his attention to the table beside him; the phone upon it. Though his hands were bound now, he could, given a few minutes, reach that phone. His hands were bound before him. He reached the table, toppled the phone onto his knees and gave the phone number of the Police Commissioner. As he did so the coal bin door crashed in and Satan fell with it.

SATAN STAGGERED, pulled himself erect. Was he too late? Then, directly before him was the long black coat; a coat which, because of its length, had difficulty in drawing itself into the wide opening that must lead above. One quick glance convinced Satan that the rest of the bin hid no one. He raised his gun, half closed a finger upon the trigger and said:

"Turn around, Mr. Other Man, and take it head on."

The black cloak moved, wiggled further into that hole, and Satan's fingers half tightened again. Murder that? His teeth parted. Green eyes slanted.

Satan stepped forward, grabbed at the black cloak, jerked hard, felt flesh beneath his fingers. It felt as if something held the body there. Then he jerked again. The body in that black cloak was out on the floor standing upon its own feet. Satan's breath came fast. His lips were a single broad red gash.

He swung the cloaked body around, gripped both its shoulders, and gasped as he looked into the startled white face.

Almost roughly he pushed the figure from him. It was not the Other Man. It was the girl, Lynda Nostrom. The girl he had risked his life to save. He was surprised, angry, disappointed. He had been so sure his strong, long fingers had sunk deeply into the shoulders of the city's greatest danger; the Unknown Menace—the Other Man.

The girl spoke.

"He went up there." She indicated the wide opening in the side of the wall. "He put this coat on me and dragged me behind him in case you came and shot. But he was going to kill me. He had to kill me."

"Why," said Satan, "did he have to kill you?"

She clutched at her throat now, and Satan saw the marks of fingers on the white skin. "Because he said I was the only living person who had ever seen his face as that of the Other Man."

Satan clutched at her shoulders, stopped, raised his gun and whirled around. There was a crash in the cellar beyond. "Wait," Satan told her, turned quickly, and was out in that cellar, slamming the coal bin door shut. After saving the girl, he did not want a stray bullet to kill her. The cellar would soon be full of bullets.

The door above the cellar stairs was still closed. Nothing had changed except that Nostrom was now on the floor, the table on top of him, the telephone jarred from its cradle. His final efforts at that phone had upset his chair.

"It's all right," Nostrom said as Satan lifted the chair up again. "There's a knife there by the bottom step. Cut these ropes, man! I got the Commissioner on the phone and he's on his way here."

"You know the address—know where we are?" Satan said as he found the knife and cut Nostrom free.

"Yes, they made no attempt to hide that. And my daughter, Lynda—she safe?"

"Yes—safe. Lynda!" Satan called out as he walked leisurely toward the coal bin. "Lynda." And when there was, no answer he opened the door and entered. The coal bin was empty! Lynda Nostrom was gone!

Plainly Satan heard feet beating against wood on the floor above. When he reached the opening the beating of heels had died away. Something else took its place. That something else was the roar of a gun, and the spatter of bullets into wood; into wood where Satan's head, might have been if he had stuck his head through the window leading to the stairs above.

SATAN STAGGERED back out of the coal bin. The bullets caromed off the side of the bin and struck him. He hadn't felt the sudden stab of lead in his own body. Yet, he felt funny; groggy. He knew that Nostrom caught him, was holding him, easing him into a chair. Then Nostrom crossed to the tubs. Satan heard him drawing water.

Satan looked down at his bare chest and arms. The cuts made by the whip had given, him a bloody shirt. There was no way to tell if he had been shot or not. They'd have to look inside of him to find that out.

From the appearance of his body he might very well have been riddled with lead.

Nostrom was back, giving him water, talking. Satan tried to pick out the meaning of his words. It had suddenly become hard for him to sit there with the gun dangling in his right hand, and his brain frantically trying to piece things together.

Nostrom was saying, "What's wrong? What's wrong? Where is my daughter—where's Lynda?" Nostrom backed away from those blank, staring, unseeing crystals of green that were Satan's eyes. He too ran to the coal bin, entered it. He didn't cover that little square opening that Bed to the floor, above with any single look, though he knew the truth with that first glance. He ran from wall to wall, and despite the fact that there was no possible hiding place, kept calling "Lynda—Lynda!"

Then he ran back to where Satan sat. Back to that chair just as Satan's great red body started to slip sideways. Nostrom caught him, straightened him, threw water in his face. He saw the dry blood start to move again, roll slowly down Satan's face.

"Satan! Satan!" Nostrom cried over and over. Lynda—she's gone. She's not there! What did you do with her?"

"Lynda!" Satan gasped. "She—" He came to his feet, swayed, gripped the back of his chair with one hand, pounded the other against his forehead. "Lynda—she's—I don't know. I don't understand it." The heel of Satan's left hand pounded three times heavily against his forehead. His right tightened on the chair. The gun dangled loosely from his index finger. He was exhausted.

Nostrom stared straight at Satan for a full minute. He tried to talk, but couldn't. Something in Satan's eyes stopped him. They held an empty look. They were blank and unseeing. Nostrom was puzzled for a moment. And then he did know. The green eyes flashed the truth. The beating Satan had taken so stolidly had knocked something inside of him off balance. Something behind his eyes—in his head—in his brain. And Nostrom knew the truth. He cried out the words in a loud fear-filled voice:

"Satan, you're mad! You're mad!"

CHAPTER XXX

THE BODY ON THE STAIRS

NOSTROM BACKED SLOWLY across the floor now, his eyes glued to Satan's eyes. Satan followed him, staring blankly, wildly. Nostrom backed against the wall, raised an arm to protect his throat from Satan's outstretched bare, red arms with red hands on the ends of them.

But Satan didn't grip Nostrom. He stood before him, staring blankly. His voice was like a child's, a frightened child groping in the dark, as he said:

"I'm Hall—Hall—Satan Hall. I'm here for a purpose. Why am I here?" And lips tightening, words almost inarticulate: "Why? Tell me! Tell me quickly. Why am I here?"

"You came here to save my daughter." The words were forced from Nostrom's throat. He knew that Satan was mad, yet added:

"The Other Man has taken her and will kill her."

"Why will he kill her? Why—" Satan started and stopped. Nostrom saw the eyes changing slowly. They were just as bright, just as hateful, but there was life dawning in them again. And though the madness was gone a terrible burning hate remained. Satan nodded, said:

"I know why he will kill your daughter—because she has seen his face. She knows who the Other Man is."

Satan was once more himself. Nostrom sighed in relief. Satan paused, jerked up his gun. Nostrom spun too, listened. A voice was talking, a low metallic voice, there in the room with them. Yet they saw no one.

Satan stepped quickly forward, lifted the phone that lay upon the floor, put it to his ear. He heard the words distinctly. A voice that he recognized was saying:

"Stutt is dead. Morgan is dead. Frank Wheeler was shot to pieces—blasted right out. Yes, that mad killer, Satan. He's trapped in the cellar, but I don't know how badly he's hurt. Bring four of the boys—the best. And burn up the road."

The voice was the voice of Chester Preston, head of the Preston Detective Agency. He was talking from the upstairs connection.

Satan laid down the phone. The floor beneath him still felt strangely unfamiliar. Satan's eyes passed over the bodies on the floor without show of emotion.

"He's calling for more gunmen," Satan said grimly. "But the Commissioner should be here by then to greet them. But your daughter—she must—"

Satan broke off and dashed quickly up those cellar steps, threw himself against the door above, felt it shake. Quickly he dropped flat on the steps. Simultaneously a gun roared. Lead made holes in that door as if it had been made of paper, bullets cracked against the stone of the cellar, high up.

Satan slid to the bottom of those steps, pushed Nostrom toward the coal bin, said:

"That door—keep throwing things at it. Wood, the shovel— anything. There may be only one man in the house now—the Other Man—and I think I know who he is. There may be one other. Hardly more or they wouldn't call for help. If the Other Man is alone he'll have to protect that door. I'll try the exit from the bin. While I do that, you keep his attention on that door."

"It'll mean your death," Nostrom protested.

Satan looked at Nostrom steadily now.

"That was what you wanted once—demanded of me. It may save your daughter's life. Inaction now means her death. If that hole in the coal bin is guarded from above it will mean my death. But I take a lot of killing, and a lot of killing takes a lot of time."

GLENWOOD E. NOSTROM did try to detain him. Satan seemed in anything but a condition to attempt to save his daughter. He gripped the swaying detective. Satan shoved him away. For a moment he watched Satan. Then he went into the main part of the cellar and proceeded to attack the door with anything he could find.

Nostrom was gratified by the instant response of pistol shots. He stood well to one side, throwing at a decided angle.

Satan didn't hesitate now. He went head first into that hole in the wall. Almost at once he was on a small platform of wood where a man could stand erect and his entire body be hidden from the coal bin below.

He stood listening, then stretched his hands into the dimness before him and felt the rungs of a ladder. He gripped it, climbed noiselessly, moved quicker when the shots came from above the cellar steps. Then he saw light. It came through a square opening above him. So the Other Man, in his anxiety to escape, had not even bothered to close the exit above? Or had he left it open purposely, so as to blow Satan's head off when he came up. For he must have figured Satan would come up. Satan knew that.

One thing was certain. The Other Man had returned to that coal bin, thrown his hand across that girl's mouth and dragged her into the hole, onto the platform and so to the floor above.

It was a desperate act, but a necessary act. Satan had hunted the Other Man a long time; every man on the Force had hunted him a long time. Now a young girl had simply to raise her finger, point it at him and he burned to death. The Other Man knew that. One of them must die. The Other Man and the girl, Lynda Nostrom, could not both remain alive.

Satan Hall looked straight up at that opening, bent his head so as to survey it from an angle. Yes, a trap door was raised. It looked as if it were made of heavy steel; solid thick steel! It could be closed flat down even with the floor, of course, and a rug put over it. But it was open now.

Satan's blood-stained shoulders shrugged. He felt the pain of them for the first time. He gripped his gun tightly in his right hand, gripped the rung of the ladder. Just a single step up, two at the most and he would pop from darkness into light—and into trouble. But there was little use to think about that. He couldn't help the girl as long as he hesitated and clung to that ladder.

His foot raised, dropped back again. He didn't make that step that might mean a bullet in the head. He stood silent listening. Somewhere far distant in that house a woman screamed, cried out shrilly for help. Satan knew that voice. It was Lynda Nostrom.

But that cry had only made Satan hesitate for a split second. It was the sound that followed the cry that held his foot. A man above him, beside that open trap door, had cursed softly. Satan heard feet scrape by the square of light above, and a voice call out to the man who was guarding the cellar door. The voice said:

"It's that damned girl. To hell with that cellar door. Satan can't get through it. Come and lock this steel trapdoor in case he does try it. I won't have time for it. Damn it! I should have killed that girl." And the speaker must have kicked the trapdoor down, for there was a crash—then darkness.

Despite the hurried words there was nothing human about that voice—nothing natural. It still talked into its owner's arm. It was the cleverly disguised, almost impossible to recognize the voice of the Other Man.

After that Satan heard the sound of running feet that seemed to pound upward upon uncarpeted stairs. Then other feet that were coming from the entrance to the cellar to lock that trap door. They meant to leave Satan in the cellar below and the girl in some room above, helpless; ready for the death the Other Man had grimly promised to inflict on her.

DETECTIVE SATAN HALL went into action. He bent his head, took that step, took another one, and pounded his shoulders against the heavy steel. Then he followed through that pound with his own rising body. The trapdoor crashed open. A gun roared behind Satan. Satan plainly heard the pellets of lead against hard steel. He swung his body; his gun. This was a lucky break—this steel door. That square, strong steel trapdoor gave him his chance.

Then the lights went out. The dull click of a button, then darkness. Satan jumped through the open trap, crouched low in that darkness, and waited.

Breathing close to him? Moving feet? He was not sure. At least sure of the breathing. But he was sure of the moving feet. He thought that those feet were moving toward the stairs.

He could see the stairs now; the dull outline of them; the uprights that supported the bannister near the top where the light came from. Then he heard a step squeak. He moved quickly to where he thought those steps must be, and the breaks of luck went heavily against him.

He fired quickly into the blinding brilliance of the electric torch that, through some freak of chance, lit suddenly straight upon his face. There was another shot too. A shot that tore at his arm. But there was only one shot from the figure that held the torch.

The light wasn't a bad target. Satan had fired as he always fired; instinctively and accurately. The light went out. There was panic after that. Racing feet upon the stairs; feet that Satan followed, as he grabbed the newel post at the foot of the stairs and swung toward the main flight. And then he saw the man running. The figure turned, a black gun shone against the white of a hand. Above it the blotch of white that was a face.

Satan saw the blotch of white for the tenth part of a second before he closed his finger and shot it out of his vision. He pressed his back against the wall as the tumbling body sped by him, cursed as a heel cracked against his right knee cap. Then he was dashing up those stairs.

The girl was still alive. She had cried out again, and this time her words were loud and clear. She shrieked:

"Don't—don't kill me! I'll never tell you are the Other Man. Never!"

CHAPTER XXXI

THE LAST SHOT

GLASS CRASHED SOMEWHERE below Satan. Heavy bodies pounded against the front door. If it were the police or the help the Other Man had sent for, he didn't know. The girl was still alive. She knew the Other Man. The Other Man was there with her.

Satan swung along the hall, saw the door at the end and the light there. It came from a small lamp above a bed. And on that bed with a man's hand pressed tightly against her throat was Lynda Nostrom. But it wasn't the hand against her throat that Satan noticed. It was the other hand; the hand that was forcing a gun, a long barreled revolver, between her teeth into her mouth.

No chance to shoot the man's wrist. No chance to shoot the gun from the man's hand. No chance simply to wound him. For Satan suddenly remembered that he had but one shot left in that gun. He remembered also that upon that cellar floor other guns lay—one a machine gun. Yes, he remembered them now as he saw the fingers of the white hand tighten. He saw the trigger start to lift. Satan raised his eyes and saw the whiteness of an ear below a black felt hat.

It never entered his head that he would miss as his finger closed.

A dozen men might have crept up on him then and attacked him from behind. A dozen men might have dashed up the stairs after him, and he would have been unaware of it. Satan was intent upon one thing—he must shoot before the Other Man pulled that trigger. And he must not miss. He didn't know he had been holding his breath until he let it go out in one great blast. His was the only shot that echoed in that room. The burnt smell of powder that bit into his nostrils came only from his gun.

A light flashed, a hand rested on his shoulder.

"I saw him fall," said a voice, "as I came down the hall. Was it the Other Man, Satan? He's lying there on his face." And suddenly seeing Satan's blood covered body, "Hell's fire! What did they do to you, Satan?"

Satan said, "Frank Wheeler beat me—and he's dead. The Other Man gave the orders and he's dead."

"Who is—who was the Other Man?" The Commissioner hardly breathed the words.

"The man I first guessed at. The man who knew so much about everybody in tire city. The man who was in a position to know." Satan moved toward the still black figure on the floor. "A man who for over twenty years guided a detective agency that protected from blackmail the pasts of people; then kept those pasts to use in the future. The Other Man was Chester Preston."

The Commissioner's eyes widened. He started to speak but a noise behind the policeman, on the stairs, stopped him. The man on the stairs moved aside. Glenwood E. Nostrom came up those stairs. His eyes searched wildly, saw the girl, and he ran to take his daughter in his arms.

"There are others coming." Satan recalled the telephone message he had heard, and told the Commissioner of it hurriedly.

The Commissioner gave quick efficient orders. Then, turning back to Satan, the Commissioner stood beside that body that lay flat on its face, the right hand out, still gripping the long-nosed gun.

"Who did you say the Other Man was, Satan?" the Commissioner asked.

Satan pointed. "He's there at your feet. Chester Preston," he said.

"Chester Preston," said the Commissioner, "lies dead at the

foot of the stairs. I saw him as we came in. Someone shot him high up in the forehead."

Satan didn't hear any more. He dropped to his knees, grabbed the back of that dead head, twisted it around into the light. The Commissioner was standing beside him.

Satan turned and looked up at the Commissioner, his eyes were amazed. "It's Maxie Rosen!" he said.

"It is. It is." The Commissioner stroked his chin. "He had the same opportunities to collect facts over the years and use them in the future as did Preston. He used Preston. A lawyer for the criminals for years, friend of the politicians until he got disbarred, close to police officials and crooked judges. Maxie Rosen had all Chester Preston's knowledge and ten times his brains.

"Of course, we didn't suspect him, Satan. Our best men failed to catch Maxie meeting the Other Man, for Maxie, himself, was the Other Man."

HALF AN hour later Preston's picked men arrived in their own car and departed again in police cars without firing a shot. The girl told her story.

It was one of terror and horror. A frenzied terrible fear of that grave. Then came Satan and hope of freedom. Then being dragged up that ladder from the coal bin to the hall above. Maxie Rosen had taken her to the room on the second floor, placed a gun against her head. Why he didn't kill her then she didn't know. It was because Preston had called from below, but she didn't know that. Maxie Rosen had looked toward the window and the girl thought it was the sound of the shot being heard on the street that he feared. But she did know that he had struck her on the head with the gun.

"Maybe my head is hard." She tried to smile, but failed dismally. "Later I suddenly became conscious, realized that I was not dead after all, and cried out. After that—"

"After that," said the Medical Examiner, Doctor Robert Joyce, as he walked suddenly into the room, "Satan shot him directly through the ear, the bullet lodged in the base of the brain and he's a very dead man indeed. The only trouble with your shooting, Satan, is that the criminal is never in a position to make a confession."

"Nor beat the rap or cost the State anything for electricity." Satan pulled the blanket over his shoulder, winced under the pain.

Alone with the Commissioner and Satan later, Doctor Joyce talked as he rolled down his sleeves.

"The bullet in your arm did a little damage, Satan. It's a bad flesh wound, of course, but I'm remembering the way you personally ignore such wounds. But those whip lashes across your body will keep you in bed for six weeks at least. Those cuts are going to be very painful."

Satan came to his feet, scratched a match along the wall and stuck the blaze to the end of his cigarette.

"That's what you think, Doc. I don't like to be on my back, and what I don't like, I don't do."

The Commissioner said, "Say the word, Doc, and I'll make him go straight to the hospital."

Doctor Joyce placed a hand over his mouth, rubbed at his lips.

"Well," he finally said, "There are five dead men in this house. I wouldn't be the one to tempt Satan to make it an even half dozen. But if I were you, Commissioner, I'd report him for gross carelessness with the taxpayers' money. Mind you, five dead, yet he used up six bullets."

Satan smiled at that. Then he tossed off the blanket disclosing his torn back. "If the District Attorney wants evidence against these men to show to a jury I'll be that living Exhibit A that lawyers like to rave about."

Doctor Joyce said: "You'll remember them for a long time, Satan. They'll stay with you for life, those scars."

Satan's laugh was not pleasant. He said: "I'll remember them forever—and enjoy the memory of each one of them."

www.ingramcontent.com/pod-product-compliance
Lightning Source LLC
Chambersburg PA
CBHW030514020726
47494CB00004B/1094